AN ALP
CHRISTMAS
(3-Book BWWM SET)
BY
STACY-DEANNE

Readers: Thanks so much for choosing my book! I would be very appreciative if you would leave reviews on retailers when you are done. Much love!

Email: stacydeanne1@aol.com
Website: Stacy's Website [1]
Facebook: Stacy's Facebook Profile[2]
Twitter: Stacy's Twitter[3]

To receive book announcements subscribe to Stacy's

mailing list: Mailing List[4]

---

1.   https://www.stacy-deanne.com/

2.   https://www.facebook.com/stacy.deanne.5

3.   https://twitter.com/stacydeanne

4.   http://eepurl.com/dFGzTL

BOOKS INCLUDED IN THIS SET:

Hawaii Christmas Baby

When Talia, a beautiful, black, independent, make-up artist wakes up from an enchanting night in billionaire Jody's arms, she has no idea that she's slept with her new stepbrother, the estranged son of her mother's new wealthy husband, Ben.

Even though Talia is convinced their affair is wrong, Talia and Jody can't keep their hands off each other. Meanwhile, Ben is running for mayor in Hilo, Hawaii, and feels Talia and Jody will jeopardize his campaign.

Just when Talia tries to end things with the lovesick Jody, she finds out she's pregnant and must choose between satisfying Ben and her mother's best interests or being with the man she loves.

A Savior For Christmas

Because of his parents taking out a loan before they died in an accident, Zach will lose the family ranch to the bank if he doesn't come up with the money to repay.

Unfortunately, the only person who can help him is Mariah whom he embarrassed by leaving her at the altar a year earlier.

Mariah has never gotten over how Zach broke her heart and has wanted to confront him all this time. But the minute his dusty cowboy boots march into her office, Mariah's hit with a thunderbolt of emotions she's not prepared for.

On the flip side, seeing the love of his life again has Zach's heart doing cartwheels, and he's forced to face the mistake he made by letting her go.

The Best Christmas Ever

All hell's breaking loose in the Bible Belt.

After getting out of prison, 23-year-old LJ McCormick settles in Beluga, Georgia for a fresh start. That won't be easy thanks to Beluga's bible-thumping residents who have issues with LJ's past and him being an atheist. Everything the community doesn't like about LJ makes him irresistible to Ginger, the wild and flirtatious daughter of Reuben and Nola Ryder, the pastor and first lady of the church.

Sick of being seen as just the preacher's daughter, Ginger finds solace in LJ, and the two fall in love despite the obstacles in their way.

Meanwhile, 45-year-old Nola is desperate to get her marriage back on track but her world turns upside down when she meets Quinn Moretti, an ex-con with a heart of gold, who gives her the attention and passion she's not getting at home.

HAWAII CHRISTMAS BABY
CHAPTER ONE

"Mm." Thirty-five-year-old Talia Frank awoke snuggled in mystery man Jody's strong arms. "So I'm not dreaming?" she whispered.

"Hm?" Jody moved his hard body against her buttocks. "Morning, Beautiful." He turned her flat on her back and gave her another hungry kiss, reminding her of how he took her body the night before. "What did you say?"

She stared into his ocean-blue eyes. "I thought I was dreaming." She glanced around at the wicker furniture of his bedroom. "Last night and now this..." She rubbed his soft arm. "It can't be real."

"It is real." He planted kisses upon her naked breasts, and she loved seeing his plump, pink lips against her dark-brown skin.

"You swept me off my feet." She giggled. "One moment we're at a Christmas luau in downtown Hilo, and now we're in bed together. It was so magical. How our eyes locked amongst the glare of the red and green Christmas lights. I didn't wanna go in the first place, but I'm glad I did."

"I didn't even want to move to Hawaii." Jody propped up on his elbow, staring into her eyes. "Was sick to death of my dad begging me to, but if I'd known I was gonna meet you I'd have come the moment he asked." He kissed her again. "But I don't wanna talk about parents or anything else. Like last night, let's keep the conversation on us."

"I like that." She wiggled her legs under the cover. "I could stare into those beautiful blue eyes all day."

"And I could hold you in my arms forever." He held her, a hint of the grapefruit cocktail from last night still on his breath. "What's happening to us, Talia? I've never fell for a woman this way before. Contrary to what you might think, it's been hard for me to find the right woman."

"I'm supposed to believe that?" She pinched his cheek. "You're a gorgeous, charming billionaire, and you've lived all over the world. What woman in her right mind wouldn't want that?"

"That's the problem." He stuck his hand under the cover, caressing her. "Most of the women I've met are more interested in money but not me to go with it. This might sound cliché, but it's hard to find a woman who wants you for more than your money. I knew you were different."

She smiled.

"You didn't know I had money. All you saw was a guy at the luau and you danced with me." He closed his eyes, tangling his fingers within hers. "And holding you close felt so right, and I got afraid because I've never felt so strongly for a woman in all my life."

"You're thirty-seven. Surely you've been with at least *one* woman who wanted more than your money."

He kissed her nose. "You'd be surprised how many greedy women there are in the world."

"I understand resenting money." She stroked his smooth pecks. "I was raised by a single mother who thinks a life without money isn't worth living."

He wiggled his flat nose. "What happened to your father?"

"Your guess is as good as mine." She chuckled. "He left when I was six, and we never heard from him again."

"That's terrible." He shoved his fingers through her bushy, raven-black fro. "Sorry you had to go through that, sweetheart."

"But Momma and I didn't struggle a day, no," she mocked. "She had an image to maintain, and that was always her first priority." She rolled her eyes. "My mother is sixty-three and has never had a job because she's always found a man to support her."

He gaped.

"Not any man, rich men. She was blessed with good looks and sex appeal that stops men in their tracks—"

"Like her daughter?"

She half-smiled. "She has no commonsense, but she knows how to get a man." She waved her finger. "Oh yeah she could teach a class on getting wealthy men."

He bit his lip. "In other words, your mother is a gold digger?"

"She used to say she did it to support me and because she wanted me to have a great life but that was bullshit. She never wanted anyone to see her without a diamond on her hand or without Armani, Gucci, or Prada. I don't know why she's like this, but she is. And me..." She shook her head. "She loves to remind me how much of a screw-up I am."

Jody's mouth wrinkled. "Why on earth would she think that?"

"Because I don't live up to her expectations." Talia pulled the sheet over her breasts. "I don't care about money or status, and I'm not materialistic. Give me enough money to live on and I'm happy. Having more than what you need is just greed."

He lowered his head, pinching the pillow.

"No offense." She touched his chin. "People like Momma throw money away and don't even deserve it. She's gone through rich man after rich man and tries to tell me *I'm* in the wrong with *my* life." She poked her chest. "Who is she to criticize me when I work for everything I get?"

"My dad's the same way." He pulled at the tan sheet. "He planned my life out before I was born."

She stroked the curly ends of his short, honey-blond hair. "I only brought Momma up to show you I'm the last one who would be with someone for their money."

"I know that." He pushed his fleshy lips over hers. "I wish we could stay in bed forever." He lay his head on her chest, squishing her size-Cs. "Just listen to the water from the shore and the birds sing. How long have you been living in Hilo again?"

"Five years." She ran her fingers through his hair. "I moved from Philly and Momma followed when she found out about all the rich men who vacation in Hawaii yearly."

"*No.*" He raised his head, grinning. "You're making that up. She can't be *that* bad."

"She is. I'm telling you. Shit, she moved up here when she found out about all the billionaires who live here and low and behold, she hooks her one."

"Let's stop talking about her." He kissed her chest, causing her to shiver. "It's getting you upset. Let's enjoy this moment."

"I wish I could." She lifted her wrist, glancing at her gold watch. "But I gotta be at work in about thirty minutes."

"You said you're a make-up artist, right?" Jody lay his muscular arm over her, keeping her in place. "For that local talk show?"

"*Good Morning with Okalani,*" she boasted the title of the show, named after host Okalani Paoa.

Talia had little in her life but at least she loved her job.

"You'd be surprised how hectic it can get on set." She flung off the cover. "I love my job."

He grinned. "I can tell with how your eyes light up."

"Part of that's *you.*" She patted his head. "I was saying even though I love it, being with you makes me feel so good I might quit." She grinned.

"You *could.*" He guided his soft lips down her arm. "I'll take care of you."

"That's sweet." She laughed, snorting. "But, I don't need a man to take care of me."

"I want to." He thrust his lips over hers again. "Talia, all you'd have to do is ask, and I'd take care of you for the rest of your life."

She moaned as he sucked her shoulder. "Ooh boy, stop." She pushed him away, getting out the bed. "Shoot, I'm gonna be late. I gotta go to my place and freshen up first."

He stood. "Wait."

"There's no waiting, Jody." She got her white, cotton underwear and striped black and white summer dress off the wicker chair. "And stop looking at me." She slipped on her panties. "Something about those eyes makes me lose control. That's how we ended up in bed."

"Come on. You can take off from work." He held her from behind, and she melted in his arms. "Let me make you feel good all day long."

"Jody." She leaned back as he gripped her breasts, her nipples hardening. "I want to more than anything, but I gotta go." She moved from him and put on her bra.

"When can I see you again?" He dropped on the bed, lips poked out. "You haven't left yet and already I'm mad that you're gone."

"How about tonight around seven-thirty?" She slipped on her dress. "I'm having dinner with my mother and stepfather, and I can't stand being around them and watching them kiss and cuddle like teenagers." She grimaced. "They just got married, and it's sickening, but you could make the night less excruciating for me. Would you like to come?"

"I wish I could, but I got plans too." He sighed. "I'm meeting *my* dad's new wife for the first time tonight."

Talia slipped on leather flip-flops, loving that in Hawaii it stayed warm all year long. "Are you looking forward to meeting her?"

"Not really concerning the circumstances of them getting together."

"What do you mean?" She got her comb out of her purse.

"Never mind. I don't want to get into my family drama."

She stood at his mirror and doused *African Pride* hair conditioner on her fro. "I have a feeling you're enjoying Hawaii it so far." She smirked, picking her hair with the comb.

He jumped and grabbed her. "I'm not letting you leave." He nibbled the back of her neck. "I forbid it."

"Just look at it this way." She got her earrings off the dresser. "The faster you let me leave, the sooner you get to see me again."

"Ah, man." He slumped back to the bed, sighing. "You're torturing me here."

"Trust me." She smoothed her hands over her curvy hips. "If I could stay here forever I would."

CHAPTER TWO

"Ooh, girl. You tramp!" As soon as Talia got into the television studio, her best friend of five years, Vincent aka V, pulled her into the door and led her to the make-up area. "Spill it, child." The chunky, gay Hawaiian sat on the stool and crossed his legs.

He always wore loud, floral shirts and khaki shorts. For someone who'd crowned himself the "Diva of Hilo", he had horrible fashion sense.

"Come on now. I want the T." He wiggled his neck, sticking his lips out as if he'd sucked a lemon.

"And I'd like you to stop acting like you're on *Housewives of Atlanta* for once in your life." Talia secured her purse in the locker in the back of the room. "The show starts in an hour and we gotta get Okalani's guests dolled up. Lord knows she'll have a conniption if the guests' make-up isn't right."

"Who cares?" V flicked his hand, cheeks glimmering under heaps of concealer. "Stop avoiding the issue. All night I wondered how things were going with you and that fine, tall hunk of man you left the luau with."

Talia smiled, thinking of how delicious Jody looked naked let alone in his suit.

"I'm your best friend, am I not?" V batted his thick, fake eyelashes. "How you gonna leave with that gorgeous vanilla bean and not even call me all night?"

"I didn't have time to call you." Talia smirked, sitting on the stool. "A sista was kinda busy."

V leapt out of the chair, grabbing her with those hefty hands. "You slept with him?"

Talia blew on her fingernails. "I can't say either of us *slept*."

V squealed, stomping around in a circle. "I can't believe you did that."

9

"Me either."

"You slept with a man on the first date?" V slid on the stool, tapping Talia's knee. "I want the details."

"It was like a dream." Talia leaned back, laughing. "Our eyes locked, we danced, and then—"

"What?"

"We walked along the beach and talked for hours." Talia wondered if she had that silly, dazed expression women in love got. "He's so charming and sweet. He cares about what I have to say and he pays attention. Men rarely pay attention to what women say."

V stuck his angular nose in the air. "Maybe he was just trying to get some."

"I thought about that too but something told me he cared."

"But how did you get from the luau to bed?"

"He asked me to go to his place." She shrugged, crossing her leg. "Now, you know I don't go off with strange men, but I was in a trance or something. It was like I couldn't control anything I did." Talia exhaled. "Something about his eyes. All I do is look in them and I'm helpless."

"He did have beautiful blue eyes." V moaned as if he'd orgasmed. "Get to the loving." He snapped his fingers. "How was he in the sack?"

Talia straightened up, acting prissy. "A lady doesn't kiss and tell."

"Girl, don't play with me. He looks like he could fuck the hell out somebody. Can he?"

"And then some." Talia laughed.

"Oh!" V sat up straight. "I hate you. Why couldn't he be gay and into sexy, plus-sized men like me?"

"Guess you'll have to get your own."

"What kind of lover is he?" V's eyes widened as if he were eating his favorite, cherry-filled donuts. "Is he patient and slow or rough and greedy in the bed?"

"He was amazing." Talia fanned, still getting hot flashes from the moves Jody had put on her. "You know how you're nervous the first time with someone?"

V nodded.

"Well, I wasn't nervous at all. It seemed like the most natural thing in the world."

"Talia." V covered his mouth. "You're in love with him, aren't you?"

Talia felt her warm cheek. "He's hooked me, but I'm not sprung now." She stuck her index finger in the air. "Don't get it twisted."

"Hm." V looked her up and down.

"What I can't believe is he wants *me*." Talia gazed at herself in the mirror. "Me with a billionaire." She shook her head. "I can't believe it. Why would he want me?"

"You better stop downing yourself like that." V patted Talia's fro. "You're the prize and don't forget it. Now call him and ask him if he has a rich, single friend, heifer."

Talia laughed then shrieked.

"What's wrong?"

"I don't know his number." She turned left and right. "Hell, I don't even know his last name!"

"What?"

Talia cringed. "I don't remember if I told him mine either."

"Wait, a minute." V squinted. "You guys had sex but didn't exchange last names or numbers?"

"He knows where I work though." Talia gripped her head. "How could I be so stupid? What if I never see him again?"

"If the sex was as good for him as it was for you, trust me, he'll come calling."

"What is wrong with me, V? I had sex with a man, and I don't even know his last name." She groaned. "I don't do shit like this."

"Maybe it's time you did."

Okalani charged through the hall, parking her wide-hips in the doorway. "Well." She had her chin stuck so far in the air it almost touched the ceiling. "Back here gossiping when you should be working?" The ends of her sentences always reached a higher pitch due to her Hawaiian accent.

"None of the guests are here yet," Talia said. "The show doesn't start until nine."

"Maybe you both should put in some extra practice before they get here." Okalani straightened her white blazer, but it kept riding up over her hips. "V, you put so much powder on my last guest's face he looked like the Pillsbury Dough Boy. What kind of make-up artist are you?"

"Excuse me?" V scoffed. "Honey I worked in Hollywood for years and have a list of references to prove it. I was Brookee Shield's make-up artist."

Talia rolled her eyes hoping they could go one day without V bringing up how he worked on *Suddenly Susan* for three episodes.

"Must we hear about Brooke Shields every day?" Okalani threw up her arms. "You did the extras' make-up. You didn't get nowhere near Brooke Shields."

"That's a lie." V's bronze face got redder. "Call Brooke and she'll tell you I was the best."

"And that show's been off the air how many years?" Okalani asked. "You haven't done nothing worth mentioning since. If you were so great how come you're no longer in Hollywood?"

V. crossed his arms, huffing.

"This is *my* show," Okalani said. "Everything about it reflects on me, and I can't have my guests looking crazy." She rattled off, cursing in Hawaiian, then focused on Talia.

"Did you get my text last night?"

"Nope." Talia glanced at V who grinned. "I was busy."

Okalani said, "I want an exclusive about Ben running for mayor. It's the biggest story going on in Hilo right now."

"I'll run it by him again." Talia faked a smile. "Beyond that I can't make any promises."

"I have to get him on the show." Okalani stomped her feet with balled fists. "The producer's been on my ass for months. We've lost a chunk of our viewers. The ratings got to get better or we'll all be out of a job."

"Honey, I'll always have me a job." V looked through his make-up kit.

"Okalani, chill," Talia said. "I'll ask Ben about it tonight when I see him for dinner, okay?"

Okalani snarled and walked away.

"Heaven's sake." V smacked his lips. "Would someone please tell her to stop squeezing that size twenty-two body into those size sixteen suits?"

"To tell you the truth, I never even talked to Ben about him being on the show. How am I'm gonna get through dinner with him and Momma tonight? I can't stand his ass."

V pulled out tubes of eyeliner.

"He cheated on his wife with Momma so how can she expect him to be faithful?"

"You know Daphne." V's arched eyebrow rose higher. "As long as he got the green I'm sure she's happy."

CHAPTER THREE

"So?" Ben McCall took off his shades, glancing around. "Haven't decorated for Christmas yet?" He walked under the wood-trimmed ceiling of the sitting room in Jody's beachside mansion. "I'm surprised seeing how it's your favorite holiday."

Jody sat on the wicker couch filled with fluffy, white pillows.

"Remember those Christmases in Aspen?" Ben's fat cheeks spread as he smiled. "Us on the sky slopes? We had so much fun in those days." He sighed. "What happened to us, son?"

"It's just us now, Dad." Jody clasped his hands, sighing. "We don't have to pretend, do we? No one is here to witness your act."

"It's not an act, son." Ben sat in the chair beside the little, round table. The sunlight from the curtains bounced against his big, bald head. "I want nothing more than for us to make amends and let all the animosity go."

"And you think that could happen?" Jody grabbed his lukewarm can of soda and sipped. "There was a time I could talk to you but that was a long time ago."

"I don't understand why you resent our good fortune. Any other son would be happy to have the money we have and you act like something's wrong with it. Do you know how lucky you are?"

He sighed. "I'm sure you'll remind me."

"I did something extraordinary, and it made us a lot of money. It's helped you become the man you are now, and its allowed you to live all over the world. Why do you hate me becoming rich?"

"Please. I don't hate you because you invented some weight loss pill in the eighties and became rich." Jody scoffed. "I don't hate you, but I don't *like* you anymore because since you've gotten rich, that's all you care about."

"No, it's not."

"You ignored me for my whole childhood because you were too concerned with your 'new' money."

"That's not true."

"Dad, our relationship is so fucked up I preferred to travel the world for the last two decades instead of being around you."

Ben sat back with a stunned expression.

"But have you cared about that? You never once reached out to make amends but now you want to because you're running for mayor. Just admit it."

"That's not true, Joseph. I love you and I want you in my life."

Jody grumbled. "I hate it when you call me 'Joseph.'"

"It's your name. Besides, I've always hated that nickname 'Jody.'" Ben grimaced. "I've never gotten used to it even when you were a kid. I can't do anything right where you're concerned. Why are you so bitter?"

"And why are you so damn selfish?" Jody scooted to the edge of the couch. "You only care about you and what you want."

"I asked you to move to Hilo to start over." Ben sighed. "It's been over twenty years we've been like this and I'm tired of it. Aren't you? I want us to be like we were before the money. I love you more than anything."

"Didn't you use to say that to Mom?" Jody scratched his head. "And then you cheat on her and leave her for some woman you barely know?"

"I didn't come here for this." Ben stood, grabbing his shades. "You think everyone ought to be perfect like you think you are."

"No, I expect my father to be more than a lying, manipulative cheater."

Ben inhaled. "I've said a million times to you and Michelle that I was sorry for how things turned out."

"Sorry?" Jody stood, shaking his head. "How can you be sorry for cheating on a woman you were married to for over thirty years then leaving her for the first slut that came along?"

"Stop it." Ben shook his finger in Jody's face. "You've never even met Daphne. You wouldn't come to the wedding."

"Are you surprised?" Jody yelled. "I'm supposed to come to your wedding when you cheated on my mother?"

"What do you want from me?"

"I want you to be a better father and better person." Jody clenched fists. "Until then I can't see us being any closer than we are right now."

"Tell me something then." Ben propped his shades on top of his head. "Why did you move here if you hate me so much?"

"Because you're my father and it meant a lot to you for me to come."

Ben's face relaxed.

"That's the difference between you and me, Dad. I'm not selfish. I do things for others before I do them for myself. I want a relationship with you but not if you continue to play games."

"Okay, a part of me wanted you here for the image of it." Ben touched Jody's arm. "But that doesn't change how much I love you and how much I want us to get past this. Tonight will be a beginning for us. I know Daphne and I caused you and your mother pain, but we fell in love before we realized it. You ever experience a love so strong that it withstands all doubt and even sense?"

"Yeah." Jody remembered how soft Talia's lips felt against his. "I have."

"It's not an excuse for what I did, and I'm sorry. I loved your mother, but we'd grown apart before Daphne came into my life. Please don't take what I did out on her. She's been so excited to meet you."

Jody held his arms behind his back. "Not sure I'll be up to it."

"Her daughter's gonna be there. She's not too happy about us being married either so maybe you two will hit it off." Ben chuckled. "I might not deserve your compassion, but will you please try to be open-minded tonight? If you don't want to ever have dinner with us again, then you don't have to."

"I said I'm coming and I'll come." Jody slipped his hands in the pockets of his shorts. "Unlike you *my* word means something."

CHAPTER FOUR

"Talia, I don't get why you're always so defensive when I try to help you out." That night, Daphne McCall dipped her spoon into the huge pot of beef stew and tasted it. "You're my daughter, and I only want what's best for you."

"No, you want me to choose a life and career *you* want me to have." Talia got the bowls and plates from the cabinet, humming to "Deck the Halls," playing from the living room. "I'm sick of this conversation every time we get together, Momma."

V got the tray of green and red Christmas cookies off the table. "Let's not argue all right, ladies?"

"Who's arguing?" Daphne twisted toward the food cabinet with her flimsy, summer dress that left nothing to anyone's imagination.

Talia couldn't blame her mother for her revealing style of dress though. If she'd spent thousands on bigger breasts, curvier hips, and a Brazilian butt lift, she'd show it off too.

"I've never been able to talk to Talia without her getting all up and arms for nothing," Daphne stated with her long, Eurasian weave sweeping her back.

"Bullshit, Momma." Talia slammed a plate on the counter. "Bull...shit."

"Talia." V grabbed her by the shoulders. "Don't get upset," he whispered. "Just try to get through this evening."

"If you want to waste your life away..." Daphne pointed the long, stiletto nail of her index finger at Talia, diamonds dripping from three out of five fingers on her right hand. "Go right ahead, but is it a bad thing for me to want more for my daughter after all the sacrificing I've done for you?"

"Sacrificing?" Talia almost dropped one of the bowls. "What sacrifices? Chasing men for money?"

"Talia," V said, his mouth full of green and red cookie mush.

"Look, I admit I care about money," Daphne said. "But who doesn't? People need money to survive, Talia. I wish you'd get off that pedestal you live on. If it weren't for me chasing rich men, where would you be?"

Talia rolled her eyes as she rinsed out the bowls and plates.

"You wouldn't have been able to go to those private schools, lived in the beautiful homes we've lived in, and had everything you wanted by just asking."

"Momma—"

"I'm talking now so listen." Daphne frowned. "Would you rather have been on welfare and food stamps? Me going from dead end job to dead end job? What the hell is so wrong with me wanting you to be the best and have the best? I don't get why you chose a career that's not up to your standards."

V glared at Daphne, obviously taking Daphne's opinion of Talia's career personally.

"Okay, that's it." Talia felt her forehead, sighing. "You can think all you want about me but you're disrespecting V now too."

"No offense, Vincent," Daphne said.

He shrugged, licking cookie crumbs from his fingers.

"Get this through your head, Momma." Talia walked toward Daphne, pointing. "I love my career. Being a make-up artist makes me happier than anything, and I won't apologize for that."

"What about the rest of your life? When are you getting married and having kids?"

Talia held her breath. "Whenever *I'm* ready to."

The doorbell rang.

"My son's here," Ben called from the other room.

"See, your new stepbrother is here now." Daphne straightened Talia's teal halter dress, which flowed at the bottom. "Honey, I love you. I might not love you the way you want me to, but I do. Will you ever see that?"

Talia sighed, not knowing what to say.

****

"Come on in, son." Ben pulled Jody into the front hallway of the luxury, oceanfront home with the travertine exterior.

Jody followed his father into the living room in awe of the bright color choices and retro décor. "Where are your servants?"

"Gave them the night off." A beaming Ben stood in the middle of the hardwood floor in black flip-flops. "I wanted tonight to be for family. What do you think of the place? It might not be your style, but Daphne has quite a flare for decoration." He pointed to the regal, iron statues and gaudy, tie-dye curtains.

"Uh..." Jody glanced around the room, littered with red Christmas garland and African art.

"I'm so glad you're here, son." Ben gave him a strangling bear hug. "You don't know how much it means you came."

Jody backed away from Ben, not in the mood for the mushiness. "It's fine, Dad."

An aroma of coconut erupted from the candles on the table beside the poinsettias.

"So where is Daphne and her daughter?" Jody asked.

"Getting dinner ready. Sit down and relax." Ben showed Jody to the couch, alive with red and white Santa pillows. "Daphne is definitely high maintenance, but she's quite the little homemaker too." He giggled, his large belly wobbling. "Aren't these cute?" He grabbed a Santa pillow. "She picked them out."

"No comment." Jody tossed the tacky pillow aside and sat.

"When did you get to be such a scrooge?" Ben smacked his lips. "I'll go check on everything. And remember to keep an open mind, okay?"

"Sure." Jody shot his thumb up in a nonchalant manner. "Looking forward to it," he lied.

CHAPTER FIVE

Ben dashed into the kitchen, grabbing Daphne's hand. "Joseph's here." He kissed her cheek. "I can't wait for you two to meet."

Talia cut her eyes to V who'd eaten half the cookies.

"Look at you." Daphne patted Ben's chubby cheek. "Proud Papa, huh?"

"I want nothing more than for us to be a family." He picked her up and swung her. "Come on and let's eat." He left the kitchen.

Daphne glared at Talia, clutching her pronounced hip.

"What?" Talia sighed. "There's no problem here."

"Look at your body language." Daphne grimaced. "Can't you pretend you're looking forward to meeting his son?"

"I'm here, aren't I?"

"Talia," V said. "Come on, chill."

She lifted her hands. "What more can I do?"

"Come say hi to his son and then we can eat." Daphne left.

"If Momma starts anything else tonight, I swear—"

"It's okay." V massaged Talia's shoulders. "Breathe and everything will be fine. You can get through this. Come on. You gotta be eager to meet his son."

"I could think of a million other things I'd rather be doing."

Like turning summersaults under the sheets with Jody.

Talia and V went down the hall.

"Talia," Ben said when she and V got to the living room doorway. "I'd like you to meet my son." He pointed to the handsome man in the frost-gray suit who appeared as surprised as she felt. "Joseph McCall."

"Holy...." Talia stumbled back as Jody got up from the couch with his mouth open.

"Uh-oh," V whispered.

"Talia?" Jody looked at his father then back at Talia.

21

Talia looked at Daphne who gaped at Talia as if someone farted. "What the hell are you doing here, Jody?"

"Me?" He gestured toward her, cheeks blushing red.

"Wait," Ben said. "You two know each other?"

"This is Joseph?" Talia covered her mouth, pointing at Jody. "You said your name was 'Jody'."

"It's my nickname." Jody swept his hand over his stunned face. "My god."

"This can't be happening." Talia's stomach turned. "I'm gonna be sick." She ran out the living room with Daphne screaming for her.

Talia burst out the house and ran into the yard, stooping beside the six-foot tall Christmas angel covered in lights.

V ran off the porch steps and joined her in the grass. "Girl, don't throw up on the Christmas angel."

Talia stood straight, fighting her swirling stomach.

"What the hell is Vanilla Bean doing here?" He waved his hands in a feminine fashion. "Might I add how good he looks in that suit? Ooh. It should be against the law for a man to be that fine."

"Did that just happen?" Talia shrieked. "Is Jody really in there?"

"Yep and he's Ben's son."

"How could this be fuckin' possible?" Talia tugged on V's shirt. "What is the chance that the guy I'd fall head over heels for would be my new stepbrother? V, it's obscene."

"I don't see the problem to be honest."

"How can you not?"

"So what if he's your stepbrother?" He looked at his manicured fingernails. "You're not related."

"It's not right." Talia pushed out her bosom. "Jody and I can't be carrying on being brother and sister. This is fucked up on so many levels." She struggled to find the resemblance between Jody and Ben. "Man, I anticipated tonight to be a surprise, but I had no idea."

"Let me ask you something. What if you'd found this out before sleeping with Jody? Would it have changed anything? Stepbrother or not you're into Jody. I've never seen you this crazy over a man since I've known you."

She grabbed V's meaty arms. "There is no way Jody and I can continue seeing each other."

"Everyone in that room saw how you two looked at each other." V pointed toward the house. "You can't fight your attraction to Jody and he won't be able to fight his for you."

"We have to if we intend to stay sane. Jody knows we can't be together now." Talia twisted and turned. "That's it. It's over. No negotiation."

"What's the big deal about dating your stepbrother?" V put his hand on his hip. "Shoot, I got *blood* cousins who are fucking so—"

"Is everything a joke to you?"

"You're a grown woman, Talia. It's your decision who you date."

"And I'm deciding to break it off," she shouted. "I'm not down with this. Besides, I don't wanna hear from Momma that this is just another way I've screwed up. She'd love to tear into me if she found out I slept with Jody."

"What if Jody tells them what happened? Isn't it better to be honest?"

"Trust me, he won't tell." Talia massaged her fro. "He looked about as sick as I am."

Jody walked out. "Talia, we need to talk."

"Let me leave you two alone." V started toward the house then stopped beside Jody. "Mm."

Jody pulled on his blazer, fidgeting. "Is there a problem?"

"Nope." V walked past, checking out Jody's ass.

"Jody, this is horrible." Talia flung her arms. "How can this be happening?"

"Calm down." He held her. "It's all right."

"It's not all right. We slept together."

"I remember." He grinned. "I was there."

"This isn't funny." She pushed him. "This is horrible. It's horrible, Jody!"

"Come here." He hugged her. "It's not horrible. It's a peculiar situation, and I'm as shocked as you are, but it is what it is."

"And what is it?"

"Talia, I care about you and last night was the best night of my life."

She touched the collar of his shirt. "Mine too but—"

"I don't want it to end."

"We can't see each other, Jody. It's just not right."

He kissed her cheek. "I'm not ready to let go of how good you make me feel. I know it's only been one night, but my heart won't let me walk away."

"We can't do this." She turned away from him for fear of losing herself in his eyes. "No way would this work."

"They don't know what went on. I played it off." He swung her around, touching her cheek. "Listen. We can be together, and they don't have to know."

"I don't wanna lie or sneak around. Don't we deserve more than that?"

"I'm willing to do anything for us to be together." He stood back, hands out and palms facing her. "Besides, we won't be able to stay away from each other even if we tried. My dad is just a few feet away and all I can think about is ravishing you right here in this grass."

She chuckled then remembered the severity of the moment. "We gotta be sensible about this, Jody."

"Do we?" He tried to kiss her.

She put her finger on his lips. "We can't do this."

He pulled her toward him. "Hold that thought until after we kiss."

"Jody..."

He pushed his lips against hers.

CHAPTER SIX

Daphne, Ben and V sat in the dining room eating when Jody and Talia returned.

"Um, here you go." Jody held Talia's chair out for her and sat beside her.

Daphne glanced at Ben from the corner of her eyes, sipping stew. "You two wanna tell us what's going on?"

Ben stared at them, clearing his throat.

"Um..." Talia gestured to the empty space in front of her. "Looks like Jody and I aren't eating tonight." She joked. "I'll go fix our plates."

"No." Jody stood. "You don't need to wait on me. I'll do it."

"You don't even know where the kitchen is." Ben chewed. "Sit down."

"I'll find it."

"Sit." Ben winced as he swallowed stew.

Jody sat.

"What's going on between you two?" Daphne asked.

"Okay, we've met before," Talia said.

"You're *kidding*." Ben glared. "How did you two meet?"

"Last night at the Christmas luau downtown." Talia placed her shivering hands in her lap. "We struck up a conversation, and that was it." She avoided looking at her mother.

"You never could look me in the face when you were lying," Daphne said.

"Uh-oh," V whispered.

"You two must think Ben and I fell off the turnip truck if you expect us to believe you just talked and nothing else."

"I don't care what you believe, Daphne," Jody said. "From what Talia says you've never cared much about her, anyway. Instead of accusing her of something when she's done nothing wrong, maybe you should try being a little more sensitive to her feelings."

Daphne gasped.

"What did you say?" Ben pointed his spoon at Jody. "You watch your mouth when you're talking to Daphne. This is our house and you will respect her."

Jody wiggled in the chair, smirking. "Funny to say since you didn't respect my mother."

V's bottom lip flopped open.

"Joseph." Ben clenched teeth. "We're not gonna turn tonight into some fiasco."

"Why not, Dad?" He laughed. "It is a fiasco. This entire thing is a farce. We'll never be a family and stop pretending you want us to be. You want us to get along for the media. Well, unlike you I can't pretend things are fine when they're not."

"Jody, I understand you might not like me," Daphne said. "And honey I wouldn't blame you for that. But no one set out to hurt your mother." She touched Ben's hand. "Your father and I fell in love and people can't control their hearts."

"Love." Jody scoffed, looking at Talia. "Yeah, I know what love is, but I'm not so sure that's what you two have."

"That's enough." Ben stood. "You can say whatever you want about me but you won't mistreat my wife like this. Take what we did out on me. I was the one who broke my vows to your mother."

"Yeah but Daphne didn't dissuade you, did she?" Jody spat. "No her plan was to rope you in, right, Talia?"

Oh, shit.

Talia's stomach cramped. "Uh—"

"Excuse me?" Daphne stood, glaring at Talia. "Is that what you told him? How dare you, Talia?"

"Don't blame Talia for anything. She's not the reason this so-called family is a mess." Jody stood, slamming his chair under the table. "I can't speak for Talia but no matter what happens, I'll never accept this marriage." He left the room.

"Joseph," Ben shouted.

"You and I have to talk, young lady." Daphne wiggled her finger at Talia.

"Not now." Talia ran out the room and caught up with Jody outside as he walked to his black Porsche. "Jody, wait!"

"I'm sorry." He got his keys from his pocket. "I had no right to talk to your mother like that, but Talia I can't stand bullshit. How are we supposed to sit there and pretend everything is okay when it's not? Shit, you're worrying about how they felt if they knew about us, we're the ones *they* should worry about."

She followed him around to the driver's side of the car. "I'm not angry about what you said to my mother."

He opened the door. "What?"

"I'm flattered. No one has ever stood up for me like that before, not to my mother." She became warm all over. "It proves how much you care."

"I do care." He slipped his arms around her waist. "You're so sweet and understanding. It's hard to believe someone as kind as you came from someone like Daphne."

"She's not that bad. She's still my mother and I love her. Don't you love your dad?"

He glanced at the house. "Sometimes I wonder."

"Jody."

"I love him, but I don't like him. If I hadn't met you I'd pack up and leave Hilo tonight because I'm fed up."

"I don't want you to get upset." She touched his silky hair.

"I need you tonight," he whispered. "I'm gonna burst in two if I gotta wait much longer. Being so close to you, smelling your perfume, and seeing your lips and not being able to kiss you is killing me. You gotta come to my place." He moved his lips close to hers until they almost touched.

"No." She closed her eyes, fighting the fire raging inside of her.

"You'll come." He grinned in between kissing her. "I can tell you're wet right now." He touched the front of her dress.

"Stop." She swatted his hand away.

"We want each other. Is that so wrong?"

She sighed. "A part of me thinks it is."

"You'll come." He kissed her again. "And then I'll make *you* come again, and again, and again." He got in the car and started it up.

"Talia?" Daphne stood on the porch. "Get your ass back in here. I mean it, girl."

"My place, Talia." Jody roared the engine. "And don't make me wait." He zoomed down the sandy street.

"Girl, what is the matter with you?" Daphne ran off the porch and flung Talia around to face her. "I know something's going on between you and Jody. It's obvious in the way you look at him."

"We're friends." Talia headed toward the house.

"Don't walk away when I'm talking to you."

Talia continued up the porch steps.

"If something is going on between you two, then I tell you it better end right now! He's your stepbrother and you're not making me look a fool carrying on like this."

Talia turned around when she reached the door. "Is everything always about you, Momma? Huh? When is my life going to be about me?"

"This is wrong." Daphne flounced toward the porch in her flip-flops. "And you know damn well it is."

"You mean like screwing a married man is wrong?"

Talia went inside, slamming the door.

CHAPTER SEVEN

Shirtless and in silk pajama bottoms, Jody opened the door to Talia a few hours later.

She had that same conning glint in her beautiful brown eyes she had when he brought her to his bedroom the night before.

"You are so beautiful." He stood aside for her to enter.

She slipped off her dress, giving him a kiss that made him tingle down to his bare toes.

"Hm." He moved his mouth from hers, their lips smacking. "I knew you'd come."

"I wasn't going to." She kissed him and each time her tongue tangled within his, his dick got harder. "I was at home lying in my bed and all I could think about was you." She pulled off his pajama bottoms and shorts. "And how much I want you inside of me. How much I need it." She removed her panties then undid her bra. "I don't know what's wrong with me."

"What do you mean?" He inhaled the mandarin aroma of her perfume.

"This is wrong." She threw her bra to the side, pressing her breasts against his pounding chest. "But right now I don't care." She chewed her bottom lip. "I'll probably care in the morning." She massaged his rod. "But right now all I care about is you fucking me like I've never been fucked before."

"That's what you want, huh?" He picked her up by her buttocks and slammed her against the dresser. "This is what you want?"

"Yes." She wrapped her legs around him. "I want all of you, Jody. Don't hold back."

"I won't." Jody got the condom out the dresser and slipped it on himself. He grabbed her by the neck and slid his dick inside of her, rough yet tender.

"Don't stop," she commanded with her head rocking back and forth. "You feel so good. Ooh. I want you so much, Jody."

Her throat rippled underneath his hand as she let out a screeching moan that pierced his ears.

"Not half as much as I want you." He paused making love to her and shoved everything off his dresser in one swipe.

Cologne and hair conditioner bottles rolled around on the floor. He laid her on the dresser and climbed on top of her.

"Yes," she begged. "Please yes."

He hoisted her legs high, resting her ankles on his shoulders. He rode her, the dresser dancing to their rhythm. "Right there." Her walls tightened around his cock. "Oh."

She spread her arms out, her tits bouncing. "Yes, Jody." She grabbed his waist. "Deeper."

"Ugh." He got a cramp in the back of his leg but refused to stop. "I'm gonna nut." A drop of sweat beaded up on his nose.

She raised her ass off the dresser. "Come on."

"I..." He leaned back, holding her legs by the ankles. "God." He flooded the rubber.

"Uh." She shivered, jerking. "Yes." She lay back, sweat running between her breasts. "I'm coming too."

"Ah, fuck."

"Wait." She moaned and did that cute little growl she had last night when she came. "Almost...oh!" Her eyes got wide. "I'm coming."

"I can feel it." He pumped faster, urging her. "Come on."

"Ah," she shrieked, her pussy soaking the condom.

"Whoa." He lay his head on her stomach. "Baby."

"Oh." She panted, rubbing his hair. "God."

****

"When's your next vacation from work?" Jody played with Talia's fingers as she lay with her leg on top of him in bed. "I want to take you on my yacht."

"I'd love that." She pinched his chin. "I guess all rich people have yachts, huh?"

"One of my favorite places in the world is Cancun. I love the weather, the food, and the people."

"I've never been to Mexico." She stroked the hair above his crotch. "I've been on plenty of yachts though."

"Really?"

"I told you my mother only dated rich guys. One guy took us on his yacht in Aruba."

"Aruba?" He stretched his fingers within her fro.

"Yeah and another took us on his yacht in Venice." She moved off him and lay flat, staring at the ceiling. "Another took us on his yacht in Madrid."

"Wow." He chuckled, but it stung to know she'd been to so many places when he'd hoped to astonish her. "And here I was thinking I'd impress you."

"Honey, you don't need a yacht to impress me." She wiggled her toes against his hairy leg. "You could be broke as a joke, and I'd still be here lying next to you."

He smiled.

"I loved how you stood up for me at dinner." She leaned up on her elbows.

His eyes went straight to her brown areolas. "I'll always stand up for you. Daphne should be glad she has such a great daughter like you."

"Ben should be glad he has such a great son too. Now we know who we are, I wanted to say I'm sorry."

"For what?" He slipped his arm around her sweaty waist.

"For your dad and my mother's affair. Jody, I was as mad as you were when I found out. She lied and told me they didn't date until he and your mother separated."

"They never separated. Everything was fine between them or at least Mom thought until Dad broke her heart."

"I've been in this world for thirty-five years." Talia flicked a bead of sweat off her face. "I'll ever understand why my mother is the way she is."

"To hell with both of them." He kissed her shoulder. "We can't let their bad decisions or their opinions affect us anymore."

"It's easier said than done." She wrapped his comforting arms around her.

"Not for me it isn't." He kissed her forehead.

"I don't want things to get worse between you and Ben." She examined his smooth hands. "I wouldn't want him to blame you for jeopardizing his election chances."

"He has no business running for mayor, anyway. The man has never served a day in politics all his life. What makes him think he could run this city?"

"Many people around here respect your father."

"I bet that makes his day." He got on top of her. "I could look into your eyes for the rest of my life."

"I could do the same." She raised her head, meeting his lips. "You're so handsome."

He raised a golden eyebrow. "Am I a good lover?"

"You're a fantastic lover." She put her arms around his shoulders. "There isn't a word to describe it. What about me?"

"Does this answer your question?" He rubbed his stiffness against her.

"Again?" She laughed. "We've already done it three times. You can't have anything left."

"I could never get enough of you." He sucked her neck. "Come on and open up for Daddy."

"Daddy?" She laughed so hard that she snorted. "Oh."

"I never thought a snort could sound so sexy."

"Sorry." She giggled, covering her mouth. "Another reason I'm not perfect."

"But you are." He wrapped her legs around him. "You're more than perfect."

CHAPTER EIGHT

The next day at work, someone tapped Talia's shoulder as she dug through her make-up kit.

Ben smiled, his white teeth bright as the sun.

"Ben." Talia straightened herself on the stool. "What are you doing here?"

"What? I can't visit my daughter?" He raised his hand to pat her fro.

She jerked. "Why you always like touching my hair?"

"It's so soft." He moved his hand away, wiggling his fingers. "That's Black Woman Rule Number One to hear your mother tell it." He snickered. "Keep your hands off the hair."

She glared. "Oh, I don't mind people touching my hair."

He sighed. "Just not me, huh?"

"Why are you here?"

"I was hoping to bridge this gap between us but that's not happening so I wanted to give you a warning about Jody."

She crossed her legs. "What are you talking about?"

"I love my son, and he's a wonderful person. But, he's a man, and he has his weaknesses. Jody's weakness is a weakness most men have, women."

"What are you trying to say?"

"I'm your father now." He rubbed her arm. "It's my job to protect you from getting hurt. I know it's hard for you to trust men. That's probably because your daddy ran off."

She looked away, exhaling.

"Don't let loneliness suck you into a bad situation. You're a beautiful, talented woman. You don't need to settle."

She jumped off the stool. "For the last damn time, spit it out."

"Jody changes women like most people change underwear."

"What?"

"He doesn't keep one around long and when he is seeing one you can bet he's seeing a lot more."

"That doesn't sound like Jody at all."

"With all due respect, you barely know him." He sighed, staring into her eyes. "You don't think he has women waiting for him all over the world? Did he claim it's hard for him to find a woman who cares about him for more than his money?" He shook his head. "The truth is one woman couldn't ever satisfy him."

She sat, contemplating. "If that's true then the apple doesn't fall far from the tree."

"At least I don't act like I'm perfect like Joseph." He put on his shades. "I'll see you—"

"Mr. McCall!" Okalani waddled up to Ben in another tight-ass blazer and skirt. "How are you?" She gave him a special greeting in Hawaii.

"It's nice to see you again, Okalani. Merry Christmas."

"Merry Christmas to you too. This is a pleasant surprise. Has Talia told you I've been trying to get you on the show?" Okalani grabbed Ben's hand. "You running for mayor is the biggest thing we got in this town, and I'm dying for an exclusive interview."

"Not sure about that, Okalani." Ben chuckled, removing his shades. "I've seen your show. You like to muddy the waters sort to speak." He winked. "You have a habit of twisting words around."

"Oh no, no, no." Okalani slipped her arm in Ben's arm. "I'd never do something like that to you. I respect you. In fact, I'll let you review the questions before we go on the air." Her chubby cheeks rose. "Is it a deal?"

"Well, if I'm gonna be in politics I'd better get used to these interviews, right?" He nodded. "I'll do it."

"Thank you!" Okalani hugged him. "Come on and let me get you scheduled. Bye, Talia."

"Bye," Talia mumbled as Okalani whisked Ben away.

Her cell phone rang, and she checked the little screen.

Jody

She rejected the call and laid her phone on the table. "How could I be so stupid?"

V walked into the room eating a bag of Cheetos. "Okay what's wrong now?" He waved his orange finger. "Did you and Ben get into it or something?"

"Jody's a snake." Talia tugged on her silver, hoop earring. "I'm the biggest idiot in the world. I kept saying, 'Why would a man like Jody want someone like me when he could have anyone?' He's a rat, V. He's just like all these other dogs around here."

"What are you talking about?" He ate another chip.

"He wanted some ass, and I played right into it." Talia got off the stool, fixing her dress in the back. "And I would never sleep with a man on the first date, but I did it with him like a dumb ass." She cleaned up her make-up station. "I never wanna see him again."

"I don't understand what the hell's going on." V smacked as he chewed. "It can't be that bad."

"Oh, it is that bad." Talia closed her make-up kit. "From this point on Jody and I are done for good."

****

Talia stood at her living room window the next evening watching Jody hop out of his Porsche looking fine as ever, but she didn't give a damn. Even his sexy eyes, firm ass, and powerful lips couldn't get him out this.

"Talia?" He knocked on the door. "Come on. Let me in."

She wanted to grab the lamp off the end table and smack him with it. "Why should I?"

"What's going on? I called and texted you all day yesterday and you didn't get back to me once."

"What does that tell you? Obviously, I don't wanna be bothered."

"Why are you acting this way? What did I do?"

She opened the door, the red bells of the wreath jingling to a poetic tune. "You're some piece of work. You know that?"

"What the hell you talking about?"

She grew faint, hit with his mesmerizing cologne, which smelled like dark chocolate and cinnamon. "You thought I was a fool, and I admit I acted like one, but I'll never give you the chance to use me again. I'm over it." She tried to close the door.

He held it open. "I don't even know what this is about."

"I'm talking about what Ben told me yesterday at my job."

"My father was at your job?" He scowled. "Why?"

"He told me about your stable of women and how you're the one who can't commit to them. He told me how you've been telling me the same recycled bullshit you tell every woman to get her into bed. You go after a woman then once you've used her to death, you don't want her anymore."

"That's a lie," he growled. "I'm not like that."

She stuck her nose in the air. "I *thought* you weren't like that."

"I'm serious. You know me."

"No, I don't. That's the problem, and I was a fool for trusting you."

"I swear on everything important to me." He pounded his chest with a flat hand. "I'm not the man my father said I am." Veins popped from his forehead. "That bastard. Don't you see what he's doing? He's trying to break us up and you fell for it. Shit, he's only thinking about how bad he'd look if people knew we were together."

"I can't believe anything that comes out your mouth."

"Look at me." He grabbed her. "True, we haven't known each other long at all, but we have a connection some people who've been together years don't have. It's the most amazing thing I've ever experienced. I'd never lie to you. Not *you*."

She took a deep breath. "I want to believe you—"

"Then listen to your heart and not lies."

She twitched. "I keep wondering why you'd want me when you can have all these other women."

He clutched her hand. "I don't give a damn about any other women because they won't make me feel half as good as you do. Please don't let my father win. He's playing games, and I won't let him get away with it." He pulled her close, puckering his lips.

"No." She moved away from him. "Kissing you is the last thing I want right now."

I'm lying my ass off.

"Please don't cut me out your life, Talia." He kissed her hand. "Don't ruin this when we could be the happiest we've ever been. I'm falling in love with you."

A tear fell from her eye.

"How can you expect me to walk away?"

"I don't know what to believe." She sobbed. "I wish I did."

"Talia?"

"Goodbye, Jody."

"Don't do this." He stepped back. "It's the devil trying to break us up. Don't let him, Talia."

She closed the door.

CHAPTER NINE

"You've gone too far this time!" Jody barged his way into the doorway of Ben and Daphne's home, past the female servant. "How dare you lie on me?"

"What the hell are you talking about?" Ben shouted, dismissing the servant with a wave. "I didn't lie on you."

They marched into the living room.

Daphne ran in a second afterwards. "What in the world is going on?"

"You told Talia that I have these women all around the world." Jody pointed at his father. "And that I'm using her as a conquest when you know damn well that's not who I am."

"Just calm down." Ben reached for him.

"Calm down nothing." Jody rocked. "You expect me to believe you want our relationship to heal and you do stuff like this? Every time I think you can't get any more selfish, you prove me wrong."

"Yes, I don't want you with Talia because it makes me look bad, and I can't risk my chance to be mayor for nothing. But, you and Talia are only gonna end up hurt."

"That's our business!"

"So it is true?" Daphne crossed her arms. "You and Talia have been sleeping together? Do you realize how that hurts your father's image?"

"I don't give a fuck about his image." Jody lunged at her, Ben holding him back. "When will you two get it? The world doesn't revolve around your lives. God, you're supposed to be our parents and care about what we want."

Daphne squeezed her hips. "And if you were any kind of son, you'd care about your father's well-being."

"Honey." Ben let Jody go and then grabbed Daphne. "Cool it, okay?"

Jody looked Daphne up and down, scoffing. "Talia told me you were ridiculous, but I thought she was exaggerating until now."

"Whatever." Her top lip wiggled. "I'm gonna go give Miss Talia a call. We have a lot to talk about." She left the room.

"This was the last straw, Dad." Jody looked Ben in the eyes. "From this point on I don't give a damn about what happens with you."

"You and Talia can't be together. How would that work?"

"I'm in love with her, Dad." The rage within Jody subsided. "I've never met a woman that makes me feel the way she does. You know how lonely I've been. Don't you want me to be happy?"

"I didn't intend to hurt you."

"That's the problem. All your life you've done things and were so into what they meant concerning you that you never think about the consequences of your actions. You're telling me you wanna be mayor of a town? Dad, you can't even get your own shit together."

"This is absurd." Ben clasped his hands in front of him. "How can you be in love with a woman you hardly know?"

Jody leaned to one side. "I guess the same way a man could be married for over thirty years, cheat on his wife, and leave her for a gold digger that treats her own daughter like horseshit."

Ben raised his head, swallowing.

"Stay out my business, Dad." Jody pointed at him, backing toward the doorway. "If you do anything else, then our chances of repairing this relationship is over."

He left.

****

"You keep saying I try to run your life but this is why, Talia," Daphne shouted into the phone. "It's because even at thirty-five you still make the dumbest decisions."

"I had no idea Jody was Ben's son." Talia paced around her bedroom, hating how Daphne scolded her as if she were a dumb child.

"You hooked up with some guy you don't even know. Didn't ask the man's last name or anything."

"You're the last one to be lecturing me on the etiquettes of dating with all the men you've picked up in your lifetime."

"Well, this is bigger than you and Jody. This is my husband's future. I don't ask you for a lot, but I'm asking you to stop this right now. Please. Don't ruin this for Ben or me."

Talia had always been one to stick to her decisions, but one conversation with Daphne could reduce her back to that little girl with low self-esteem who second-guessed herself at every turn.

"Don't worry about me and Jody, Momma." Talia wiped a tear. "It's over for good."

****

"This is stupid," Talia declared when V stepped into her living room two weeks later. "Why did I let you talk me into this?"

V set the plastic sack on the table and pulled out three boxes of pregnancy tests. "I got reinforcements because we're gonna do this right."

"I'm not pregnant for the last time."

"How do you know?" V leaned back, batting his eyes. "You've been fainting at work, your stomach's been crazy, and you get out of breath walking to the door."

"Nonsense." Talia sat on the couch as another wave of exhaustion hit her. "I'm just stressed. I might be getting congestion or something too." She forced a cough. "I have horrible sinus."

"Sinus makes you miss your period?"

"I didn't miss it, I'm late." Talia propped a pillow under her arm. Besides, I can't be pregnant. I stay on top of things like this, and Jody and I used protection."

V opened a test, glaring at her. "Every time?"

"Y...yes."

"Why did you hesitate?"

"Well, we'd always use protection the first time." Talia played with her fingers. "But, we do it so many times in a row that sometimes we might not have always used—"

"Talia." V sighed.

"What can I say? Passion overtook commonsense." Talia cursed herself. "But, I'm not pregnant. I'd bet my life on it."

"Prove me wrong, Diva." V threw the test at her.

"I will." Talia snatched the test off the couch. "Get ready to look stupid."

"We'll see." He followed her from the room.

CHAPTER TEN

"So, eh..." V picked up the third, used pregnancy test forty minutes later. "What was that you were saying about me looking stupid?"

"Something's gotta be wrong." Talia examined the tests again. "There has to be an answer for this!"

"Yeah, and the answer is you're pregnant." V tossed a test into the bathroom sink. "Three plusses don't lie."

"Oh god." Talia lowered herself on the toilet lid. "We used condoms every time."

"Not every time, remember?" V grabbed his hip. "Why you think using a condom the first time, then having sex eight times in a row and not using something is fine, I don't understand."

"I told you we got caught up."

"And look who's paying for it."

Talia looked at the tests yet again. "I'm not prepared for this. I can't take care of a baby."

"Why not? You're financially stable. You got your own place and a good job."

"Are you nuts? I'm an emotional wreck." Talia stroked the nape of her neck. "How the hell could I raise a child right with all the mommy issues I have?"

"Maybe that's why." V leaned against the sink. "You can take this as an opportunity to be a better mother than yours was."

"No." Talia stood, crossing her arms. "I cannot have this baby. No way."

V squinted. "This baby is Jody's right?"

"Course it is." Talia huffed, wanting to punch V for suggesting otherwise. "You know I don't sleep around. Before Jody, I hadn't had sex in five months."

V's eyes popped out their sockets. "*Five* months?"

"Not since that guy, Herman, who you made me go out with on that horrible double date."

He rolled his eyes. "How many times must I apologize for that?"

"The rest of your life." Talia paced. "The entire night was a disaster."

"It couldn't have been that bad since you slept with him," V mumbled. "It's been that long since you had sex? No wonder you jumped Jody's bones so fast." He fanned. "Ooh, child. Call the mental institution and book me as a resident for life if I don't get dick for five months."

"Can't you for once be serious?" Talia continued pacing. "Everything's not a damn joke."

"I'm trying to get your ass to settle down and see reason. This isn't bad. I mean there could be worse things than getting pregnant by a billionaire. Honey, no matter what happens between you and Jody, from this point you're gonna be set for life."

"I don't want his money," Talia said through gritted teeth.

"It's better to be pregnant by someone like Jody instead of the guy from the Seven-Eleven."

"Jesus." Talia sat on the toilet and dropped her head. "I can't even think anymore. Why is this happening?"

The doorbell rang.

"Uh-oh," V said. "You're not expecting anyone else are you?"

"Hell no." Talia raced into her adjacent bedroom and looked out the window.

Jody's car sat in the driveway.

"Shit, it's Jody." She fidgeted. "What do I do?"

"You gotta let him in." V pointed to the tests in the bathroom. "Hello, especially now."

The doorbell rang again.

V shrugged. "He's not going away."

"This is terrible." Talia pulled at her fro. "I haven't even had time to get used to this. How am I supposed to explain it to him?"

"You better figure it out."

"V—"

"Child, I'm gonna go let this man in." He flicked his hand in a dismissive way. "You figure something out." He twisted out the bedroom.

"Wait!" Talia chased him downstairs and stopped him at the front door. "Hold on."

"Talia?" Jody shouted through the door. "I'm sick of this! I gave you time to think things over, but now I wanna talk."

"Woo, he's feisty." V unlocked the door.

"Don't open that door!" Talia grabbed V's shirt.

V opened it and presented a huge smile. "Jody," he sang the name.

"Hey." He walked in and stood wide-legged with authority. "Talia, we need to talk, and I won't take no for an answer."

She huffed. "You don't give me orders, Jody."

He glared at V.

V smiled, appearing uncomfortable at Jody's demeanor. "I was just leaving. It was wonderful to see you again."

"You too," Jody said.

"Call me, Talia." V winked on his way out the door.

"I told you I don't wanna see you." Talia went into her living room on the right. "You're making an already difficult situation worse." She sat on the floral ottoman, crossing her legs.

"I miss you." He sat on the table in front of her. "I gotta know where we stand. I swear my father was lying about those other women."

"Forget all that," she snapped. "There's something going on that's much, much bigger than other women." She took a deep breath. "I can't believe this is happening."

"What is it?" He moved beside her, sheltering her inside his warm embrace. "Are you okay?"

"I didn't plan this." She wept. "Please don't think that, Jody. I didn't do this to trap you or get your money."

"What the hell are you talking about?"

"I don't want you to hate me." She dropped her head, sniffling. "Don't want you to get the wrong picture of me."

He lay his finger under her chin and lifted her head. "Nothing would make me stop caring about you. I'm in love with you, Talia."

"Already?" She wiped tears. "How can you be sure?"

"I'm sure every time I look into your eyes." He sniffed her cheek. "Or every time I smell or hold you. Trust me, there's no doubt on my part."

She cried against his chest. "I'm pregnant."

He stopped caressing her hair.

"Jody?" She raised her head, and he looked as if someone shot him. "Please say something."

He batted his eyes with his mouth open. "What did you say?"

"I'm pregnant." She scooted away from him, struggling to read his emotions. "I'm sorry."

"You're pregnant?" He swept his hand through his hair, eyes wide as tennis balls. "With a baby?"

She snickered. "No, with a horse."

His hands shook. "Are you sure?"

"I took three different tests, and they all came back positive. You want me to get them?" She stood, pointing toward the doorway.

"No." He pulled her back beside him. "I believe you." He batted his eyes. "Wow."

"I'll go to the doctor to make sure. Jody, I'm so sorry. I didn't do this on purpose."

He patted her hand. "I know you didn't."

"Are you mad at me?"

"Mad?" He cackled, cheeks flaming red. "I'm not mad at all. I'm happy!"

"Happy?"

"I've always wanted to be a father. I didn't expect it to happen like this, but I'm happy."

Talia dropped her shoulders. "Are you *nuts*?" She stood. "Did you hear what I said? I'm pregnant, Jody."

His smile grew bigger. "And it's great."

"Stop it." She walked from the couch. "Have you gone crazy? We have no business having a baby together."

"Well, looks like it's too late to worry about that now. You're mad?"

"Course I'm mad." She stomped around. "I don't want a baby."

"Why not?" He stood. "You've never wanted a child?"

"Do you know how hard it will be to change my life around to support a child?"

"You act like you're gonna be doing it all alone." He walked from behind the table. "I'll be in the picture no matter what."

"If I had a child, I never wanted it to be where I just got pregnant by some man." She touched her forehead. "I want my child to have a father."

"Our child can and will have a father if you want that." He caressed her hand. "The last thing you have to worry about is being alone. I'll never, ever leave you or this baby no matter what happens."

"You just being there is not the dream I had when I thought of having kids." She let go of his hand. "I want my child to have someone there to teach it things and spend time with it."

"You mean you don't just want me in the picture, but a part of your life?" He raised an eyebrow. "I'll marry you then."

"You're crazy."

"I'm dead serious."

"Wow." She paced, swinging her arms. "I don't know what planet you come from but here on earth, we don't do things like this."

"I don't know what you wanna hear. I'm being more sensitive than most men would be. I didn't run out the damn door, did I?"

"For me to marry you would be..."

He pulled her close, holding her waist. "The best thing that's ever happened to me."

"This is too much." She pushed him away. "I don't want the reason you marry me to be for a baby." She exhaled into her palms. "All of this is just too much, and I'm getting stressed."

"Okay relax." He guided her to the couch. "You don't need to get upset in your condition. I don't wanna pressure you."

Talia sat on the couch and curled her knees up under her. "I need time alone."

"You don't need to be alone." He knelt beside the couch. "Let me stay here for the night. You need someone to talk to."

"I'm fine." She swatted her hand at him. "I don't wanna think about this right now. Please leave."

He got off the floor, scowling. "I meant what I said." He caressed her cheek. "I wanna do what's right for you and the baby."

"I appreciate that." She managed a light smile. "I'll keep it in mind."

CHAPTER ELEVEN

"You haven't told Ben or Daphne about the baby yet?" V pulled several eyeliner pencils from his make-up kit, preparing for the day's show. "When are you gonna tell them? It's been a week since you found out you were pregnant."

"Hush." Talia glanced at the show's crew members as they passed the doorway. "What time is it?" She checked her watch. "Ben should be here by now. The show starts in forty minutes."

"So how do you feel about him doing the show today?"

"I don't care." Talia shrugged. "Got too much other stuff on my mind."

"You mean like being knocked up by his son?"

"*V.*" Talia motioned to him. "Damn, you have the biggest mouth I've ever seen."

He patted the side of his head, smirking. "That's what my last boyfriend said. You can't hide you're pregnant forever."

"I don't plan to hide it forever." Talia looked through her make-up kit. "Just until I give birth."

V guffawed. "I don't care for Daphne but she deserves to know she's got a grandkid on the way." He opened a new container of mascara. "You gonna keep it?"

"I...I don't know." Talia paused from searching the kit. "I hadn't even thought about it."

"You want to keep it?"

She stared into the mirror at her flat stomach, curious how her daughter or son might look.

She chuckled.

If it had been anyone else's baby, she'd be terrified, but she'd grown excited to become the mother of Jody McCall's child. The baby would connect them forever, and she wanted nothing more.

"Oh my god," V whispered. "Talia, you're glowing."

"What?" She snapped from her daydream. "Boy, please. Stop playing."

"I'm serious. You got the angelic, motherly glow."

"When Jody asked me to marry him, I thought it was the most insane thing I'd ever heard." Talia rubbed the front of her blouse. "But, lately I've had these visions of how wonderful life could be for the three of us. I want my baby to have the best, V. It isn't just about money. It's about having a father there who loves it."

V poked his lips out. "You're going to make me cry."

"Being pregnant has made me understand my mother better too. I'm not saying she's perfect, but I understand what she means when she says she wants the best for me. That she'd do anything to keep me from suffering. That's how I feel about this baby." She patted her stomach. "I want it to know no matter what happens I'll be always be there."

"You're gonna make a great mother." V hugged her. "What about Jody? Have you given thought to his idea of marriage?"

Talia sat on the stool. "Being married to Jody McCall isn't exactly a turnoff." She smiled, swinging her legs. "He'd be a great daddy."

****

Okalani jumped from behind the parted door where she'd been listening to Talia and V's conversation. "Holy moly." She rubbed her hands together, cackling. "Talia is having her *stepbrother's* baby? This will be my highest rated show yet!"

****

From across the set, Talia and V watched Okalani take her place in front of the main camera. She began after the camera operator gave his signal.

"Hello, everyone!" Okalani waved into the camera. "Welcome to *Good Morning with Okalani*!" She gestured to the man on the couch. "Mr. Ben McCall is joining us today, and it's a pleasure to have him here." She sat in the chair. "Thanks so much for coming, Ben."

"Thank you." He smiled into the camera.

"He's gonna blind somebody with that head," V whispered.

Talia grinned.

"Ben, you're a prominent figure in Hilo," Okalani said. "You've developed many businesses around here and put together foundations for cancer research. Where do you find the time?"

"I always make time for the people." Ben's plastered, goofy smile remained. "I feel it's our duty as citizens to always help our fellow man."

After Ben finished rattling about his charitable contributions, Okalani inquired about the weight loss pill he'd invented and his interest in politics.

"That's fascinating." Okalani beamed. "You've talked about business and politics, would you like to share about your personal life? You've recently gotten married to Daphne Frank, am I correct?"

"Oh, yes." Ben held up his hand, showing off the wedding band. "And, it's been wonderful. Every day feels like our honeymoon again."

Talia stuck her finger in her mouth, and V laughed.

"And Daphne is African-American," Okalani said. "Has it been difficult in an interracial marriage?"

"Not here in Hilo, no." Ben crossed his legs. "That's what's so wonderful about this city. It's full of people of different races from all over the world, and we encourage diversity." He lifted his index finger. "And if I become Hilo's mayor I'm gonna continue to spread the message."

"That's nice," Okalani said. "So there have been no issues in your marriage?"

Ben cut his gaze from the camera, holding that stiff smile. "I'm not sure what you mean."

"Come on, Ben," Okalani teased. "If you're gonna be mayor, then the people of Hilo must know we can trust your word. You must be transparent."

He cleared his throat. "My marriage is wonderful."

"Unlike the last one?" Okalani smirked.

"Uh-oh," V said.

Talia's mouth dropped. "Did she just ask that?"

"Is it true you cheated on your ex-wife of nearly forty years, Michelle, with Daphne?" Okalani asked.

Ben squirmed. "No, I—"

"Isn't that true?" Okalani raised an eyebrow.

"It wasn't how you're making it sound." Ben gripped the arm of the couch. "Michelle and I had grown apart."

"Then why didn't you get a divorce?"

Ben fidgeted, looking left and right. "I don't mind discussing my personal life but this has gone off the rails."

CHAPTER TWELVE

"Sorry if this makes you uncomfortable, but you'd better get used to it." Okalani fixed the tiny microphone on her collar. "If you end up mayor, then you'll have to answer tougher questions than this." She stood. "You don't want to answer that question? How about this one? Is it true that your stepdaughter Talia is pregnant by your son?"

Talia shrieked.

"Ooh." V covered his mouth.

"What?" Ben scooted to the edge of his chair. "What the hell are you talking about? That's not true!"

"Really?" Okalani scoffed at Ben. "So Talia and your son Jody aren't having an affair and she's not pregnant?"

"I don't know what you're talking about." Spit flew out Ben's mouth. "Where did you get this from?"

"I don't believe this." Talia burst into tears. "This can't be happening!"

"That Okalani," V whispered. "She should be ashamed. All she cares about is ratings."

"You wanna be mayor then you have to be honest, Ben," Okalani said.

"This is nonsense." He jumped up. "You take this show and shove it up your ass!" He ripped the microphone off his shirt and stomped off set. "Get that camera out my face." He pushed the cameraman who tried to follow him. "Talia!"

"Oh, shit." She covered her eyes.

"Talia," Ben hollered. "What the hell is going on?"

Crew members jumped out of his path as he headed toward Talia and V.

"Are you pregnant?" Ben huffed and puffed with his chest heaving. "Answer me."

"You, bitch!" Talia raced toward Okalani and slapped the hell out of her.

Okalani fell into a male crew member's arms. "How *dare* you?"

"How dare *you*?" Talia rocked with balled fists. "How could you get on TV and embarrass me and my family?"

"It's not my fault you're screwing your own stepbrother." Okalani stood straight, fixing her blazer. "What kind of sick family is this?"

"It's not like that. Jody and I love each other. How did you even find out I was pregnant?"

"So it is true?" Ben grabbed Talia and shook her. "Answer me!"

"Yes!"

"Are you crazy?" He let her go. "You and Jody don't even know each other. He's not father material and never will be."

"Who are you to talk about being father material? You've never been a father to Jody." She threw her hand in his face. "He's a great person, and I know you made that shit up about him and other women just so we'd break up."

"Listen." Ben's breathing slowed. "I didn't want you to get hurt."

"You're disgusting," Talia said. "How could you lie on your son like you did? Maybe if you'd spent more time being a father and less time thinking about your career, then you'd be a better person."

Ben stood back, exhaling. "You might be right, but it doesn't change the fact you're pregnant. You can't have that baby." He pointed to her stomach. "I forbid it."

"You get this straight, Ben." She got in his face. "You are not my father, and you never will be. Don't tell me what to do."

V crossed his arms, smirking.

"When it comes to this baby," Talia continued. "I don't care what you or anyone else thinks." She touched her stomach. "This is my child, and I'll decide what happens to it."

"Damn straight." V snapped his fingers. "You go, girl."

"How can we be a family if you and Jody have a child?" Ben grimaced.

"We'll never be a family as long as you and Momma continue to ignore what Jody and I want." Talia focused on Okalani. "And as for this show, I quit."

"What?" V dropped his arms.

"I'm sick of everyone pushing me around and expecting me to put my life on hold for them," Talia said. "Okalani, I've taken a lot of shit from you, and I tried to give you the benefit of the doubt about how you treat people. I didn't like you, but I always respected you until today. I thought you had scruples, but you proved that you'll do anything to anyone as long as you get ratings."

Okalani's eyes watered. "Talia—"

"Save it." She raised her hand. "How could I work with a woman who'd embarrass me and hurt me the way you have? As Ben said, take your show and shove it up your ass." Talia stomped to the make-up area.

"Talia?" V ran up behind her. "Hold on, girl."

"I need to get my things."

V held on to her, stopping her. "You're really quitting?"

"I love being a make-up artist, but shit I'd flip burgers before putting up with more of Okalani's shit."

"I love working with you."

"I'm tired of this shit, V." She laid her head on his shoulder. "What Jody has been telling me has sunk in."

"What?"

"That I need to worry about me and stop caring about others. We all make mistakes. So what if I'm in love with my stepbrother, and I'm having his baby out of wedlock? It's my life. I've spent too much time being perfect and not happy. I can't do that anymore."

V kissed her cheek. "All I've ever wanted was for you to be happy. If Jody gives you that, he's the man for you."

"He is." Talia smiled, feeling liberated. "I'm gonna have this baby and trust that God will make a way."

"You got my blessing."

"I have to get my stuff." Talia exhaled. "Then I'm going to see my mom. It's time we have the talk we should have had a long time ago."

CHAPTER THIRTEEN

"Well?" Daphne addressed Talia at Ben and Daphne's front door. "How could you not tell me you were pregnant?"

Talia glanced to her right as two little Hawaiian boys rode bikes up the street.

"I don't understand what your problem is, and I'm sick of this ungrateful attitude," Daphne said. "You've been walking around here with a chip on your shoulder for months. What did I ever do to you?"

"I'm not gonna talk to you from the porch."

Daphne exhaled and stood aside. "Come in."

Talia walked in and remained by the front door. "I'm tired, Momma." She rubbed her eye. "So tired."

"And I'm not tired? For thirty-five years I've worked hard to give you the life I felt you—"

"*Worked*? Do you even know what the word means?"

"Watch the lip." Daphne pointed at her. "I might not have scrubbed floors or delivered pizzas, but I worked for you to have a decent life."

"No, you dated rich men so *you* could have the best life. Let's stop the lying now please." Talia walked toward the glass table. "I need to know one thing I've been trying to figure out since I was a kid."

Daphne held her hips, neck wiggling. "What?"

Talia closed her eyes, digging deep to ask what she'd been dreading to utter for years. "Why did you have me?"

Daphne let go of her hips, mouth wide open. "What did you say?" She patted her bosom. "How could you ask me that? I had you because I wanted you. God, Talia."

Talia blinked back tears. "I've never felt you loved me."

"Oh." She grabbed Talia's arm. "Look at me."

Talia did, holding her breath.

"I did everything for you." Daphne poked Talia in the chest. "Yeah, I went after rich men, and yes I love money but I did it for you." She sobbed. I didn't want you growing up like I did, not knowing where your next meal was coming from or not having a decent place to stay. Every time you had running water, clean sheets, new clothes, and food in your stomach, it was me showing I love you. Never question that."

Talia avoided Daphne's gaze.

"I'm not perfect and I don't try to be." Daphne patted Talia's hair. "Put yourself in my shoes. You've never shown me appreciation. I don't remember you thanking me once."

"Thanking you?" Talia chuckled. "For doing what you're supposed to do?"

"Sometimes I need to hear you love me too. It goes both ways. I'm not the most affectionate person, and if that's what you needed then I'm sorry. But, you always had something I never did and I envy you for that."

Talia's lips shivered. "Why would you envy me?"

"For your strength and independence." Daphne sat on the table. "I criticize your career, but it's not because I'm not proud. I wanted you to be a doctor or a lawyer because in my mind, you deserve the best."

"But, as long as I love what I do, isn't that important?"

Daphne nodded, smiling.

"I'll never be what you want me to be, Momma." Talia sat beside her, taking her hand. "All I can be is me, and all you can be is you. It has to be good enough or we'll never have a real relationship."

"No one's ever told me I was good enough for anything." Daphne stroked her extensions. "I was determined to be the best mother. I failed at that too, didn't I?"

"It's not too late to improve." Talia kissed Daphne's cheek, her lips landing on a tear. "That includes both of us."

"I love you so much, baby." Daphne hugged her. "I'm sorry if I didn't give you what you need, but I'm going to be there for you and the baby if you let me. Let me make it up to you."

Talia wrapped her arms around Daphne's waist, reveling in the comforting, rare embrace. "That's a wonderful start."

****

Talia drove up to her house thirty minutes later to see Jody sitting on her front porch.

"Hey." She walked to the front door, swinging her purse.

"Hey." He stood up, looking gorgeous as usual in a light-blue shirt that brought out his eyes. "You look great."

"Thanks." She opened the door and invited him in.

"Am I missing something?"

"What?" She entered the living room and threw her purse on the couch.

"Well, you seem cheerful for someone who was embarrassed on a television show a few hours ago. I'm sorry about that." He scratched his head. "My dad called me cursing up a storm. He's convinced this will ruin his campaign."

She took his hand and led him to the couch. "I'm over what happened on Okalani's show, and I'm over Ben."

He sat beside her, chuckling. "Why are you so happy?"

"I spoke to my mother." She sat Indian-style.

"That must've been an experience."

"It was amazing." She propped her arm on the back of the sofa. "We spoke about how we'd been feeling. What's funny is that she didn't understand me anymore than I understood her."

He caressed her hand, sending sparks through her body. "Are you two okay?"

"We'll get there. What's great is I'm learning to be okay with my life and to stop caring what others think. I won't fall victim to emotional blackmail anymore."

"Wow." Jody batted his eyes. "Is it the pregnancy giving you this revelation?"

"Maybe." She patted her stomach, giggling. "At first I was terrified of being a mother, but I'm looking forward to it more and more each day." She stroked his thigh. "I wish you and Ben could work things out."

"He'll never change, and I don't expect him to. I've learned to accept him for who he is."

"We have to discuss what to do about the baby once and for all."

He touched her hair. "The proposal still stands."

She smiled. "It's not the right time, Jody."

He nodded. "You're right." He leaned over and kissed her. "As long as you give us a shot to do this together then I'm happy."

"We can see how things go as a couple first and who knows what will happen by next year? But, I don't want to rush anything else." She smiled. "Our relationship has been a rollercoaster, but we need to slow it down. I want to enjoy the ride."

"As long as we're together I'm fine with taking things slow." He scooted closer to her, and she put her head on his shoulder. "I can't wait until the baby is here. Don't laugh, but I've been picking out baby names."

She giggled. "For real?"

"Yep." He kissed her nose. "I picked unisex names so it'll be easier if we get attached to one before the baby comes out." He guffawed. "We won't have to change it according to gender."

"You're really excited, aren't you?"

"You kidding?" He pinched her nose. "There isn't anyone else I'd rather be the mother of my child."

"You don't know how much that means."

"Can't believe Christmas is almost here." He wiggled his leg. "I haven't picked out your present yet."

"Oh, you've given me the best present already." She rubbed her stomach. "It's more than enough."

"You'll be the best mother." He kissed her forehead. "And don't think just because we're taking it slow that I'll forget about us getting married. I won't give up until I have a ring on that beautiful finger of yours."

"Good." She wiggled her fingers. "Because I'm looking forward to being Mrs. Jody McCall someday, and I don't give a damn who has a problem with that."

"I like your style, Mommy." He kissed her as she laughed. "Our child's gonna have spunk."

"That's right, Daddy." She climbed onto his lap. "And more love than it could ever hope for."

He gave her a soft kiss that reminded her of a flower petal against her cheek. "Merry Christmas, Talia."

"Merry Christmas, Jody." She grabbed his shoulders, beaming. "I promise it'll be the best one yet."

THE END

A SAVIOR FOR CHRISTMAS
CHAPTER ONE

"I'm sorry, Zach." Barbara Bell, an associate banker at Briar Hurst, Texas' only bank, sat behind her office desk, twiddling her fingers. "Either you give up the ranch or we take it from you. It's your call."

Thirty-three-year-old Zach Carrington chuckled while straightening his cowboy hat in his lap.

"What's so funny?"

"You. You finally did it, huh?"

Barbara squinted her hazel eyes. "I don't understand what you're talking about."

"The heck you don't. You've been waiting for years to get back at me because I didn't want you in high school. It's pathetic."

"How dare you?" She straightened her scrawny, no-bosom frame in her black blazer. "I'd never use my position to get back at you. I'm over you."

"Is that why you almost threw a party when me and Mariah Phoenix broke up?"

"Oh, please." She sat back, clasping her hands. "You think I was jealous of Mariah?"

"She's beautiful, talented, and one of the best attorneys in the state." He smirked. "Why wouldn't you be jealous?"

She sighed.

"You're not getting your greedy hands on my parents' ranch. I don't care what you do."

"You act like I'm the one behind this. I just work here. It's not my fault your parents owe the bank."

"My parents haven't been dead a year!" He slammed his fist on the desk. "Yet you come to me with this. You're loving this, Barbara, because if you weren't you'd help me. Plead my case for me."

"What kind of power do you think I have?"

"You made Associate Banker in three years. You're the youngest person of authority they ever had. They listen to you."

"No, they don't."

"Barbara, please." He gripped the desk. "It's almost Christmas, for God's sake. Have a heart. Look, no matter what you think of me, that ranch is all I have left of my parents. When they died in that accident, I swore I'd do all I could to keep it in the family. You gotta give me more time."

"My hands are tied." She tapped her fingers on the desk as he sat back, exhaling. "I know it's not fair that they didn't tell you they had the loan, but you know now." She shrugged. "Either you pay or you lose the ranch."

"Where the heck am I gonna get three hundred thousand dollars? I've never even *seen* three hundred thousand dollars."

She smirked, waggling her thick, mud-brown eyebrows. "Did you mean what you said? About wanting my help?"

"Yes."

She leaned forward, her eyes glowing with sin. "What are you going to do for *me*?"

"What?"

"Come on, Zach. You're right. I still want you. Isn't it time you give me a chance?"

"Barbara, this is my livelihood we're talking about here. How can you be so selfish? I can lose everything."

"Not if you're nice to me." She looked up at him through her lashes. "If you take me out on a date, for example, I can make sure the higher-ups listen to everything you have to say."

Zach jerked out of the chair and slapped his hat on his head as he stomped to the door.

"Zach?"

"It ain't happening, Barbara. I'm not letting you use my desperation to get me into your bed."

"You're a fool." Anger lines sprouted across her narrow forehead. "Am I so repulsive that you won't take me out on *one* date to save your ranch?"

He opened the door. "You just answered your own question, didn't you?"

"Bye, Zach." She waved. "Oh, and Merry Christmas!"

****

Zach tossed and turned that night, not able to get that notice from the bank out of his head.

After giving up on trying to sleep, he shoved the covers off and went into the hallway.

Despite Christmas being his favorite holiday, he'd just thrown up some tinsel and scattered a few plastic poinsettias on the walls. Nothing compared to how the home used to be decorated when his parents were still living. The entire place would be alive with laughter and Christmas music two months before the holiday. His mother's favorite Christmas song, "Deck the Halls" would boom from the stereo while she made gingerbread cookies and eggnog.

He closed his eyes and sniffed, swearing he could still smell her homemade fruitcake.

But those days were over and he was just alone now.

The only sounds he heard were the singing of crickets and the tapping of the backdoor screen, blowing in the wind.

Memories. So many memories he'd never get back if he lost this place.

He opened the kitchen cabinet and got out the bottle of his daddy's whiskey, hearing his mother's voice in his head.

She'd always gotten on his father for taking too many shots on the weekends. But this was Briar Hurst, Texas. You work and you drank. Nothing much else to do.

He took a long sip, ripping his lips from the bottle as the alcohol seared his throat. "Jesus."

Maybe he didn't have the money to save this place, but he'd find a way. He needed help, and there was only one woman he could call. *Mariah Phoenix.*

"Damn." His hand automatically grabbed his dick, just thinking of her. He'd never wanted a woman so much where every hair stood up on his body when she just looked at him. Those sexy lips and poisonous curves that went on for days. Her electrifying tannish-brown skin.

The woman he'd left at the altar and embarrassed beyond belief. The woman who he was sure hated him more than she could hate anyone. Yet, a woman he needed more than anything and didn't know how to go crawling back for help.

He sighed, hooking his arm on the back of the chair. "Fuck."

But he had to try. No matter how bad things were between

him and Mariah, she was his only hope and it made him wanna go crawl in a cave for the rest of his life and hide.

CHAPTER TWO

Sherman City, Texas (An Hour Outside Briar Hurst)

Thirty-three-year-old Mariah Phoenix paced in her posh, contemporary-style office, cracking her knuckles.

Zach Carrington.

He'd called her out of the blue, and she still couldn't believe it. And a few weeks before Christmas, to boot. Fucking up her holiday spirit.

Supposedly he might lose his ranch and needed a lawyer to help him. Funny how the one thing that stood in between them, that darn ranch, is the thing that could ruin his life.

Someone knocked on the door and her secretary announced Zach.

"Send him in." With butterflies fluttering in her solar plexus, Mariah clenched her waist.

Even though it had only been a year since she last saw him, she hoped by some miracle he'd lost his hair and gained a pot belly. Would serve him right.

Zach stomped in wearing a tight white T-shirt, carrying that enormous cowboy hat.

Damn.

Her mouth went dry as the Sahara Desert. Toes trembled in her patent leather heels as she remembered those times when Zach had those muscular hands around her waist, fucking the shit out of her from behind.

Mm.

He was even more gorgeous than ever with eyes so passionate they made her forget he broke her heart.

At least for a second.

"Hey." He waved the hat. "Merry Christmas. How have you been?"

She glared at him.

"Yeah, okay." He closed the door, clearing his throat. "Guess my call surprised you, huh?" He ran his fingers through his dusty-blond curls, sweat trickling down the side of his face.

He'd always been a heavy sweater. He could be out for five minutes and be drenched like he'd been walking around the African jungle for miles.

When they made love, at times she'd be wearing so much of his sweat it was like she'd taken a shower and forgot to dry off.

"This is awkward." He grinned, his skin boasting a golden-tan hue from being in the sun all his life. "Say something, Mari."

Take me. Take me now.

She shook her head. "Uh, wow. Zach Carrington as I live and breathe. I thought I'd never see you again."

He wiggled those sensual, crooked lips where you couldn't tell if her were smiling or frowning.

Those lips.

She had to drop eye contact for a second because she kept thinking about the last romp they had that night in the rain and how no man had ever pleasured her from head-to-toe like he had. Shit, she wouldn't even let one try. No one could come close to Zach Carrington with passion. Not even a sexy and successful brown brotha like Dominic Haslam who most women would crawl over cracked glass to be with, but dumb ass Mariah still couldn't get Zach out of her system despite how he'd dumped her like trash.

"You hoped to never see me again, huh?" Zach winced. "And I don't blame you."

"I blame *you.*" She strutted back behind her desk. "For hurting me beyond belief."

"I don't want to get into this—"

"Oh, you're going to hear it." She pointed at him. "I've wanted to say this to your sorry behind for the last year."

He sighed, sitting his athletic, country-boy build in the chair. Jeans hugging those muscular thighs for days. "What did you want to say?"

"Do you realize how much you hurt me?"

"Yes."

"No, you don't." She wiggled her neck, crossing her arms. "How could you do it, Zach? Leave me at the altar looking like a fool."

"Mari, I told you it wasn't the right time."

"Well, you shouldn't have asked me to marry you! We both know the real reason you dumped me. It's because I'm more successful than you and you couldn't take it."

"That's not true. I was always proud of you." He swallowed, licking his lips. "I love you, Mari. You gotta know that."

"Yet you called me up five minutes before it's time for me to walk down the aisle, claiming you changed your mind, but still haven't given me a *reasonable* explanation why you did that to me in all this time?"

"I was too ashamed, but is this really making you feel good, Mari? To kick me when I'm down?"

She drew back.

"I wouldn't be here if I didn't need your help. If they take the ranch, I'll have nothing."

"Okay, fine." She sat at her desk. "But why should I help you?"

"You shouldn't." He shrugged. "But you've always been a good person, and even though I don't deserve your help, my parents don't deserve to have everything they've worked for, ripped out from under them. Whether they can see it or not."

She swallowed, avoiding his sensual gaze. "If I get the bank off your ass, which I will, how do you expect to pay my fees?"

"Frankly..." He tugged on his ear. "That's none of your business."

"Oh, I think how I get paid is my business. I don't work for free."

"You'll get paid, Mari. Have I ever not kept my word?"

She scoffed. "Seriously?"

He closed his eyes. "Okay, besides the wedding thing."

"The wedding thing? Zach, you have some nerve—"

"Okay, okay. This is serious, Mari. Are you going to help me or not?"

"Lord knows you don't deserve it." She pursed her lips. "I'll help."

Relief fell across his magnificent features, and all Mariah wanted to do was smack it off. She'd dreamed of this day, seeing Zach again and throwing her success in his face. Flaunting the fact that she was now dating or semi-dating Dominic Haslam, the son of Rick Haslam, one of the most successful black lawyers in all of Texas who owned one of the most revered law firms in the country.

Yeah.

Mariah snickered, nodding. She pushed the picture of Dominic closer to him, making sure he saw it.

"May I ask exactly why you're helping?" He grinned. "Because I really didn't think you would."

"I became a lawyer because I got sick of big companies stepping over the little guys." She straightened her gold bracelet. "And it's my job to make sure that doesn't happen."

He nodded, rubbing his thigh.

"The bad news is, this is now your debt. Your parents left you the ranch, and that includes any loans they owned on it. They didn't tell you about this?"

He swallowed, forehead wrinkling. "No."

"I just can't believe they stuck you with this."

"Well, they didn't expect for a truck to run into them head-on and kill 'em, Mari."

"Wait, I didn't mean to be insensitive." She touched her bosom. "I loved your parents too and it broke my heart when I heard they died."

"Thank you," he mumbled. "I got the card you sent. It was sweet. I hoped you'd come to the funeral, but I understand why you didn't."

"My point is they knew they had a three hundred thousand dollar loan they couldn't pay off and that you'd inherit the ranch one day. They also knew they were up in age and didn't know how long they'd be around. I just can't believe they would leave you on the hook like this."

"Yeah, okay." He waved off her opinion. "What can we do about it *now* though?"

"First, you need to sign a contract with me and then I need your financial books to see assets, how much the ranch is making, everything."

"Okay."

"You might not wanna hear my advice."

He gaped. "What?"

"I'd let the bank have it and cut your losses."

"That ranch is what my family stands for, Mari. I grew up there. It's not just a house, it's who I *am*. Shit, I came to you because I don't wanna lose it now you're telling me to let it go?"

"Have you tried working out anything with the bank? Payment plan?"

"They want too much money."

"I might can get the payments down." She drummed her

fingers on the desk. "Most times this stuff gets settled when they see an attorney involved."

"I wouldn't know." He exhaled. "I'm just a dumb cowboy. I don't know how all this stuff works."

"You're not dumb."

He rubbed the rim of his hat. "This stuff came out of nowhere. First, I lose my parents and now this."

"Well, you've come to the right place." She smiled but dropped eye contact when she caught herself staring. "Get me all the info I need. First, my secretary will give you the contract. Please fill it out before you leave."

He stood, putting on his hat. "Okay."

"Don't forget the financial info. I need everything, Zach. Even if you think it's not important. You can email, fax, mail or bring it in—"

"I'll bring it in." He clutched her fingers in his calloused hand. "Nice to see you again, Mari."

She stared at his magnificent derriere in those jeans as he marched from the office. "You *too*."

CHAPTER THREE

Mariah Phoenix.

Zach jumped into his silver-gray Ford Pickup truck and exited the parking lot of the law firm.

Wasn't it ironic? Zach left her at the altar and chose loyalty to his family, to the ranch over her, and now he needed her to keep the one thing that tore them apart.

He turned through the congested streets, the curve of the lanes reminding him of Mariah's delicious figure.

The entire time in her office he hadn't been able to control his boner, and he wasn't embarrassed at all. He hoped she'd notice. What better way to tell a woman how much you still wanted her than a hard dick?

He chewed his bottom lip, rolling his palm on the steering wheel and imagining it was the satiny skin of Mariah's thighs. God had to be punishing him because she looked better than ever, and he didn't think that was possible.

He'd only seen her online since their wedding. Yes, he'd been stalking her to see what she'd been up to from time to time.

Online hadn't done her justice. She was even more beautiful than before. And though she had that smooth skin that reminded him of a gooey caramel bar and lips so sexy they'd make a bear come out of hibernation, it had always been Mariah's confidence that attracted him. Her wit. Her no-nonsense attitude and how despite being a little black girl from Briar Hurst, Texas, she'd graduated law school with honors and had shown everyone what he always knew she was capable of.

Since they were kids, Mariah had been the only person who knew him better than he knew himself. The only one he allowed to strip him of his ego and grab hold of the self-conscious guy he hid so well.

And he knew her better than any man could. He was her first boyfriend. Her first kiss. Shit, he popped her cherry in the woods behind the railroad station. Taught her what to do with that pussy after just the third kiss. Now because of Zach's training, Mariah could lay it down and make a man's toes curl backwards.

So if the black dude in that picture was getting her good lovin' now, he had Zach to thank because Mariah couldn't even find her pussy hole before Zach first hit it.

Their relationship had been filled with years of him giving her orgasms that had her body jerking and head turning like she was Linda Blair in *The Exorcist*.

He tightened his grip on the steering wheel. Despite how upset she was with him and whoever the hell that black dude in the picture on her desk was, she would always be Zach's woman.

And now, after that long ass, painful, gut-wrenching year away from her, he'd make sure she knew it.

****

"Don't play with me, Barbara." Mariah stood in Barbara's office a few days later, scratching through her short, light-brown curls. "Honey, you couldn't tangle with me on your best day."

Zach watched from the chair by the file cabinet, loving every minute.

"You want to be stupid and drag this out?" Mariah asked. "When you know you're going to lose? So be it. That's not my client's debt, and he's not paying for it."

"You know something I don't?" Barbara chomped on a multicolored candy cane. "Want one?"

"No thanks." Mariah faked a smile. "Not good for the figure. I wouldn't eat too many if I were you."

Barbara smirked. "Zach owns the ranch now, and it means he takes on his parents' debts. Take this to court and you'll lose." She glared at Zach. "It's better if he gives the ranch to us and he can be free."

Mariah stuck her chin in the air. "I've never lost a case in my career—"

"In your *short* career?" Barbara grinned. "Keep practicing law honey and I bet you'll lose real soon."

"Fine." Mariah grabbed her Louis Vuitton briefcase. "See you in court." She twisted past Zach and to the door. "Let's go," she ordered him as she flounced out the office.

"Jeez." Barbara poured a cup of coffee. "I can see why you left her at the altar."

Zach ran out of the office and met up with Mariah by the elevator. "Don't mind her. She's trying to fight a war she can't win."

They got on the elevator and Mariah pushed the down button.

"Barbara's just as pathetic as she was in high school," Mariah said. "She's never liked me."

"She's always been jealous of you." Zach pushed his hands into the pockets of his jeans. "You were the smartest and prettiest girl at Briar Hurst High and she couldn't stand it."

She smiled, diamond earrings sparkling. "She still wants you after all this time. Guess I can't blame her."

He wanted her to elaborate, but didn't push it. "Do you think we'll go to court?"

The bell dinged, and the elevator opened.

"Maybe," she said as they stepped out of the elevator. "Maybe not."

Zach rubbed up against her as they walked. "Thought you told me having a lawyer would deter them."

She pushed open the glass door that led to the parking lot. "I got more tricks up my sleeve."

Zach chuckled as he followed her to his truck.

****

Mariah didn't think it would be so hard to take a ride out to the Carrington Ranch with Zach. But the minute they got on that desolate country road, all those memories came rolling back like thunder.

They'd take turns making innocent conversation, but the way his hands shook against the steering wheel told her he was as uncomfortable as she was.

She crossed her legs in her lavender Ralph Lauren suit, bracelets jiggling with every movement.

A grin peeked from Zach's damp lips.

"What?"

"Nice suit." His eyes sparkled. "Always had style, and it's good to see that hasn't changed."

"Worried about losing your ranch? Don't be."

"I'm not worried *anymore*." He sat back, smirking. "I have the utmost confidence in you."

"You're holding the steering wheel like it's going to fall off." She smirked. "I'm a lawyer, remember? Very observant. You're nervous about something. Is it me?"

He glanced at her, eyebrows rising in the center. "Just thinking up the words to say—"

"About leaving me at the altar?" She scoffed, snapping her head in the other direction. "Don't."

He turned his head back and forth at her and the road. "I wanted you deep within my soul, but I didn't know how to love you. I still don't."

"That's nonsense. Love doesn't have to come with rules, Zach. I'd fallen in love with you so it means you did something right."

He pressed his lips together as he made a right onto the rickety, rocky road she remembered led to the ranch.

"You didn't know how to love me?" She mocked, holding onto the rocking truck. "You've known me since I was a kid. We grew up together. No one knows me better. Admit you were afraid."

"All right!" He squeezed the steering wheel. "I didn't think I could give you what you needed."

"I needed love."

"You need a man who can take care of you. Who, when you go to fancy parties or meet up with your lawyer friends, you don't have to be embarrassed."

She gaped.

"A man who fits into your world." His eyes watered. "You're such a treasure, Mari. You were always too good for this town and everyone in it. We both know that."

"Wait, a minute." Her breath caught in her throat. "Are you saying you're not good enough for me?"

"I know I'm not." He swallowed. "I'm an ignorant country boy who only knows two things; growing food and raising animals. We're from two different worlds."

"Yes, we are." She stared at him. "In obvious ways, but that's what made us special, Zach. We're special because with us, race or class never came into the picture. I loved you. Down to your stained jeans, clunky cowboy boots, dirty hands and sarcasm." She touched his cheek. "You, Zach. I've always loved you."

"I loved you too much to let you settle."

"If I love you, how can it be settling?" She bounced when he drove over a dip. "Do me a favor and let *me* decide if I want to be with you or not."

He half-smiled. "You saying you wanna be with me?"

"I'm saying let me decide." She crossed her arms. "You owe me that."

CHAPTER FOUR

It had been a year. A whole year since Mariah had stepped foot on the Carrington Ranch and the moment she got out of the truck, she felt like someone who'd been kidnapped for years and finally returned home.

"Wow." She froze, taking in the scenery.

The house was surrounded by miles and miles of vibrant, bright-green grass with a symphony of cows mooing, chickens clucking, and horses neighing.

They walked through the dusty driveway toward the white wooden home and the first thing she noticed was no wreath on the door.

Zach's parents had made decorating for Christmas an art form. His mother reveled in covering the house with Christmas cheer.

But those days were no more, and it hurt Mariah to see the Carrington home as a shell of itself.

Entering the house after all this time felt like walking into the embrace of an old friend. Walls covered in framed memories. She was happy to see some garland and tinsel hanging, but still nothing compared to the past.

Mariah closed her eyes. She could still smell the peach and apple pies Zach's mother used to offer her when she'd come over as a kid.

She walked past the staircase, remembering the first time she had dinner with Zach's parents and how, even though she felt out of place, they'd shown her nothing but love.

"Well?" Zach stood in the living room full of wicker furniture, brightened by his mother's homemade yellow curtains. "How does it feel to be back here?"

"Seems like I was gone more than a year." She walked across the hardwood floor. "Ever not realize how much you missed a place until you saw it again?"

"That's funny." Zach threw his cowboy hat on the couch. "You hated this place."

"I never hated the ranch. It's a part of you. How could I hate it?"

He blinked, smiling.

"I need to apologize." She exhaled, stroking the suede recliner. "You did me wrong but part of it was my fault. If I hadn't made you feel you had to be someone you weren't—"

"No." He rushed toward her. "Mariah—"

"Please." She flashed her palm, sniffling. "Let me stand in my truth, Zach."

He stood back, brows heavy with concern.

"All this time I blamed you because I refused to see my faults." She walked past the chair and to the coffee table. "It was unfair to pressure you."

"Mari, I didn't blame you for anything."

"Maybe you should've. Because I *was* ashamed of you."

He grimaced.

She closed her eyes, sobbing. "I was, and I hate myself for it."

"But I left you," he whispered, reaching for her. "You didn't deserve that kind of cowardice. Especially not from me."

"I treated you badly and you didn't know it. Lying to you about not going to a work meeting because I was embarrassed you'd show up looking like you'd been plowing all day. Making up excuses why you couldn't meet my boss. I wanted to be with you but didn't want you in my world."

"Mari." He tried to hug her, but she moved away.

"No, let me sit in it. Let me sit in what I should've been honest about from the beginning. I'm not the prize here, Zach. You are. You're a wonderful man. You're loyal and honest." She held out her manicured hands. "Look at me. I'm so selfish. All I cared about was my career. My image. Because that's all I thought I had. But I lost something that's more important than anything. I lost you, Zach." She cried into her hands. "I lost *you*."

"You didn't lose me." He pulled her into a hug. "We both made mistakes."

"Mine were worse."

"Okay." He snickered. "If you insist."

She managed a chuckle, wiping her tears on his T-shirt.

"You don't have a selfish bone in your body." He sandwiched her face in his hands. "If you did, you wouldn't be helping me now."

"I'm so sorry, Zach." She caressed his muscular forearms. "I waited so long to hear those words when I was the one who should've been saying them too."

"You're saying them *now*." He tightened his embrace, smashing his lips over hers.

Like the ranch and house, his lips felt so familiar. Like they'd never broken up.

He moaned, caressing her hair as they turned their heads. They bumped noses and foreheads a few times and laughed.

Funny how you could be with a man for so long, but had to get used to kissing him again.

He squeezed her tighter as she spread her fingers across the flexing muscles in his back.

Her breathing quickened the longer the kiss lasted. All she could think about were those powerful arms pitching piles of hay and wrangling cattle back to pasture.

In his arms, just like before, she felt safe and wanted.

Zach carried her upstairs to his bedroom and yanked off her blazer and blouse.

She trembled because it had been so long since they'd seen each other naked, and she wasn't sure if she'd disappoint him or not. She was a stickler for fitness. Did all she could to stay in shape, but it was different being confident when she looked at herself as opposed to being naked in front of the only man she ever loved.

"What?" He pulled her close, breathing on her forehead before kissing it. "You're beautiful."

Of course, Zach knew her thoughts without her saying them. That's how they'd always been.

He stood back, staring at her breasts, tucked away in her lacy black bra.

Her first instinct was to wrap her arms around herself to hide, but she didn't want to anymore. She felt a power she'd never felt before when she saw how weak in the knees he got just from looking at her.

"You're trembling." She grinned. "I thought I was supposed to be nervous."

"It's just funny." He blushed. "That we've made love so many times, but it feels like the first time. Every time with you is like the first time."

She took his large hand and laid it on her shoulder, slid it down, lowering her bra strap as she did. Her breast bounced as soon as they released it.

Again, she didn't have to tell him what to do because he bent over quickly and latched his mouth onto her breast, sucking her nipple while tickling her areola with his tongue.

"Ooh." She ran her hands through his sodden hair, amazed at how much sweat he had trapped in it but that's what happened when you wore a hat in Texas weather all day. "*Yes*. Your mouth feels so good on me."

"I can make it feel even better. My tongue..." He moved to her other breast and slurped. "Where do you want it? I'll put it anywhere."

"Oh." She rocked, gliding against him. "You know where I want it."

Grinning, he undid her pants and slid them off.

"Mm." She bit her lip, massaging her breasts. "Yes."

Zach placed her leg on his shoulder, kissing the warmth in between her thighs.

Mariah writhed, bending over, as he stuck his tongue inside her wetness.

"Oh, yes." She gripped his head, moving it at the pace she wanted. "Yes, left to right. Like that...ooh!"

Moaning, he licked inside her labia as if it were a taco, delivering long, measured strokes that made her toes curl.

"Yes!" By this time, she was bouncing so hard her tits nearly hit her chin. She grabbed them, pinching and kneading her nipples. "That feels so good."

She was glad to see his tongue game still on point, but that wasn't the reason it felt so good. It felt good because they knew each other so well. At least she had that because she sure as hell didn't trust him anymore.

But right now she didn't care because she was here with him. *Zach Carrington.*

The man her body and heart had ached for, for a year. The man who had the power to turn her entire world upside down. She still hung on his every word and felt absolutely pathetic for worshipping him after how he'd hurt her, but tonight she'd gladly be a fool. She'd relish being a fool if she meant he'd make love to her at least one more time.

"Ow, wait." Zach stopped licking, exercising his tongue. "My tongue's hurting."

"Who gives a fuck?" She shoved his head back into her cunt, nearly falling over as she was about to come. "Yes, right there! Right there, Zach."

This was ridiculous, because the more he sucked, the hotter she got. With any other man she'd come by now, but how her body held out was proof how badly she wanted him.

"Ooh!" She pressed her fingers into his head. "Oh, God. Keep licking. Just like that. Yes!" She quivered, her muscles seizing and pussy tightening.

He moved his head and placed his finger where his tongue had been. "Come on, Mari. Come on!"

She bounced, riding his finger. Her pussy was so wet she almost digested his hand.

"Fuck me." She squeezed her eyes closed, squealing as a tsunami of ecstasy filled her gut. "Yes... oh. Ah, yes. Yes!"

She busted, coating his finger with silky cum.

CHAPTER FIVE

Zach sat in the rocking chair across from his bed, staring at the gorgeous woman immersed in his cotton sheets.

She slept with her head turned away from him, depriving him of looking at a face that brought more rays to his heart than one thousand suns.

She'd come harder than he thought possible; on his finger, in his face, against his dick. She'd been an animal, unleashing the same inhibited passion and desire he had for her.

Now he knew, no matter what she'd try to say, she wanted him. The mouth could lie, but the body... no way.

He knew he could help her get over her broken heart and trust him again, but his concern was if she was with someone else. He had one question; who was that handsome black guy with the slick smile in that picture on her desk at work?

Mariah whimpered and wiggled as she turned toward him.

"Hey." He smiled, only wearing his boxer shorts. "Now, please don't tell me you do this with all your clients."

She grinned while rising on her elbows, the sheet hiding her bosom. "What time is it?"

He looked at the antique Howard Miller clock on his dresser. "Nine."

"At night? Damn. I've been here since two in the evening?"

He nodded. "Guess time flies when you're having fun."

She sat against the headboard, exhaling. "What did we do, Zach?"

"Mm." He squinted, pretending to guess. "We made the best love I ever had. Now, if you forgot, I'm losing my touch."

She smiled, her curls flattened at the back. "You know what I mean."

"No." He spread his toes against the cool wood floor. "Why don't you tell *me*?"

"This was wrong on so many levels."

"Who says?" He leaned forward. "Don't do this wishy-washy shit with me, okay? One minute you say you regret what happened between us, make love to me, and now you're acting like I'm some random guy you took back to a motel."

She scowled. "I don't take men back to motels."

He sat back. "You know what I mean."

"Maybe I'm afraid of being hurt again, Zach. Is that so hard to understand?"

"I can't change the past. Either we move on from it or we just move on for good."

She froze, those sexy eyes digging into him. "Maybe we *should* move on for good then."

He groaned, knowing better than to argue with Mariah, because he'd never win. "Who is that guy in the picture on your desk?"

She ran her fingers through her hair, moving her eyes left and right. "What guy?"

"The black guy." He dropped his shoulders. "The one in the fancy suit that looks like a sleazy politician."

"Wow." She scoffed. "He's Dominic Haslam. The son of Rick Haslam."

He gaped. "Rick Haslam? That big-time lawyer?"

She nodded, scratching under the sheet.

"What's with you two?"

"Nothing."

"I don't have pictures of women on my desk if it means nothing." He clasped his hands. "Be honest. I mean, we aren't together, are we—"

"Hell no." She waved her finger. "No, no way. This was just something that happened. Take it as us getting each other out of our systems."

"From the way you were screaming, you enjoy me in your system."

She rolled her eyes.

"So what is this dude to you, anyway?"

"Just a friend."

"Does he know that?"

"This isn't your business, Zach. I didn't ask you who you're fucking."

"I'm not fucking anyone." He shrugged. "I'm too busy trying not to lose my family's ranch and ruin my parents' legacy to worry about women."

She smirked, turning on her side and propping her arm under her. "Not all women it seems."

"The Haslams are big news. How did you get involved with them?"

"Dominic is a criminal attorney at his father's firm and we crossed paths at a business function." She laid her head on the pillow. "We struck a conversation and became friends. That's all."

"How long have you known him?"

"What's with the interrogation?" She sighed. "I've known him for a few years but we didn't go out until you and I broke up."

He wiggled his lips. "You knew this guy when we were together and didn't tell me?"

"Why should I?"

"Because now you're dating him."

"So?"

He jumped out of the chair. "You think I'm stupid? How do I Know you weren't with him when we were together?"

She sat up. "You're accusing me of cheating on you? The man who dumped me like old shoes? How dare you, Zach? I never once looked at another guy when we were together."

He held his waist. "But you were attracted to him, weren't you?"

"I never cheated on you. You got some nerve. For all I know you left *me* for another woman!"

"That's not true."

"How do I know?"

He rushed to the bed. "I want you back, Mari."

"Oh, Jeez." She turned her head, chuckling. "Are you crazy?"

"Of course I'm crazy because I left you at the altar." He held her face. "You're the best thing that ever happened to me and I'm not letting you go again."

She moved from his kiss. "You got some of this loving and now you're hooked again? Forgot how good it was?"

"It's not about sex." He grimaced. "I love you, Mariah, and we belong together. You think us making love this quickly after seeing each other is not a sign? It's fate."

"I don't trust you."

He took her hand. "Let me earn your trust again."

"Hell no."

"Why not?"

She took her hand from his. "Because you can't."

"I just want a chance."

"Too bad." She fixed the sheet over her breasts. "That's a

privilege you don't deserve. You know why I slept with you, Zach? So you could see what you're missing. So I could hurt you almost as much as you hurt me. I planned this whole thing."

"Liar. We made love because we both wanted it. Because we couldn't stop it—"

"We're just business, Zach." She pushed his hand from her face. "We deal with this bank stuff and after that we go our separate ways and never have to see each other again."

He stood, glaring down at her.

"I've moved on with Dominic and you gotta accept that."

"Do you love him?" He raised an eyebrow. "Say it then. Come on, Mari. Lie through your teeth. You're a lawyer so you're used to it right?"

She squinted. "How dare you? Take me home right now."

"Fine." He rolled his eyes on his way to the hallway. "You didn't even have to ask."

CHAPTER SIX

Of course Zach wouldn't give up pursuing Mariah. It wasn't his way, but it sure was funny that he tried to be so tough with her a few days ago now he stood in her kitchen, washing her load the dishwasher and she didn't understand why.

Not to mention she was in that damn bonnet but he'd caught her off-guard and her hair was a mess.

She knew what he wanted, but Mariah couldn't go back to him. She loved Zach more than she'd loved any man, but she'd never be vulnerable around him again and that's exactly what she'd always be unless she could trust him.

"Man." Zach sat at her marble top island, whistling. "This place is clean. I mean spotless. You always was a neat freak."

"I'm a neat freak because I pick up after myself like a grown person should?" She chuckled, placing a plate into the dishwasher. "What do you want, Zach?"

"To look at the most beautiful woman in the world."

She glanced at him, rolling her eyes. "Surely you didn't drive all the way to Sherman City at eight at night just to watch me load dishes."

"Why not? I can't think of anything better to do." He took off his hat, and she imagined brushing her fingers through those flattened curls like she had the other night when they made love.

"You have no idea how much I appreciate you helping me, Mari. Shows what a wonderful woman you are."

She closed the dishwasher and started it. "Just trying to do the right thing." She got a cup out of the cabinet and went to the fridge. "Want some lemonade? It's homemade."

He nodded. "I wouldn't mind some, sure."

She poured the juice into the cups and handed him one. For a moment, they stared at each other while sipping, her trying to read his mind like she did any client.

He drank, chuckling. "What?"

"You asked me about Dominic, well *I* want to know some things. It's been a year, so I know you hooked up with someone."

"I haven't been with anyone, Mari." He rubbed his hands. "You can believe it if you want, but after hurting you, my heart died. You don't understand it was just as tragic to me what I'd done. I hated myself for hurting you. I still do."

She tilted her head.

"I didn't trust myself around women. I didn't want to get involved with anyone else because I felt like I'd hurt them too."

"So you've felt guilty?"

"Course I have. You've been like a cloud over me. Every move I make, I think about what I did."

"When did you realize it was wrong?"

"Our wedding day. The second I hung up the phone after telling you I wasn't coming, I knew I'd made the biggest mistake of my life." His lips shivered. "I was just down the street from the church."

"What? When you called?"

He nodded. "I thought I was ready. Had my tux on and I was elated when I first got in the car, then by the time I got to the street by the church, I pulled over and called you. Just within seconds, I just couldn't do it."

"You mean you were at the church the whole time?"

He nodded.

"I thought you were still at home and hadn't even gotten dressed."

"I left my house intending to marry you that day but then I got this fear I never experienced and it was like someone took over my body because the next thing I knew I was calling you and you were cursing me out and crying." He dropped his head. "It's hard to look at you when I go back to that day."

"I just don't understand how you could let me go through a wedding day; getting dressed, being excited, going to the church with all our friends and family, and you called it off. How could you do that to me, Zach?"

"I don't know." He flinched, dropping eye contact. "But it was never about you. I got scared, Mari."

"Of what?"

"That I wasn't good enough. That you deserved more than what I could give you."

"All I wanted was for you to love me." She set her cup on the counter by the sink and crossed her arms. "That was it."

"Yeah, but Dominic fits your image better than I do." He clasped his hands. "I mean, I'm sure your parents would agree."

"This isn't about Dominic. All I needed was you. I didn't care about anything else."

"But now I can let go of the pain I caused you and breathe again. Because I've gotten a second chance to make things right."

"What are you talking about?"

"You know what I'm talking about." He licked his lips. "You wanted me the other day at the ranch and you still do."

"Stop." She got her cup, staring into it so she wouldn't have to look him in the eyes. "I told you what that was."

"Yeah, you said it was to get back at me." He scoffed. "Show me what I've been missing, well I already knew that, Mariah. I didn't need any reminders."

She drank, but the lemonade didn't go down as smoothly as before.

"You wanted me then, and you want me now."

She shivered, looking into his feverish gaze. "Don't give me that look."

He squinted. "What look?"

"That look you get when you wanna fuck. Is that why you came over here, Zach? To get me into bed again?"

"Yes."

She jerked back, batting her eyes.

"I've been hard ever since you left my place because I can't get you out of my head. All I want to be is inside you again. It was so magical, Mari. Better than before and it proved you still love me."

"Course I still care about you but that's different from trusting you."

"You trusted me enough to fuck me."

She swayed against the sink. "I had a weak moment."

"Then have another weak moment." He got up and crept toward her.

"Zach." Her hand shook as she set the cup on the counter. "Don't."

"Don't what?" He stood close to her, his breathing being the rope that bound them. "Don't stand close to you?" He touched her face. "Don't touch you, like this?"

She groaned, closing her eyes. "I hate you."

"Yeah." He inched his lips to hers. "I *know*."

Fuck.

Here she was again, letting Zach kiss her like a fool and she

knew she'd let him do more because it felt too damn good to stop him.

She couldn't keep doing this. She knew she had to be honest with him and let him know they had no future, but it wasn't so easy to say when she was in his arms.

He tossed her to the tile floor and snatched the bonnet off her head.

"Hey." She laughed. "Don't be grabbing my bonnet like that."

He grinned, pitching it on the table.

Now, unlike other women, it wasn't her fantasy to be thrown down just anywhere. Sure, she loved it that Zach wanted her so much, but doing it on the floor was uncomfortable and disgusting. Her floor was clean enough to eat off, but Mariah *was* a neat freak and laying on these germs made her skin crawl.

Then when she looked in the opposite direction, she saw the trash can.

"Ugh." She wiggled. "This is... man. You really wanna do this *here?*"

"Stop whining. Your kitchen is spotless."

"Yeah, but I'm looking at the damn trash can."

"Then look at *me.*"

"You know how many germs can be on a floor though? A gazillion. You wouldn't believe it."

He sighed. "Mari—"

She raised her head. "I read on the Internet once that a toothbrush can have over one hundred million bacteria. One hundred million, Zach! Now imagine how much a floor has."

He pushed her back down. "I don't give a fuck." He ripped his belt open and slid his jeans down to his knees. She loved he wanted her so much that he couldn't even take his clothes off before fucking her.

He shoved his hands up her house dress and slipped her panties down.

"Wait." She rose on her elbows. "We need—"

"Sh." He pulled out a large-sized, ribbed condom. "I got it covered."

She laid back down, smiling, glad he didn't take offense that even though she still cared for him, she wasn't ready to be anybody's momma.

He put the condom on, and she leaned up to see that dick she'd missed so much. It was perfect. Not too long or thick, but equipped to hit every angle just right.

She laid down, legs rattling and fingers shaking.

Why in hell was she so nervous? They'd had sex a million times but now she felt like a teen taking the driver's test.

"Sh." He lowered his lips to hers, gently opening her mouth with his tongue before tasting her breath. "I love you, Mari. I've always loved you."

She just lay there, staring and melting into the floor.

Now she knew for sure he still cared, and he wasn't just fucking her out of nostalgia or loneliness. But the biggest questions were, could he ever commit? Could she ever trust him again?

She wondered and she hoped, but as soon as he was inside her again, nothing else mattered. His touch erased all doubt or apprehension, at least for this moment.

Before they'd started fucking again, she'd forgotten how wide his dick got when he stroked. He was a great size but it felt much bigger than it looked, and she flinched unintentionally every time he pumped.

Maybe it was her body getting used to him again.

"You okay?" he asked, humping with sweat dripping off his forehead already.

"Y...yes." She relaxed, gyrating to his pace. "Right there. Oh, that's good."

"Ah." He moaned. "Your pussy's like fine wine, Mari. Worth the wait."

She grinned, covering her mouth. "Now that's just corny as hell."

He laughed. "You like my corniness, don't you?" He thrust harder and faster. "You missed this dick, huh?"

"Ooh, yes." She rocked, his sweat sprinkling her. "Faster, Zach. Fuck me."

He increased his pace, their bodies thrashing together while the scent of man sweat mixed with the aroma of lemon Cascade overtook the room.

"Ooh." Zach groaned, his rod tightening against her walls.

"God, yes!" Mariah raised up, sweat burning her eye. "Yes, baby. Come on, Zach. Come on!"

"I'm coming." He gyrated as her ass burned because of the friction from the tile floor. "Yes, Mari. Yeah!"

CHAPTER SEVEN

The next two weeks were unbearable for Zach. Almost as bad as the night he found out his parents died. Perhaps others couldn't tell how miserable he was because he kept up with his usual routine; tending ranch, feeding the animals, running errands in town. He'd exchange greetings with townspeople, a phony smile plastered on his face while making useless conversation.

Christmas would come and go in a few days and this overwhelming emptiness, and even a shot of his daddy's whiskey every night didn't shake the pain he felt.

He lay in bed in the middle of the night, wide awake yet again, tucked in self-pity. He barely slept because every time he tried to, he thought of making love with Mariah. Smelled her rose perfume on his pillow. Could feel the softness of her skin whenever he closed his eyes.

Torture.

They hadn't made love since in her kitchen, and she'd been avoiding him ever since. He'd get her voice mail almost every time he called, and if he didn't, she only stayed on the phone for a minute. She'd ramble through about the progress of the case and then hang up before they could talk about anything else.

He sent her flowers that she didn't acknowledge. Sent her loving emails and texts filled with heart emojis and smiley faces.

He knew she didn't like that shit. Mariah wasn't into the emojis and stuff. She thought it was elementary, but his plan had been to annoy her enough so she'd at least tell him he was getting on her nerves.

Nothing.

Many times, he wanted to charge into her office, grab her, and demand she speak to him. But what right did he have after what he'd done?

He didn't care what she said. He just wanted her to speak to him. Even if it was to curse him out. He'd take anything just to hear her voice. But to be locked out like this? It was the worst feeling in the world to have her shut him out of her life as if he was some stain or mistake she wanted to erase.

Seeing her again and holding her after months only to have her give him the cold shoulder was killing him.

Yet he'd created this misery. He could've had her a long time ago. The day she waited on him at the altar, but he did what she said he'd do, chose this ranch over her.

He looked around his bedroom. Everything dripped in pathetic despair. He had no one to blame but himself.

He could've been living the dream with Mariah starting a year ago. Could've had a house full of kids running around. Could've been in bed with the love of his life every night, staring into her precious eyes.

He tucked his arm under his head, swallowing.

But no. He'd clung on to that Carrington pride. Told himself this ranch and life in Briar Hurst was all he'd ever need, but that was far from the truth.

"Man, you fucked up, Zach." He turned over on his side. "I gotta get her back." He sighed, slapping his pillow into shape. "I just got to."

****

"It is true!" Zach's best friend and "sometimes" ranch hand, Mitch yelled over the phone the next morning. "I saw it on the news last night. How could you miss it?"

"This can't be real." Zach cracked another egg into the sizzling butter in the cast-iron skillet on the stove. "You've played some evil tricks on me before, but this is fucked up, Mitch."

"I'd never joke about the ranch with the shit you're going through. It's true, man. The bank's being investigated by the Feds for money laundering, fraud, and illegal loans."

Zach tossed the eggshell into the sink. "You gotta be kidding me."

"Shit, I can't believe it myself. That little ass bank is Crime World Central." Mitch cackled. "Who would've guessed a scheme like that happening right here in Briar Hurst, and we didn't even know? So you know what that means. They sure as hell won't be coming after you for your parents' loan." He chuckled. "That's one hell of a Christmas gift if you asked me. Still can't believe you didn't know."

"I skipped the news and went to bed early." Zach yawned. "Why I don't know since I never sleep."

"Mariah didn't call you?"

"Nope."

"Maybe she thought you saw it."

"She's not talking to me. Fuck!" Zach roughly stirred the eggs with the spatula. "I fucked up, man. I don't think I can get her back."

"Well, she's still open for you if she fucked you, so that's a sign, right?"

"I thought so but women play so many damn games they can have you thinking one thing is happening while they're doing another."

"Yeah, and they say men are the players. Bullshit."

"Hell yeah. They *invented* the game. I gotta be the dumbest motherfucker." Zach snatched the dishtowel off his shoulder. "How can a man be so stupid and lose the woman he loves *twice*? This was my last chance."

"Wait, are you giving up? Because the Zach Carrington I know *always* fights for what he wants, regardless."

"I can't *make* her want me."

Mitch laughed. "The hell you can't. Anyway, she wants you or

you wouldn't have gotten down and dirty in her kitchen that night. Ewe," he teased. "Getting ass on the kitchen floor. Zach, my man. Didn't know you had it in you."

"You'll never understand." The eggs scrambled. "The longest relationship you've had is getting blow jobs from Kim at the post office when she delivers your mail. What the fuck do you know about relationships?"

"I know you can't just give up, and I'm jealous as fuck."

Zach turned off the eggs. "Of who?"

"You. You think I don't want a real relationship sometimes?"

Zach grinned. "I think you're quite happy fucking half the

town."

"I'm serious, man." Mitch sighed. "Sure, the variety is fun but I'm in my thirties now and it scares me sometimes to think I might be alone for the rest of my life."

Zach reflected on Mitch's words as he reached for the crispy bacon that had been draining on a paper towel.

"I wouldn't mind having a little shawty to come home to at night, talk to her about my day, and she rubs my feet when I'm tired."

"Shit, ain't no woman gonna be touching *those* dogs."

"I love my freedom, but it gets lonely too. You got a chance at something real, Zach. You gotta fight, and you can't let her go. No matter how hard you gotta push this."

"I don't know, man." Zach got a clean plate from the dishwasher. "I mean, maybe she really has moved on. She's with that Dominic cat now."

"Aw, that shit ain't real. He's just somebody she got with so

she wouldn't be thinking 'bout you. She ain't even fucking him."

"How do you know?"

"Because I know the woman Mariah is, and she doesn't fuck

men she doesn't love and she don't love Dominic. If she did, would she have fucked you the second you came back into her life? She sure didn't hesitate, did she? Naw, man. Mariah's a great woman. She's beautiful, she's fine, and she's successful. A sista too? Shit. If I had Mariah, I'd wife her ass up tonight." Mitch chuckled. "I don't know what she wants your country ass for."

Zach scoffed. "She's country. Whether she wants to admit it or not."

"Take it from a brotha who's been around and around and around. You gotta fight for a woman like that. A woman like that don't grow on trees, especially not around here."

"You're right." Zach stood straight, tossing the towel on the table. "Shit, Mari is *my* woman. I ain't letting that slick ass attorney have her."

"Hell no. Fuck that chump."

"Shit, he doesn't deserve her, anyway. He's probably gotten everything he's wanted his whole life, well he ain't getting Mariah Phoenix." Zach dumped the eggs and bacon on a plate. "I must be out of my mind thinking of giving her up. I'm not some punk whose gonna roll over and let this fool take my girl."

"Yeah," Mitch howled. "Now that's the Zach I know and love! Go get your woman and show that fool who she belongs to. You got this, bro. Go get her, man. Go!"

"Fuck, yeah." Zach marched out of the kitchen. "I sure as hell will."

****

Soon as Zach got off the phone with Mitch, he headed to Sherman City only to have Mariah's secretary inform him she wasn't there.

"What do you mean, she isn't here?" Zach checked his watch. "The firm just opened thirty minutes ago."

"She shouldn't be long." The woman smiled, popping raisins into her mouth. "You're free to wait—"

"Hell no." He waved off the suggestion. "I need to talk to Mariah *now*."

She switched her eyes back and forth. "She's on a breakfast date with Dominic Haslam. You know who that is, right? His father is Rick Haslam of the Haslam & Benedict Law Firm. That's one of the most successful law firms in the country. Surely you've heard of Rick Haslam—"

"I know who Dominic is." He lifted his hat so she could see his eyes and know he wasn't in mood for cute games. "Where are they?"

The secretary swallowed. "The Fadora Café."

****

Mariah sat at the little lace-covered table in the Fadora Café, the "it" place for Sherman City's most influential people. Everybody who was anybody came here to "bask in the ambiance".

Mariah swayed to Luther Vandross' smooth version of "Have Yourself A Merry Little Christmas". She looked around at all the elegant, well-dressed people sitting at the tables decorated with Christmas bows and poinsettias, partaking in upscale brunches and over-priced, fancy cocktails with names Mariah couldn't pronounce.

Dominic sat in front of her, rambling about something she couldn't care less about.

This place, this scene, and Dominic was what she *should've* wanted. A life full of luxury and status with Dominic, a gorgeous, single and successful black man who belonged to a respected family.

Mariah faked smiles in between sipping her nonalcoholic cocktail; a tart, sugary mixture of cranberry juice, grapefruit juice, and maple syrup.

Yes. This was the life she should've wanted. But she didn't. At least not without Zach.

"Earth to Mariah." Dominic's moist lips spread, revealing his white-as-piano keys teeth. "I know I can't compete with Luther, but you're a million miles away."

"Oh, sorry." She chuckled, setting her glass on the table. "I was listening, I assure you."

"Then what is your answer?" He clutched his long, milk-chocolate fingers on the table.

"Um, to what?"

"See you weren't listening." He grinned, sexy wrinkles appearing in the corners of his onyx eyes. "I just made a full-blown pitch of why you need to talk to my dad about a position at Haslam and Benedict."

She groaned. "Oh, this again."

He raised his eyebrows, making his wavy hairline shift. "It's a wonderful opportunity that could catapult your career within a year."

"I like where I am besides..." she exhaled. "I don't practice criminal law, remember?"

"There's not much difference between it and civil. A case is a case and you're a darn good lawyer." He tilted his head, his milk-chocolate cheeks blushing. "I believe in you, Mari. You haven't made your mark yet." He took her hand, sticking his long fingers in between hers. "You got so much more to do."

She faked a smile.

"Isn't this the life you want? I thought it was." He snickered, eyes flashing. "It's the one you *deserve*. Let me give it to you."

She faked a smile as he kissed her hand.

CHAPTER EIGHT

Zach rushed into the glass doors of the Fadora Cafe' with everyone looking at him as if his clothes dripped with cow manure.

The feminine bald greeter skipped up to him from behind a gold-trimmed counter.

"Excuse me?" The man grimaced as he overlooked Zach's wrinkled shirt and jeans. "Um, are you a guest of someone here?"

Zach observed the dining area, overtaken for a moment by the soothing sounds of Luther, but then remembered where he was and scoured the uptight, stiff people eating until his eyes found the most beautiful woman in the room.

Mariah sat across from Dominic, who moved so smoothly he looked like he'd slipped off a magazine cover.

Zach groaned, clutching his waist.

"Sir," the bald man shrieked. "You can't dine here without a reservation. What is your name? Are you a guest of someone here?"

Zach bolted to Mariah's table.

"Sir," the man yelled. "Stop, or I'll get security!"

Everyone stopped eating, gasping and gaping at the dirty cowboy who dared to grace them with his uncouth presence.

Zach marched to Mariah, who looked just as shocked as the rest of them.

"*Zach*?" Mariah's golden earrings swung as she swiftly turned her head in his direction. "What are you doing here?"

Damn, she smelled good. Just like a Creamsicle and it knocked Zach off his game for a second.

"Hello?" Mariah wiggled her neck. "What are you doing here, Zach?"

"Huh?" He shook out of his trance. "Oh, uh, you know why I'm here, woman. Let's go."

She grimaced. "Excuse *me*?"

"Yeah, you heard me." He clutched her wrist. "We need privacy. I got something to say."

"What the hell?" Dominic scowled. "Uh, Mariah who is this?"

"Don't worry about who I am." Zach jerked on Mariah's arm.

"Let's go. Get up, Mari."

"Get off me, fool." She jerked free. "You crazy? Who do you think you are coming up in here and grabbing on me? What the hell are you doing here, anyway?"

"*Who* is this, Mari?"

"I'm Zach," he snapped at Dominic. "Is that clear enough for you?"

"Oh, wow." Dominic cackled, throwing his head back. "Zach Carrington, huh?"

Zach smirked at Mariah, who looked like she wanted to slip under the table and hide. "She's mentioned me? Course she has."

"Oh yeah, she's mentioned you." Dominic's forehead lowered. "Mentioned how much of a coward you are. What man lets a woman get dressed and go down to the church to get marry then just calls her and breaks it off? You must be out of your damn mind."

Zach clenched his teeth. "You don't wanna go there with me."

"I don't?" Dominic stood.

"Dominic." Mariah reached for him. "Please, just sit down. People are watching."

"Uh, please don't trouble yourself with this person, Mr. Haslam," the jumpy greeter said. "I've called the police."

"The police?" Zach grimaced. "Because I'm just *standing* here?"

"Because you barged in here..." The man looked at Zach from head-to-toe. "And you obviously don't belong."

"Now wait a minute," Mari said. "He can come in here if he wants, but he needs to remember his manners."

"No need for the police." Dominic approached Zach, slipping his hands under his blazer to put them in his pockets. "I can handle this."

"I don't have any beef with you but you need to just back off."

Dominic grinned. "Back off of what?"

"Of Mari," Zach said. "She's *my* woman."

"What?" She got up. "How dare you? I'm not your woman. Get out of here, Zach!"

A lady at the next table grinned in between sips. "This has more drama than last night's episode of *Grey's Anatomy*."

"I'm gonna tell you this just once," Dominic said. "Get your sweaty, country, horse wrangling ass out of here."

"You're insulting me?" Zach chuckled. "Wonder what all those big time clients of yours would say? I mean, you judge me just because of how I look and what I do?"

"No, I'm judging your ass on how you hurt Mari."

"Dominic." She grabbed his arm. "Please don't do this here."

"No, ever since you told me about this coward, I've wanted to stick my foot up his ass."

"I wish you'd try." Zach snatched his hat off. "You don't know how bad I wish you'd try."

"Not the hat." Mariah grabbed it. "Dominic, he took the hat off. You don't want this. Remember, he wrangles horses and cows."

"Please, I'm not afraid of this bum," Dominic said. "He can be tough now, but wasn't man enough to tell you he couldn't marry you? How could you do that to her, Zach? How?"

"I don't know!"

Dominic backed up, batting his eyes.

"For a year, I've asked myself that same question. How could I hurt someone I love so much?" Zach looked at Mariah. "I've apologized the best way I know how and I can't take the pain I caused away." He turned to Dominic. "You wanna hit me because of what I did? Trust me, I wanted to do much worse to myself. You could never bring me more pain than I brought myself."

Dominic squinted, taking small pants.

"You're perfect for her, man." Zach grabbed Dominic's lapel. "You got the fancy clothes, expensive cars, high-class family, the life she's always wanted. Isn't that right, Mari?"

"Zach," she whispered, tears filling her eyes. "Don't—"

"It's okay if you want that but I'm not giving up unless you tell me to." He stood back, sticking out his chest. "If you want me to leave and never come back into your life, just tell me. And I'll do it. It'll kill me but I'll do it."

"Oh." A server covered her mouth, sniffling. "This is so beautiful."

"It's on you, Mariah," Zach said. "I can't keep chasing you and even though I wanted to, I can't drag you out of here and make you be with me so..." He exhaled. "You want me out of your life for good then tell me."

"Yeah." Dominic glared at her. "Tell him, Mariah. Tell him he had his chance and you're building something with me now." He walked around the table to her. "Tell him." He scowled. "*Tell* him."

She dropped her head as she laid Zach's hat on the table. "I can't."

"W... what?" Dominic scoffed. "What the hell you mean, you can't?"

The women at the tables gasped while the men they were with rolled their eyes.

"I'm sorry, Dominic." Mariah kept her head low. "I am so sorry for wasting your time, but I don't love you." She lifted her head and directed her gaze to Zach. "I love Zach. I've always loved him and I always will."

Dominic's shoulders fell. He looked at the table, then at Mariah. "*Bitch*," he shrieked.

Everyone gasped, including Mariah.

"You had me spending all this goddamn money on your ass, buying you dinner and all this shit and you don't know what the fuck you want any damn way."

"Wow," Zach whispered.

"Wait, a minute, fool." Mariah grabbed her waist, wiggling her neck. "Who the hell you calling a 'bitch'? You better get your ass out of here while you can still walk."

"Yeah," an old, dapper man at a table said. "You better leave. I don't think you want to mess with *her*."

The greeter gasped, clutching his pearls. "I concur."

"Get out of here!" Mariah lunged at Dominic, and Zach ran and grabbed her. "I guess I didn't know your ass at all. So much for good breeding and class."

"Fuck you. I don't need this shit." Dominic took out his wallet and threw money on the table. "On second thought, let your ass pay, shit." He snatched the tip. "I can see why he left your ass at the altar."

"Someone's gonna be leaving your ass at the cemetery if you don't get out of my face!" Mariah charged him as Zach held her back. "You better go on now!"

Dominic scoffed as he marched toward the entrance and left.

"Can you believe that clown?" Mariah straightened her blazer. "He called me a bitch."

"Yep." Zach got his hat off the table. "I'd have socked him but something told me you had it covered." He grinned.

"I can't believe him." She glared at the entrance. "You think you know somebody."

"I need to talk to you, Mari."

"Okay. We can talk on the terrace."

"Oh, *no*," a woman whined. "We want to see."

Zach grimaced at her.

The greeter jumped in front of Zach, barely reaching Zach's chest. "You need to leave. You've caused enough trouble."

"It was Dominic causing the trouble," Mariah said. "Now move, Pete." She pushed him. "Come on, Zach." She took Zach's hand and pulled him to the terrace.

"Damn." Zach broke out laughing when he got outside. "I thought you were gonna kill Dominic. Man, seeing you all mad like that turned me on." He grabbed her waist. "Can I get a kiss?"

"You can kiss my ass." She shoved him and shut the double doors. "Have all the men in Texas lost their minds or just you and Dominic?"

"What's wrong?"

"*Both* of you are assholes. *You* come stomping in here like

some caveman and grabbing me like you've lost your mind..." She waltzed past him, waving her arms. "And Dominic jumps up like he's ready to throw down and then calls me a bitch!"

"I shouldn't have grabbed you like that, but Dominic was the

one acting a fool. It's *your* fault." He licked out his tongue mockingly. "See the effect you have on men?"

"It's not funny, Zach. You both embarrassed me."

"Oh, who cares about those people in there? I sure as hell don't."

"That's because you don't have to work in this city and get clients."

He whistled, sniffing the snootiness in the air. "The Fadora Cafe', huh? Even the air smells rich."

She combed her fingers through her curls. "*What* are you doing here, Zach?"

"Came to right all the wrongs I've done to you."

"Ha! In five minutes? I doubt it. Get out." She sashayed to the doors.

"Don't you want to hear what I have to say?"

"I've heard enough." She twisted back over to him. "You have no class. You pop in here and embarrass the heck out of me in front of everyone—"

"You said you loved me in there."

She scoffed, fidgeted, and crossed her arms. "So? Just because I love you it doesn't mean we belong together." She looked at the diamond-outlined face of her watch. "I gotta get back to the office. I got business."

He blocked the doors. "I gotta get you back or I'll die."

"You should be happy. You get to keep the ranch and everything. The bank's in shit and can't come after you now."

"Well, I'm not happy." Sadness broke through his voice. "Because I realize what good is a ranch if I'm lonely?"

She gaped, swallowing.

"I'm the dumbest son of a bitch on the planet. I'm sorry, Mari."

"Jesus, stop apologizing it's annoying."

He chuckled. "Is it getting to you, though?"

"You being sorry isn't the issue. I know you regret what you did." She pointed to her chest. "It's me trusting you that's the issue."

"Well, you gotta give me a chance at least to see if you can trust me again, right?" He touched her cheek as a cool breeze swept through.

She looked up. "It's cloudy."

"Yeah, rain's in the forecast." He clutched her face in both hands. "What do I have to do to get another chance? I'll do anything. Walk over cracked glass barefoot. I'll run down the street naked."

She grinned.

"I'll give up meat. I'll eat dog shit. But I can't lose you." He put his arms around her waist, pushing his forehead to hers. "I was a coward before, but I'll never be again. You'll have to kill me to get rid of me, girl."

She parted her luscious lips.

"I've missed you." He gave her a peck on the nose. "I've missed you so much."

"I didn't know how much I missed you too until we went to your place." She touched his face, sniffling. "When I set foot back into your parents' house, it was like I'd missed an old friend. It's when I knew I belonged with you and then we made love and..." She looked into his eyes. "And everything felt so right, but I knew you'd hurt me again. I knew it."

"No, honey. I'll never hurt you again. Listen." He kissed her hand and squeezed it. "You're my lady. I wanna give you the life you deserve whether it's here in Sherman City, Briar Hurst or the moon."

"Why should I trust you and give you another chance?"

He shrugged. "Because you want to?"

She smiled, and he held her tighter, afraid she'd disappear if he let go.

"You're everything to me, Mari, and this time I'll make sure you know it every day."

Hooting and hollering erupted from inside. Zach turned to see the women in the café clapping and cheering.

"What the fuck?" Mariah whispered.

Zach laughed, shaking his head. "I don't know *what* the hell's going on."

The women giggled and gushed as they snapped pictures of the couple on their phones.

"Jesus," Zach said.

"Well..." Mariah threw her arms around his shoulders. "If they want a show, let's give them one they'll never forget."

She laid her soft, velvety lips over his, and it felt like someone had hooked him up to an oxygen machine because finally... after all this time, he could breathe again.

THE END

THE BEST CHRISTMAS EVER
CHAPTER ONE

Beluga, Georgia

"Come on, I dare you." Da'Kuan Wells drove alongside Tisha Eason's station wagon. "You won't do it!"

"I won't do it?" Twenty-two-year-old Ginger Ryder shouted back, tumbling into Tisha's backseat with her skirt flying. "Who won't do it?"

"You won't do shit." Da'Kuan and his friend Ronny laughed. "You so big and bad then let me see."

"Tisha, level this piece of shit up." Ginger inched her lean waist out the back window.

"No." Tisha struggled to keep the car straight on the desolate road. "Ginger, stop."

"Shut up." She laughed, holding her arms out to Ronny, who sat on the passenger's side of Da'Kuan's teal Toyota Corolla. "Catch my hands, fool."

Ronny reached for Ginger's hands, wobbling as Da'Kuan swerved. "Man, slow down, shit."

"Slow down nothing." Da'Kuan cackled, increasing his speed.

"Those fuckers are going faster, Tisha." Ginger almost slipped out the window. "Ah!"

"Holy shit." Ronny elbowed Da'Kuan in the chest. "Slow down so I can get her."

Ginger fell into Tisha's backseat, laughing. "They are so stupid."

"Ginger, what the hell is wrong with you?" Tisha stared at her best friend through the rearview mirror, her chocolate face torn with worry. "You're gonna get yourself killed. Settle down."

"This Negro dared me to do something and I never walk away from a challenge."

Ginger threw her bust out the window again. "I'm gonna surf with one foot in Da'Kuan's car and the other in here."

"*What*?" The station wagon veered as Tisha glanced back at Ginger. "Girl, get your black ass back in this car."

"Grab my hands, Ronny." Ginger reached for him. "Hold me until I get my leg out and grab my foot."

Ronny watched with his mouth open and eyes wide, his kinky twists blowing in the humid wind. "This bitch crazy, D."

"You shouldn't have dared me." She laughed. "Grab my hands!"

Ronny hesitated then took both Ginger's hands.

"Oh god." Tisha swerved off to the side. "Ginger."

"I swear Tisha, you can't drive for shit." Ginger got one long leg out the window. "Ronny, grab my leg." The wind blew the loose curls of her thick, jet-black hair. "Shit, messin' up my hair. Grab my damn leg, boy!"

"Ginger, please," Tisha shrieked. "Get back in the car. This isn't funny."

Ginger laughed as Ronny caught her by her white Ked sneaker. "Hold me." She slid more of her leg inside Da'Kuan's car as her other hung out Tisha's back window.

"I don't believe this." Tisha jerked in the driver's seat. "I always knew you were crazy, but this is too crazy even for you."

"Shit, a car's coming." Da'Kuan yanked the toothpick out his mouth, laughing. "Bitch, you're out of your damn mind, Ginger."

"Never dare me to do something, motherfucker." Ginger wobbled as she sat upright with both legs in the each vehicle.

"Woo, hoo, hoo!" Ronny laughed, gripping Ginger's skinny leg. "What you on, girl?"

"She gon' be on *me* tonight." Da'Kuan licked his pink tongue out at Ginger. "Pull her ass in here."

"Oh, shit." Tisha struggled to steer the car.

"Jesus, girl," Ginger shouted. "Stop swerving. You trying to kill me?"

"This ain't funny." Tisha clutched the steering wheel. "Please, get back in the car."

"I'm surfing, woo!" Ginger waved her arms in the air as a white; Subaru came from the opposite direction.

"Fuck." Spit flew out Ronnie's crooked mouth. "Get in here, girl. Stop playing."

"Shit, that's Mrs. Moore's car," Tisha shouted. "She'll tell Pastor Ryder, Ginger!"

"I don't give a fuck." Ginger gyrated her tiny hips from side to side, licking her tongue at the Subaru. "Faster, you guys. Drive faster!"

"Ginger, please." Tisha hit the steering wheel. "Please, get back in the car."

Ginger swung her arms, roaring, "This is amazing!"

"What if your daddy saw you, huh?" Da'Kuan yelled. "He'll snatch a ditch in yo' black ass. Stop playing."

"Please, Ginger," Tisha screamed.

Ginger locked eyes on the fear in her friend's face. "All right, pull me in, Ronny."

"Better hurry," Da'Kuan said.

"I got to get out this lane," Tisha said. "The car's coming!"

"Pull me in," Ginger shouted. "Now, Ronny!"

Ronny grabbed Ginger by her waist and pulled her 5'7 body into his lap.

"Ah, ha!" Ginger flicked the finger at Mrs. Moore who cruised by, staring with her old face in a deep scowl. "Fuck you, Mrs. Moore!"

"Girl." Ronny moved her off his lap and in between he and Da'Kuan, the stench of weed filling the car. "Shit, what's wrong with you, Ginger?"

"No wonder you always begging me for the chronic." Da'Kuan laughed. "Guess it's the only thing that calms your ass down."

"Mm." She put her arms around the neck of his dingy T-shirt and kissed his sweaty, dark-brown skin. "Showed you, didn't I?"

She climbed into the backseat and laid on the plaid seat covering.

****

"Yo, LJ?"

Twenty-three-year-old LJ McCormick lifted his head from the musty hood of the '86 Chevy Silverado pickup as his cousin stalked through the jungle of old, dead cars.

"There you are." Rocco made his way to LJ, scowling as if someone farted. "It stinks like shit out here."

"It's a junkyard." LJ grabbed a screwdriver from the pile of tools beside his feet. "You expect it to smell like roses?"

"I think you farted before I got out here." Rocco fanned.

LJ laughed, combing his oily fingers through his straw-yellow hair, cut low on the sides with the strands wild at the top.

"You did, didn't you, Luther-James?" Rocco wiggled his hawk nose. "You farted."

"Don't blame *me*." LJ leaned under the hood in his sleeveless, white shirt and jeans. "I told Aunt Felicity not to put all those onions in the stew."

"Good God Almighty. Smells like death." Rocco held in a grin. "Oops. Didn't mean to say

the G word in front of you."

LJ rolled his narrow, emerald eyes. "Don't start."

"Start what?" Rocco's short, blond hair stuck out the sides of his dirty baseball cap. "Not my fault you hate God—"

"Drop it, man." LJ explored the old engine. "And atheists don't hate God. How many times I have to explain this?"

"Oh, right." Rocco's bushy eyebrows rose. "Y'all just don't believe in him."

"You know..." LJ sighed. "I've been in this town only three weeks and I've gotten more shit because of my beliefs here than I ever did in Chicago."

"This ain't Chicago, son." Rocco straightened his cap. "This is Beluga, Georgia, the Bible Belt. Folks here don't understand people like you. Shit, I love you and even I don't understand you. How can you doubt God's existence?" He raised his arms wearing an opened plaid shirt and white T-shirt under it. "He's all around us, LJ. You don't need no book or lessons to know it."

"I wish everyone here would respect my beliefs like I respect theirs." He got the flashlight from the ground. "Like I don't get sick of seeing Christmas decorations or hearing church music every damn where I go around here. Don't see me complaining."

"We were here before you, sucker." Rocco poked LJ's sweaty arm. "There's a difference."

"I don't care what people think of me."

"Well, that's a lesson you'll learn in this town." Rocco leaned against the dent in the navy-blue truck. "Here, everything is everyone's business. People will judge you, talk about you, gossip. Especially a newbie." He grinned. "Those church folks wanna run you out with pitchforks."

"Let 'em try." LJ shrugged. "I survived two years in prison." He lifted his head from the hood, winking. "I can survive the folks of Beluga, Georgia."

"I don't know about that, pal." Rocco peeked under the hood. "See, in Beluga, it's all about religion and the church. Pastor Ryder is more powerful than the Mayor is to these people, hell more powerful than the president even is. Everything in this town begins and ends with God. The sooner you realize it, cuz, the better." He hit the truck. "Come on; let me buy you a hamburger. Maybe I can get you out this junkyard for once and you can meet some ladies."

LJ got the rag from his back pocket and wiped sweat off his neck.

"That's another thing." Rocco squinted. "Been here three weeks and you ain't hooked up with nobody yet?"

"I'm the atheist, remember?" LJ nudged him. "No girl in their right mind would be seen with me. Plus, I've been in jail and that's a huge no-no around here too."

"Hasn't anyone caught your eye?"

LJ snickered as Ginger Ryder's gorgeous, honey-brown eyes and sleek curves came to mind.

"Ah, yeah." Rocco pointed at him. "Someone's caught your eye. Who is it? Megan who pierces ears at the mall?"

"Megan?"

"The blonde with the big cantaloupes." Rocco laughed. "I introduced you two the first day you came."

"Nah." LJ pressed his hands against the truck.

"Then who is it?"

"No one, man." LJ tossed the rag on the ground. "Said you were buying me a burger." He put his arm around Rocco's shoulders as they walked.

"Tell me." Rocco poked LJ's stomach. "Who is she?"

"It's no one."

They made their way to the gate.

"Stop lying." Rocco laughed. "Tell me who she is."

"No *one*." LJ closed the gate behind them. "No one at all."

CHAPTER TWO

"Paula, I'm not depressed." Nola Ryder stood by the island of her U-shaped kitchen filled with stainless steel appliances that brought out the warmth of the ivory walls. "Want another piece of cake?"

"No, I want you to stop changing the subject." Paula Long's round, brown eyes shined against her caramel skin. "We've been friends for over twenty years." She pursed her full lips, crow's feet hinting to her age of 49. "You've been in a funk for months. You might can fool Reuben but not me."

Nola scooped chocolate frosting off her slice of cake and licked it from her fork. "It's that obvious?"

"Girl, a blind person could see there's a problem with you." Paula's graying braids wrapped around her head in a maze. "I hate seeing you like this." She reached across the island and took Nola's hand. "You can tell me and you know it won't leave this room."

"I'm miserable and bored." Nola smoothed the side of her auburn hair, styled in a a fluffy, jaw-length bob. "I'm only forty-five and I feel like I'm one hundred years old. Like there's no life left in me."

"Nola, you have a wonderful life. You're married to the most revered man in town, you're the First Lady of Beluga Baptist Church, and you live in this huge house." Paula snickered, sipping black tea. "Shoot, around here you're royalty."

"You made my point." Nola tapped her long, polished nails on the laminate countertop. "Everything you named has to do with Reuben." She sighed. "For twenty-five years of marriage, I've sacrificed my identity."

"That's not true."

"It is true." She hit the countertop. "I don't even know who the heck I am, Paula. It doesn't help that my world revolves around a man who ignores me." She sat on the stool and stuck her fork in the cake slice. "Who only remembers I'm around when it's time to make public appearances, when he needs clean drawers, or when he wants someone to go to the store."

"Are we looking at the same marriage here? Reuben adores you. He fawns all over you. You know how many women would kill for their husbands to show them an ounce of the attention Reuben shows you?"

"None of you see what happens behind these doors. We come in this house and we turn into strangers. He's always off doing his sermons and tending to the needs of the congregation but can't sense what *I* need." She touched her large bosom. "I need a man, Paula. Not a preacher. I need someone to make me feel like a woman because I swear I've forgotten what that's like."

"Then you should remind Reuben. Shoot, Jamell and I ran into some rough patches a few years back. He was just like Reuben, got to where he never had time for me anymore. We went to marriage counseling and realized it was both our jobs to correct the issue. Now we have designated date nights to make sure we spend time together. You gotta put the effort in."

"Reuben won't go to counseling because he thinks he knows everything." Nola stroked her medium-brown hand. "It's not time that's our issue. Reuben doesn't *see* me anymore. Girl, I walked into the room the other day with a see-through negligee on and he didn't even look at me."

Paula grimaced.

"Didn't notice. I could've been buck naked and Reuben wouldn't care. The only thing he cares about are his sermons." She propped her elbow on the counter. "I'm thinking of leaving."

Paula spit out tea. "You can't leave Reuben. You crazy?"

"I love him, but I can't take twenty more years of feeling like this." Nola made fists. "I wanna feel alive and for him to see me as a beautiful woman again." She huffed, lips wiggling. "I want him to fuck my brains out."

"Nola." Paula covered her mouth, giggling. "What if people heard you?"

"I'm tired of worrying about other people. They go home to spouses that pay them attention while my needs get ignored." She stood and straightened her silk robe. "I'm every bit as attractive as I was when Reuben and I got married. I need more than sitting in this house and getting old."

"Your life doesn't just revolve around Rueben." Paula pouted. "What about all the charity work you do and the organizations you work with? Your legacy is every bit as important as his. I'm sick of this moaning and groaning."

"You asked what was wrong."

Paula hopped off the stool and took Nola's hand. "I got an idea. It's the Christmas season so forget this bah humbug stuff. You can help me at the soup kitchen."

"The soup kitchen?" Nola chewed cake.

"I've signed on to take over the duties there this season." Paula smiled. "Mrs. Farias will be out of town for the entire holiday so she can't do it this year so she asked me."

Nola licked crumbs off her mouth. "The soup kitchen, huh?"

"What would make you feel more valuable than serving the needy and bringing some Christmas spirit into their lives?" Paula beamed, dimples sprouting from her cheeks.

"That's a great idea." Nola smiled, a warmth brewing inside her she hadn't felt in months. "When do I start?"

****

"Ginger?" Da'Kuan turned from the counter at the burger joint, chewing that toothpick. "What did you say you wanted again?"

"Lord, have mercy." She sat with Tisha at the booth by the soda dispenser. "I want the double bacon cheeseburger and curly fries." She rolled her eyes whispering to Tisha, "I told him five times before we got in here."

Tisha chewed gum. "Girl, men don't be paying no attention."

Da'Kuan patted Ronny's shoulder and Ronny took out his wallet.

"Look at Da'Kuan." Ginger smacked her lips. "He never has money yet always showing off."

"For someone who sells weed how come he's always so broke?" Tisha turned sideways and laid her feet in the booth. "It's dead as hell in here. Nobody in here but us. I'm tired of this boring ass, country ass town."

"You?" Ginger checked her lipstick in the napkin dispenser. "Shit, I've been ready to go since I was born."

Rocco sped toward the building blasting Brad Paisley from the stereo. He and LJ laughed as they got out Rocco's red pickup.

"Hold on." Ginger sat back, eyeing LJ through the window as he entered. "Take that back. Might be a reason to stick around this sorry town."

"There you go." Tisha shook her head as the guys passed their booth. "You've been lusting over LJ since he got in town." She turned, gawking at him too. "What's with you, Ginger?"

"You're looking harder than I am." Ginger stared at the imprint of LJ's ass in his jeans. "He's something else." She licked her lips, a tingle warming her crotch. "Don't say you ain't interested."

"I ain't." Tisha turned back around, grimacing. "He's cute but I don't see what's so special. Plus, I don't want no jailbird."

Ginger cocked her head to the side, chewing her lip. "He's different."

LJ and Rocco got in line at the counter, talking and laughing.

Ginger sighed. "I'm sick of the same old shit and the same old lame ass boys."

"Thought you and Da'Kuan were serious."

"Girl, please. I'm just with him for the weed." Ginger propped her elbow on the table, gazing at LJ. "Wonder what Rocco and LJ doing after this. Think they'd like to party with us?"

"I'm not partying with no God hater."

"LJ doesn't hate God." Ginger straightened, sitting back. "He doesn't believe in him."

Tisha lifted the saltshaker. "Atheists are into all kinds of weird stuff like witchcraft and voodoo."

"What are you talking about?" Ginger grinned. "Atheism has nothing to do with witchcraft. You talking about devil worshipping."

"So?" Tisha grumbled. "How you know he's not into that?"

"I don't *care*." Ginger wiggled. "He's the only thing in this sorry ass town that's got people talking. That's something, isn't it?"

"Your daddy would flip if he knew you were even thinking about LJ McCormick. Besides, LJ doesn't even like you."

"All guys like me." Ginger stuck her chest out.

"He's the only guy in town that don't fall on the ground with his tongue wagging when you speak to him." Tisha laughed. "He run like you the law or something."

"I only said hi to him once."

"And he didn't even speak."

Ginger patted her hair. "Some men get tied-tongue around beautiful women."

"Tied-tongue my ass. You scare him to death."

Ginger blinked. "What do you mean by that?"

"Some guys don't like forceful girls like you. You have to admit, you can be intimidating."

"Better than being boring." She kicked Tisha under the table.

"Ow." Tisha threw a napkin at her. "I'm not boring. Just because I don't fling what I got in every man's face."

"Yeah if a man wanted it you would." Ginger gripped the table. "Nothing wrong with a woman going after what she wants. How come the man gets to always make the moves?"

"I was just saying why I think LJ doesn't talk to you."

"He's just standoffish because he was in jail."

"That's another thing." Tisha scowled. "Don't know what he did in there. Probably tossing salads and stuff."

"Girl." Ginger guffawed, slapping her hand over her mouth. "No, he wasn't."

"How do you know?"

"Anyway." Ginger fanned her hands, chuckling. "He likes me. Even if he didn't, he *will* like me. I bet you that."

"Be quiet. Here come the guys." Tisha cleared her throat. "Leave that white boy alone."

Ginger smirked as Ronny and Da'Kuan made it to the table with the food.

CHAPTER THREE

"Here you go." The woman behind the counter passed LJ his burger and fries. "Merry Christmas."

He groaned, following Rocco to a booth in the back of the restaurant. "You ever notice how people say Merry Christmas like they assume everyone celebrates the holiday?" He unwrapped the double cheeseburger. "It's such a double standard."

"In what way?" Rocco chewed with his mouth full.

"How weird would it be if I assumed everyone was like me?" LJ took the top bun off his burger and squeezed ketchup onto the cheese. "It gets me how Christians think the world revolves around them."

"That's not fair." Rocco smacked, rolling his eyes. "She was just being nice. People say Merry Christmas to be friendly. Everyone is not out to offend you, LJ."

"Fuck off!" Ginger slapped Da'Kuan's hand from her thigh. "You don't own this."

"I don't?" Da'Kuan cackled, pulling Ginger into his lap. "Give me a kiss."

"What's her deal?" LJ bit into the juicy burger.

"Ginger?" Rocco shrugged, dipping his fry in ketchup. "Preacher's daughter is all."

"Why does she act like that?"

"It's dead in here." Ginger jumped out the booth with her pleaded miniskirt riding up her ass. "Y'all ain't got no radio?"

"Sit down, girl," Tisha said.

LJ scoffed, shaking his head. "She sure doesn't act like the preacher's daughter."

"You got that right." Rocco smirked. "I could write a book on the stories I've heard about her."

"Woo!" She danced in front of Da'Kuan, gyrating her slender hips, the skirt rising with each movement.

"Damn." Rocco's mouth hung open. "Look at that."

Ginger swung around, lifting her leg to where LJ could see the seat of her pink panties.

The workers from behind the counter watched in awe.

"If *she's* supposed to be a Christian, then God's more of a ruse than I thought." LJ chewed. "There's gotta be a reason she acts like that."

Ginger sat on Da'Kuan's lap and wiggled as he held her waist.

"She's rebelling against her daddy." Rocco took another huge bite out his burger. "Pastor Ryder is so strict and you can't imagine the pressure she's under being his daughter in this town."

LJ stared at Ginger's long legs.

"Why so interested in Ginger?" Rocco raised an eyebrow, laughing. "It's her, isn't it? She's the one you're interested in."

"Shut up, man. And, you couldn't be more wrong."

"Bullshit. You can't even eat because you're staring so hard." Rocco glanced at her. "Can't blame you if you want a shot but get in line. Every guy in this town wants Ginger."

"Even you?"

"Too wild for me." He wiped his mouth. "Though I can't say I haven't been tempted."

Ginger turned around, making eye contact with LJ.

"Shit." He looked at his plate.

Ginger slid off Da'Kuan's lap and sashayed toward LJ and Rocco.

"She's coming over here." Rocco laughed. "I'm gonna tell her you like her."

"You better not tell her that." LJ set his burger on the plate. "I don't want nothing to do with her."

"Liar." Rocco snickered, covering his mouth with his hand. "I'll tell her, watch."

LJ sipped his soda, breath quickening.

"Hey." Ginger pressed her hands to the table and leaned forward, her boobs hanging out the plunging neckline.

"Ginger." Rocco smiled. "How you doing today?"

"I'd be better..." She looked at LJ. "If your cousin wasn't so rude."

"How am I rude?" He sat back, widening his legs.

"When I spoke to you before, you didn't say nothing." Her round, ebony eyes narrowed. "Kinda took that personally."

"I'm sorry." His gaze fell to the heart-shaped belly button ring in her navel. "I guess I didn't hear you."

"Hm." She moved closer to him, smelling of sweat and cocoa butter. "So, you're the bad boy."

"From what I've seen I'm not the only one who's bad."

Rocco snickered underneath his hand.

She tossed her head. "What does that mean?"

"You seem to be a resourceful young woman." LJ licked his lips. "You tell me."

She leaned over on her elbows, blouse exposing more of her white bra. "Heard you like to fix cars. I love cars."

LJ tapped his foot. "Do you?"

"You be at your uncle's junkyard a lot." She stood straight. "Maybe you can show me around some time."

"You sure have been paying a lot of attention." LJ sipped more soda. "Guess I should be flattered."

Rocco turned his head, grinning.

Ginger glanced at him then focused back on LJ. "Something funny?"

"No." LJ gave her a once-over. "Sad, actually."

She stood back, crossing her arms. "What's sad?"

"That you think you got to act like this to get attention from guys. You're selling yourself short."

"How would you know?"

He leaned into her. "Because any decent man would want to know the real you and I don't think this is her."

"You'd be wrong." She ran her fingers through his hair. "And, I'd love to show you more of the real me to prove my point."

"Ginger?" Da'Kuan called to her, smacking food. "You eating with us or them?" He glared at LJ. "Man, leave them suckers alone and get yo' ass back over here."

"You don't own me." She walked away, pulling at her skirt.

"Wow." Rocco gaped, fixing his cap. "Looks like she gave you the green light, my man."

Ginger got back into the booth beside Da'Kuan.

LJ wiped his mouth. "I bet there isn't a man in this town she *hasn't* given it to."

****

"Hey, boy." Judson McCormick walked through the junkyard that night, carrying a flashlight.

"Hey, Uncle." LJ sat beside the Silverado truck on an upside down paint bucket wearing goggles and cleaning the truck's carburetor.

Judson hobbled toward LJ on bowlegs. "How you doing?" He'd been skinny if not for that beer belly. "Cleaning the carb I see."

"Yep."

The 50-year-old leaned over LJ, sweating. "Did you soak it first?"

"Uh-huh but it was so much gunk on it soaking it made it worse." He sprayed cleaner into the holes. "What can I do for you?"

"You ate dinner and then run off." Judson took his blue baseball cap off and dabbed sweat from his forehead. "Goodness, it's hotter than the devil's living room tonight."

"It's hot every night in this town."

"Your aunt wanted me to come out and check on you." Judson set the flashlight on the truck. "Felicity's worried about you. You seem closed off."

"No reason to worry." LJ smiled, showing teeth. "Just trying to stay out of trouble and mind my own business."

"I'm wondering if you have a fetish for these cars." Judson laughed. "You're in this junkyard every time I turn around. Been here three weeks and spent no time with your aunt and me."

"You're no better." LJ grinned. "Spend all your time at the car shop."

"That's my shop though, I have to be around cars all day. Felicity and I want you to come to us, okay?" Judson clutched LJ's shoulder. "If something is wrong."

"Chill." He laughed, cleaning the jets. "I'm cool."

"Met any girls yet?" Judson stuck out his barrel chest. "Rocco mentioned you haven't dated anyone yet."

LJ sipped from his can of dark soda. "Hear me complaining?"

"You're a twenty-three-year-old man who spent two years in prison. You'd think all on your mind would be women." Judson's eyebrows wrinkled. "Did something happen in jail? I mean—"

"No, no one assaulted me or anything." LJ sighed.

Judson shrugged. "Concerned is all."

"These cars bring me more pleasure than people would." LJ looked toward the security lights that lit up the junkyard. "They give me peace, you know?"

"Level with me." Judson squinted with crust in his hazel eyes. "There has got to be one woman in this town you're attracted to."

LJ got the towel and wiped cleaner off hands. "If I tell you, will you keep it between us?"

Judson winked, clicking his angular jaw.

"I don't want Rocco teasing me and stuff." LJ straightened his butt on the bucket. "I think Ginger's interesting."

Judson's furry, brown eyebrows rose. "The preacher's daughter?"

"But something about her rubs me the wrong way. She's beautiful, sexy and has a great body, but I don't know."

"Ginger can be a little flirtatious." Judson laid his callused hand on the truck. "Does it turn you off?"

"I'd like to get to know *her* and not this persona."

"What makes you think it's a persona?"

"Come on, Uncle. No one acts like that for real. Even Rocco says she's rebelling because of her dad. I don't know." He swatted a gnat. "Forget it."

"Wait, a minute."

"Nah, the last thing I need is to get into trouble and a woman like Ginger is nothing but." He put the carburetor back together. "Besides, I need to concentrate on my future. Anymore thought to letting me work at the shop?"

"Uh—"

"I'm just as good as those trained mechanics you got working for you."

"I'd love nothing more." Judson fidgeted, rocking on his heels. "But, it's a bad time with Christmas and all. We've been slow."

"You didn't look too slow yesterday." LJ chuckled. "Had people waiting in the street for service."

Judson pulled his suspenders.

"Oh." LJ's shoulders dropped. "The church people wouldn't like it, is that it?"

"LJ, I love you, but your aunt and I are longtime members of the congregation and the bulk of my clients are from the church—"

"Unbelievable."

"Look, you're my little sister's boy and anything I can do for you I would but it's a sticky situation."

"It's cool." LJ snorted. "I wouldn't wanna jeopardize your business."

"I'll help you find a job, I promise."

"In *this* town?"

"Anywhere." Judson patted LJ's head. "When your mother died, I swore I'd look out for you and I will until the day I die."

"It's funny. In prison, I worked my ass off learning how to be a mechanic. I took classes on how to score points at job interviews and learned etiquette. Yet, not one thing prepared me for the truth. Whether it's Beluga or not, no one wants to hire a thief." He looked his uncle in the eyes. "Not even you."

"That's not true, son." Judson exhaled with his lips tight. "I don't see you as a thief. You made a mistake, and you paid your dues. Here in Beluga, it's more that you don't believe in God than your record."

"Prison's like a revolving door, you know? People get out on Tuesday then back in on Friday. You wonder how they can be so stupid but now I see." LJ did a lazy nod. "What else is there when doors keep slamming in your face?"

"You're not thinking of doing something illegal are you?"

LJ scratched his neck. "The thought's crossed my mind."

Judson knelt beside him. "Remember how miserable you were in there. How much you wanted your freedom. Don't throw that way."

"I don't see things being any different now. People shun me or ignore me, and they won't even let you give me a job. Aren't I still in prison?"

"Don't let them win, LJ." Judson touched his cheek. "You're too smart for that."

"I'm destined to be like dear old dad." He tinkered with the carburetor. "He's been in prison all my life. How do I know that's not what's in store for me?"

"Because I won't let it be." Judson stood, pointing at himself. "You hear me. No matter what, you're not going back to prison. Your aunt and I invited you here to help you get on your feet. Be patient."

"Yeah."

"It's times like this that believing in something helps." Judson turned the wedding band around his finger. "You should give thought to choosing a faith."

"Are you going there?" LJ closed his eyes. "Using my moment of weakness to get me to be a Christian?"

"I said choose a faith, not become a Christian."

"No thanks."

"LJ, you gotta believe in something to get you through. God gets me through the hard times.

Who does that for you?"

He stood and lifted the hood of the truck. "Me."

CHAPTER FOUR

"Coming!" Ginger ran downstairs in her pajamas as someone banged on her door. "Who the hell is it this time of night?" She scampered across the peach carpeting of her neutral-blue living room and looked through the window.

Fifty-one-year-old Reuben Ryder stood on the wooden deck of her white porch, clasping his huge, saddle-brown hands. His fat wedding band sparkling under the porch light.

"Shit." Ginger pulled on her clothes and opened the door, awaiting yet another strenuous lecture. "Hi, Daddy."

He stomped inside, his size 13 wingtips sinking into the carpet. "Why do you keep embarrassing me and doing your best to tear down everything I've worked for?"

"I'm not trying to embarrass you, Daddy." She sat on the peach sofa with the matching footstool.

"You could've fooled me." Reuben's close-set, brown eyes penetrated her, the muscles in his square face contorting.

"Let me guess." She curled her leg underneath her. "Mrs. Moore told you I was car surfing again?" She grinned, but it disappeared when her father's frown got deeper. "Sorry, Daddy. But, must I remind you again that I'm grown and can do what I want?"

"What are you talking about?" Sweat crept to the edge of his low flattop. "Car surfing?"

"Shit." She bit her lip. "I suppose you're talking about something else I did?"

"You were car surfing again?" he bellowed in his Sunday-sermon voice. "I was getting on you about getting everyone riled up at the burger place. I didn't know about this other stuff." He leaned back, rubbing his forehead. "Lord, please help us."

"Some church person called you, right?" She exhaled, shaking her head. "Course they did."

"Said you put on one heck of a show and all you needed was a pole."

Ginger laughed, covering her mouth.

He leaned his 6'4 body over her. "This isn't funny."

She reverted to the intimidated specimen that sat by her mother in the front row of church while her father quoted scriptures.

"Just tell me why, Ginger." He sat beside her, gripping the back of the sofa. "Why do you act like you do?"

"It's who I am." She swept her hand across the back of her hair, which she'd wrapped into a bun for bedtime. "No more and no less."

"This is not who you are. I didn't raise my daughter to act like this."

"Well, this is what you got." She pushed her hands between her thighs. "I do more than enough playing the part in church and everywhere else when we're together but you're not telling me how to run my life anymore."

"Who are you speaking too, young lady?" He scooted closer to her with his legs wide open. "The devil is inside you and it's plain as day."

"There's nothing wrong with having fun."

"When I was your age I was being groomed to step into the shoes of my daddy." He closed his eyes. "God rest his soul. I wasn't car surfing, hooking up with different men or dressing and acting like a stripper. The stuff you're doing..." He pointed his long, thick finger at her. "It's gonna get you in trouble."

She laid her head back. "Trouble is the only thing to look forward to in this town."

"Okay, who'll clean up the mess though?" He scratched his wide nose. "Yeah, me and your mother once again are the ones who will have to fix things when you screw up."

"You and Momma don't have to do shit."

He pulled his arm back and slapped her so hard her teeth shook.

She clenched her jaw, panting.

"Don't you ever curse at me, little girl." He stood. "Who do you think you are? Being twenty-two doesn't give you the license to be disrespectful." He pulled at his black slacks. "Here I am coming from the church where I've been practicing my upcoming sermon and I have to get another call about you acting a fool."

She squeezed the muscles in her face but tears snuck through, anyway.

"You ain't grown." He scoffed. "You're out the house but who pays your rent in this place? Who pays the note for that car you drive?" He pointed to the front door. "Who still pays for your medical insurance and everything else your job at the ice cream shop doesn't take care of?"

"Just go." She stuffed her crying face into her palms. "You hit me."

"Damn right I did. I'm trying to knock sense into your sinful behind." He quoted a scripture, but she didn't even register which one. "Here's the deal. Until you act like you're grown and pay for this house, that car, and everything else we pay for, then you do what I tell you to do. You call it playing a part well you make sure it's the best part you've ever played." He straightened his shirt. "If you're not a child, then stop acting like one." He went to the door and opened it. "I better not receive another call about you or you'll be wishing a slap is all you get."

He slammed the door so hard he shook the pictures on the wall.

****

Three days later, Nola entered the Love and Hope Center and greeted the woman at the front desk who was a regular from the church. After the woman praised Rueben's last sermon and doted over the hat Nola wore in church Sunday, the woman showed her into the dining area.

Inside the giant, white room were multiple cafeteria tables with Santa Clause place mats and minimal Christmas decorations on the sad walls.

"This is it," the woman said. "It'll get crowded by lunchtime." She checked her watch. "We wrapped up the breakfast shift an hour ago. So glad to have you here, Mrs. Ryder. It's a true honor."

"The honor's mine."

"Nola." Paula sprung from the side door. "I'm so glad you made it." She hugged her, playing with Nola's curls. "Girl, this is a soup kitchen not a magazine shoot."

The front desk woman smiled and went on her way.

"Seriously." Paula propped her hands on her waist, wearing a lopsided white apron and hairnet. "You look like you're on the red carpet on Oscar night."

"I can't go out looking any kind of way." Nola grinned, though it annoyed her having to play to expectations. "If I walked out the house looking a mess, I'd never hear the end of it."

"This is gonna be so much fun." Paula shimmied.

"I'm ready to get started."

"Well, we're getting lunch together now." Paula walked Nola through the hall and stopped at the kitchen where two women with hairnets prepared food. "Today's special is macaroni and cheese, fried chicken and creamed vegetables."

"Mm." Nola rubbed her midsection. "Sounds better than a Sunday meal."

"We go all out." Paula held her head high. "Just because someone is needy doesn't mean they don't deserve an adequate meal."

"Amen." Nola entered the kitchen. "Which do you need me to cook? You know cooking's my thing."

"And, you're one of the best in Beluga but we don't need you to cook." Paula pulled Nola out the door. "We could use help with cleaning."

"Cleaning?" Nola's excitement faded. "Not what I had in mind. I thought I'd be cooking."

"We need you to clean and serve." Paula took Nola into a smaller, mustier room with dirty dishes stacked on the table and in the stainless steel sink. "Disappointed?"

Nola stared at the mess. "This is for the needy." She smiled. "Whatever you need me to do, I'll oblige."

"You can put your purse back here." Paula put it in the two-door cabinet by the antique payphone.

"It's been a while since I've seen one of those phones." Nola picked up a wooden spoon with dried egg particles on it.

"I tripped out when I first saw it." Paula tapped the phone. "It works and everything." She stood at the table. "You're disappointed, aren't you?"

"It's just a lot of dishes."

"Yeah, and we need them cleaned by noon for lunch." Paula handed Nola an apron. "Good news. You don't have to wear a hairnet until you serve." She winked. "Here are gloves." Paula got a box of latex gloves from the drawer. "If you need any supplies, they'll be in these cabinets or this drawer."

Nola nodded as Paula handed her the gloves.

Paula snickered.

"What's so funny?"

"You didn't think you'd be doing this alone, huh?"

"What do you mean?"

"You'll have help."

"Thank goodness. Who is it?" Nola wiggled her fingers in the gloves. "Someone from the church?"

"Eh, not exactly." Paula rocked on her heels. "In fact I'm betting this guy hasn't set foot in a church in years if ever."

Nola grimaced. "Who is it, Paula?"

"You don't know him. He's new to Beluga...and here he is right here." Paula ran to the door as a tall, white man with an olive complexion and greasy, black hair slumped in the doorway.

CHAPTER FIVE

"Hey." The stranger gawked at Nola, his shocked expression mirroring the way she felt. "What's up?" He parted his sausage lips. "You must be Mrs. Ryder. The First Lady of the Church? I'm Quinn Moretti." He held out his sweaty hand.

Nola glanced at it.

"Sorry." He wiped his palm on his jeans. "It's hot as shit out there today and I'm one hell of a sweater." He extended his hand again, his gruff tone suggested he'd been smoking for years. "Trust me, I don't bite."

Nola took his leathery hand, staring into his shifty, brown eyes. "Nice to meet you." Her attention locked on the black hawk tattoo on his forearm with its wings spread.

"You're the first lady." He pulled his hand back, smirking. "Ain't supposed to lie."

"Excuse me?"

"You said it was nice to meet me." He straightened the satchel on his shoulder, the short gold chain strangling his thick neck. "But, that ain't the truth."

"Course it is." Nola forced a smile, hands shaking. "I just wasn't aware you were coming. Paula forgot to mention you."

Paula grinned, avoiding eye contact.

"Well." Nola scanned the small red stain that looked like ketchup right where Quinn's T-shirt bunched up over his flabby belly.

He wasn't fat but probably hadn't been to a gym in the last decade either.

"I've lived in Beluga all my life," Nola said. "I've not heard of any Morettis."

"He's not from here, remember?" Paula stated. "Quinn's from Atlanta."

"I've been to Atlanta many times for church events with my husband."

Quinn nodded and Nola couldn't tell if the sheen on his forehead was sweat or from that gunk in his hair.

"Atlanta's much faster than Beluga that's for sure." Nola giggled. "I'm helping out here because I love charity work. Nothing like helping the needy during the holidays."

"Nola's a saint when it comes to helping the less fortunate." Paula tapped Nola's shoulder.

"I have a higher calling in everything I do in life." Nola cleared her throat, checking out Quinn's tattered, leather lace ups. "What brings you here, Mr. Moretti?"

He set his satchel on the table next to the pile of bowls. "Prison."

Nola did a double take. "Prison?"

"Yeah." He pushed his hands into the pockets of his dingy jeans, a whiff of aftershave and tobacco floated in Nola's direction. "I got out a few weeks ago and want to do something worthy with my time to stay out of trouble." He slumped to the sink, sliding his feet, which already got on Nola's nerves. "Guess we should get started." He plugged up the drain and turned on the sink.

"Eh, just a minute." Nola dragged Paula out the room. "Are you out of your mind? What did you get me into?"

"What?"

"Don't act innocent. Paula, why didn't you tell me about this man?"

"Because you'd have cold feet if you found out an ex-con would be working with you."

"You darn right." Nola peeked into the room as Quinn put the dishes in the rising water. "I can't do this."

Paula exhaled with a condescending expression. "Why not?"

"This isn't a good idea."

"Let me get this straight. You're the first lady of the church but can't see when a lost soul needs your guidance?"

"That's not a lost soul." Nola pointed to the doorway. "That's a Soprano. Look at him. He's probably a gangster or something."

"A gangster?" Paula batted her eyes. "You're judging him because he's Italian?"

"I'm judging him because he gives me the creeps." She got in Paula's face. "How can I work with someone if I'm constantly checking my purse?"

"Fine." Paula shook her head. "If you don't wanna do this, then go in there and tell him. So much for the Christian way."

"That's not fair."

"It's also not fair for you to judge Quinn. He happens to be a nice person, and he's here to better himself. Anyway, this is about feeding the needy not liking the person you work with. You don't have to like Quinn but can't you put up with him a few hours of the day?"

"You're right." Nola sighed. "I should be ashamed of myself. God put him in my path for a reason."

"Exactly. You might be his beacon of hope."

A loud rumble followed by a high-pitched squeak, escaped the room.

The women stuck their heads in the door.

"What was that?" Paula asked.

"Oh, excuse me." Quinn fanned his butt. "Those damn enchiladas I had last night."

A sour, doo-doo scent smacked the women in the face.

"Uh-uh, Paula." Nola covered her nose and mouth. "I'm supposed to put up with that?"

"Oh my..." She gagged, fanning her face. "It's for the needy."

Nola fell against the wall, funk charging through her nostrils. "Lord, have mercy."

****

"What the?" LJ arrived at the junkyard to find Ginger sitting in her shiny, silver Mazda Miata with the top down.

"Ha, ha!" She hopped out wearing denim booty shorts and a white, off the shoulder, ruffle crop top. "I surprised you, didn't I?"

He unlocked the gate.

"What?" She moved from the car. "You can't even say good morning?"

He clenched his knees together, hoping to subdue the growing hard-on. "What are you doing here?" He walked past, keeping his eye on the Silverado ahead.

"What do you think?" She hopped in behind him and flicked his ear.

He stopped and faced her. "I got a lot of work to do."

"I don't mind." She twisted toward the truck, thumbs hooked into the belt loops of her shorts.

"How does someone who works at the ice cream shop afford a brand new Mazda Miata?" He put his keys in his jeans. "Let me guess, dear old mommy and daddy?"

"How come you don't have a car?" She gave him a once-over.

"I do now." He patted the Silverado truck. "Soon as I get this carburetor clean, she'll be ready to go."

Her little nose flipped into the air. "This old thing?"

"This is a classic, girl. I'm gonna paint her and everything. She'll be like brand new."

"Why not something more stylish?" She pointed to the banged up, black Camaro sandwiched between two other cars. "Now *that's* style. Why don't you fix that up?"

He glanced at it. "The Silverado needed the less work out of everything here."

"Ah." Her striking features contorted. "You didn't fix the truck because you like it but because it's in better shape."

"I like it."

She wagged her finger. "A guy like you needs a car with style and this big thing right here..." She patted truck. "Ain't it. What's with you and this obsession with cars, anyway?"

"I love working on cars." He sat on the paint bucket. "It's peaceful."

She blew a breath, making her high cheekbones more pronounced. "How long you been into cars?"

He got the carburetor while sneaking a glimpse of her legs. "Two years."

Her eyes held a catlike glare. "Did you get into them in prison?"

He nodded, scraping debris off the carb with a wire brush.

"I see now." She threw her head back. "Guess in prison cars were your salvation?" She leaned on the truck, stretching her arms over the hood. "Your escape?"

"Prison can kill you mentally unless you have something to take up your time. I signed up to learn auto mechanics and there was a garage some of the inmates worked in. We repaired cars for the prison staff and I got my certification."

Her face lit up when she smiled. "That's cool."

"Thanks." A warm tingle went through him. "I want to be a master mechanic so I plan to go back to school and get a degree in automotive repair."

"That's great." She rocked. "At least you got a plan." She looked at her fingernails. "That puts you ahead of most that come out of jail."

"Not sure about that." He scratched around the silver stud in his right earlobe. "The main reason I came out here was for my uncle to put me up at his shop but the church folks got to him and—"

"No need to explain." She sighed, grimacing. "That's a damn shame. Welcome to Beluga where no one minds their own business."

"I won't let anything stop me though." He scrubbed the carburetor. "I can't allow myself to get lazy or lose focus. If so I'll end up right back where I started."

She moved to the front of the truck and leaned in a seductive pose. "You're too smart to go back to jail."

He chuckled. "Too bad I wasn't smart enough not to go in the first place."

She fanned a fly away. "What was it like?"

"It was lonely." An old CD sparkled from inside the grass. "You'd think a place with so many people wouldn't be so lonely."

"I heard your Momma died." She tucked in her lips. "Sorry."

He nodded. "It's been a while. I've dealt with it."

"Is it true your daddy is in prison?"

"You've been asking about me, huh?"

"Info flies fast in this town."

"Yeah, my pop's in prison." He blew debris out a crevice of the carb. "For robbery."

She whistled.

"That's the stock I come from." He winked. "You better run. I'm bad news if you haven't heard."

"I like bad news."

They stared into each other's eyes until LJ broke the trance. "I don't hate God."

"What?" She held her waist.

"Just answering before you asked." He brushed dirt off the thigh of his jeans. "Why do you believe in God? Since folks always asking me why I don't."

"Preacher's daughter, remember?" She flicked her hair behind one ear. "I was brought up in the church."

"You sure don't act like it." He grabbed the screwdriver from the grass.

"That's an unfair judgment seeing how you don't know me." She moved closer to him, shaking her leg. "But, if you took the time to judge me it means you care."

He scoffed, picked up a bolt from the ground and when he got back into position, Ginger stood right in front of him with her denim crotch in his face.

"Why don't you like me?" She licked her glossy lips.

He cleared his throat, pretending to concentrate on the carb. "What I'd like is to see the real you."

"What do you mean?" She slid up on the truck and lay flat on her back. "You wanna fuck?"

"This is what I'm talking about." He gestured to her. "It was cool just talking and then you go back to flirting."

"This is me." She turned toward him, leaning on her elbow.

"Bull." He scratched his head. "Until you stop hiding the woman underneath this image..." He stood. "I ain't interested. Get up." He pulled her off the truck.

"Hey." She snatched her arm away, digging her shorts out her crotch.

"Those get any shorter they'd be a shirt."

"You've been looking though, right?" She rubbed his back. "Come on, LJ."

He dug under the truck's hood. "This is my private time, and I'd like to be alone."

"Fine." She backed away. "You keep acting like this and you'll be alone for the rest of your life."

He watched her over the hood. "That's my business, right?"

"I got to go anyway." She pouted, looking damn cute doing it. "Got errands to run before work."

"When do you work?"

"From two until closing at ten." She held her waist. "Why?"

"You like working at the ice cream shop?"

"Guess it's my sanctuary like you and this place." She turned around, walked a few steps and then stopped. "Why don't you come by? I'll give you a free cone."

LJ grabbed a wrench from the red toolbox. "I bet you want to give me more than ice cream."

"If you want to see me, stop by around closing unless you got something better to do." She waited as if she expected him to answer but he didn't. "Bye." She ran out the gate, shorts hugging her plump ass as she got into her car.

LJ gripped his throbbing middle. "*Fuck.*"

CHAPTER SIX

Quinn sat on the concrete steps in front of the center smoking a cigarette when Nola exited the building that evening.

She walked down the steps, flashing him a quick smile. "Well, have a good evening."

"I surprised you, didn't I?" He flicked cigarette ashes on the pavement.

She held the purse strap to her shoulder. "Excuse me?"

"It wasn't so bad working with me, right?" He took a drag from the cigarette.

"I'm confused." She walked back to the steps. "Why would I have an issue working with you?"

"You got that 'first lady' stuff down pat, don't you?" He tapped his foot, fanning stinky smoke. "Just go through life wearing this facade."

"Wait, a minute." She took another step forward. "You know nothing about me."

"And, you knew nothing about me but it didn't stop you from judging."

A woman jogged past with her Chihuahua.

"I don't care what you think of me, lady."

"You seem to care or else you wouldn't be upset."

He touched his necklace. "I'm a person just like you are and if I treat you with respect, then you should do the same."

"Where is this coming from?" She took her purse off her shoulder. "You misunderstood something I did."

"Which time? When you called me a 'Soprano' or when you said I gave you the creeps?"

She closed her eyes, condemning herself.

"There's nothing wrong with my hearing, Nola." He glanced at the tip of the cigarette. "That's one thing I can say."

147

"I'm sorry, Quinn." She touched his shoulder and let go when he glared at her. "I apologize."

"You're no better than me."

"I agree." She held her palm out to him. "It's commendable that you're working here."

A lazy smirk covered his thick lips. "That your car?"

She looked at the cherry-red Cadillac XT5. "Yes."

"I love Cadillacs." He sucked the cigarette. "My first car was a Cadillac."

"Really?" She sat beside him, placing her purse in her lap.

"*Yeah.*" The word slithered from his mouth with rhythm. "A nineteen eighty-five Eldorado when I was sixteen."

"You had an Eldorado?" she gushed. "My uncle had an Eldorado. Goodness, I loved riding in that car. It always smelled like mothballs though. His was maroon, and he always drove it with the top down."

"Mine was a yellow son of a bitch." He cackled. "With rims and tinted windows as black as my hair." He moved his arm as if he were driving. "Used to lean back and cruise through the neighborhood bumping El DeBarge."

"Get outta here." She laughed, covering her mouth. "I loved El DeBarge. 'Rhythm of the Night' was the jam." She wiggled, snapping her fingers until she noticed him watching. "Sorry. I'm being silly."

"Sometimes it's good to be silly." His arm rubbed against hers when he put the cigarette back in his mouth. "Man, I haven't thought about that car in ages."

"What are you driving now?"

"The bus." He laughed.

She flinched. "Sorry."

"It's just until I get on my feet. That's why I was late getting here. Damn bus driver taking her sweet time." He checked his watch. "Bus should be here in a few minutes."

"You say you were sixteen in nineteen eighty-five?" She figured the numbers in her head. "That means you're forty-eight now?"

He nodded. "How old are you?"

"Forty-five." She rubbed the knees of her slacks. "I hope I look younger."

"Shit, younger than what?" He crossed his arms over his knees. "You're hotter than a lot of twenty-year-olds today."

"Stop. It's not nice to lie."

"You kidding me?" He licked his lips, gaze falling to her blouse. "You could give these younger chicks a run for their money."

Her stomach grew anxious and her heart sped up. "Thank you."

He winked at her. "You're welcome."

"I..." She stood, wobbling.

"You okay?" He raised his arm as if to catch her.

"Yeah. I have to go." She hurried off the steps. "See you tomorrow."

He flashed a smile, igniting fire to her most intimate parts. "See you, Nola."

****

The little bell rang above the door of The Icebox Ice Cream Shop, alerting Ginger of a customer.

"Merry Christmas," she answered with her back to the front counter. "What can I get for you?" Her heart stopped when she turned around to see LJ at the counter with a teasing grin. "You came." Those fearless, sexy green eyes gave her hives.

"Well, well, well." He chewed his lip, gazing at her baby-pink apron that matched the walls. "Aren't you cute?"

She straightened the little hat she hated wearing. "Don't tease me."

"I'm serious." He watched her with more enthusiasm than she'd seen from him since he arrived in Beluga. "I like seeing you like this. Gives me more perspective."

"Into what?"

"Let's me see the real you."

"We're back to that again." A strand of hair hung from her French roll. "I close up in a few minutes."

"Is that a hint for me to go?"

"No." She chuckled, flustered. "I told you to come. Why would I want you to leave?"

He scanned the stainless steel containers of various ice cream flavors. "Can I get that cone you promised?"

She nodded. "What would you like?"

"Mm." He stuck his lips to the side. "Scratch the cone and give me cookies and cream in a cup."

"Cookies and cream?" She got the scoop out the half-gone cookies and cream and grabbed a plastic container. "This is my favorite flavor." She dumped scoops into the cup. "I love butter pecan and vanilla too but I could eat this every day."

"On Fridays, we always got ice cream in prison." He took a breath in between smiling,

touching the glass divider. "See in prison, you appreciate the little things. Like just walking down

the street when you want or taking a bubble bath. Things everyone takes for granted."

She swallowed, taking in the solemn declaration. "Sprinkles?"

He shook his head, taking out his wallet.

"I said it's on me." She set it on the counter.

"Only if you let me buy you one too."

She smiled. "You don't have to do that."

He took his container and got a plastic spoon from the dispenser. "Give me another cookies and cream full price."

She dished up the treat, he paid for it and they sat at the table by the soda machine.

LJ tasted the ice cream. "Hm." He sat back, eyes rolling in the back of his head. "That's what I'm talking about."

"Jeez." She laughed. "Looks like you're having an orgasm." She stirred hers. "I like it when it's melting."

"This is delicious." He moaned, eating more. "You guys make your ice cream?"

"Yep. This place has been here since nineteen fifteen."

"You're shitting."

"Nope. It's a Beluga landmark. Back then it was The Icebox and the church." She chewed an Oreo cookie chip. "Those are the two places that define the town."

LJ scraped ice cream off the side of his cup.

She giggled, chewing cookies. "You didn't walk all the way over here from the junkyard just to see me, did you?"

"No, I'm in the truck."

"It's good to go now?"

"All I had to do was clean the carburetor. I'll paint it soon as I get my hands on some money." He smacked as he chewed. "My uncle will help me out."

"You're real close to Judson and Felicity? They're very nice."

"Judson is my momma's older brother. When we found out she had cancer, he made a promise to her that if something happened, he'd look after me. So, I'm here."

"What kind of cancer did she have?"

"Lung." He chewed slow, staring at the table. "And, never smoked a day in her life."

"I'm sorry, LJ. When did she die?"

"Three years ago. I'd just turned twenty." His eyes watered. "She had cancer for about six years and at one while she was doing good but took a turn for the worse."

"It's rough. Both sets of my grandparents died of cancer."

"My mom's folks were dead before I came along and I don't know my daddy's family." He licked cookie pieces off his lip. "Shit, I barely know my dad."

She held in a chuckle.

"You're an only child?"

Ginger nodded.

"I had a little sister, but she died when she was a baby. She had SIDS."

"Crib death?" She touched her bosom. "That's horrible. When?"

"I was about twelve." He squinted. "My momma got pregnant by one of her deadbeat, abusive men. Still, I couldn't wait to be a big brother."

Ginger smiled.

"I had dreams of protecting my sister and being the father figure for her I never had."

"What happened?"

"Momma put her down and the next morning, she was blue and stiff."

"My god." Ginger covered her mouth with both hands. "LJ, I'm so, so sorry. I can't imagine how that felt."

"Momma never got over it."

"Life threw you a load, huh? Your sister dies, your mother dies, your father's in prison and you were in prison." Ginger exhaled. "And, you're only twenty-three-years-old. May I ask you a question?"

He nodded with a withdrawn expression.

"Is that why you're an atheist?"

He winced. "Maybe."

"For what it's worth, LJ, I can't blame you. Had I gone through all you have I might not believe in God either."

"I've lost everyone in my life." He scraped the bottom of his container. "What has God done for me? Except taking everybody away? And why did he pick me to have this kind of life?"

They were silent for a moment before Ginger spoke, "Can I interject another way of looking at it? God keeps putting people in your life too, right? While others leave, you've had others who cared like your aunt and uncle. Instead of looking at it like God taking people away, appreciate the time God gives you with others."

"What about my dad? I've never seen the man outside prison, Ginger. Spoke to him ten times in my whole life because my mother couldn't stand taking me to see him."

"You're grown now and you can change that. You can see your father whenever you want. Have you tried?"

"What good would it do now when I don't need him?"

"Why you say you don't need him? Just because you're grown doesn't mean he can't have a place in your life. He might feel horrible about not having a relationship with you."

"I blame him for the mistakes I made. If he hadn't been such a screw up I wouldn't have taken the wrong path."

"Is it fair to blame your dad for your mistakes?"

"Hell yes." He pouted.

She giggled at how cute he looked with his lips poked. "Well, as a Christian, there's nothing you can't forgive."

"No offense, Ginger." He finished his ice cream and laid the spoon in the container. "I don't see it that way."

She shrugged a shoulder, swaying her head. "That's fine."

He grinned, avoiding eye contact.

"What?" She closed her mouth. "Do I have cookie chunks in my teeth or something?"

"You're the first person who didn't try to change my mind about God. Every time people find out I'm an atheist I get a bunch of questions that turn into accusations rounded out with pity. Then they always wanna preach about how empty my life will be if I don't change."

"I'd never do that, LJ." She took his hand, a warm sensation coming over her. "It's not my place to change you and I wouldn't want to. Don't you see? I'm attracted to who you are. I don't care you don't believe in the Lord. It doesn't make a difference."

He laid his other hand over hers. "Thanks."

CHAPTER SEVEN

"Nola?" Reuben busted into he and Nola's third-floor bedroom, the strap of his black Tote bag falling off his shoulder. "Whoa." His bottom lip dropped. "Are you all right?"

"Do I look all right?" Nola lay on the queen-sized bed in a black, baby doll negligee with lace trimming on the bottom and side panels. "Well?" She sat with one leg stretched out and the other with her knee propped, knowing Reuben could see the sun, moon, and the stars from underneath the skimpy ensemble. "You gonna just stand there?" She lowered a shoulder strap, fluffed her hair and lay back on the brown and white spotted pillows. "Come over here."

"Nola, what's going on?" He dropped his satchel at the door and rushed to the bed. "I thought something happened. You called and demanded I come home."

"Yeah." She shrugged a shoulder.

"That's all you can say?" His bottom lip grew moist as he stared at her legs. "Um, I was working with Pastor Marroquin so we can do a joint sermon Sunday."

"Who?"

"You know." He moved his hands around. "The pastor from Augusta I told you about. She's the guest pastor for this week."

"Oh, right." Nola wiggled her shoulders. "I didn't mean to interrupt but this was more important."

"You're just lying in the bed." His nostrils flared. "I thought something had happened to you, woman."

"I want *you* to happen to me." She glided off the bed and inched toward him on her newly polished feet. "Like my toes? Frosted-blue, your favorite color."

"Um." He looked at her toes as she unbuttoned his shirt. "Nola."

"You gotta be hot in these clothes. We can get hotter without them."

"Nola." He grabbed her hands. "What are you doing?"

"If I gotta explain it then something's wrong." She stood back, snapping her neck. "Has it been that long? Scratch that, it has."

"You tricked me?" He sat on the brown and white bedding. "How could you be so selfish?"

"I'm selfish?"

"Nola, Pastor Marroquin is one of the most revered pastors in the south. She's getting her own access preaching show in Augusta."

"Well, whoop-dee-doo."

"She's not just someone I admire but she can open a lot of doors for the church and for our futures." He took her hands and pulled her to him. "I can't mess this up. I have to be my best Sunday or she'll never want anything to do with me."

"Reuben." She grabbed his face with both hands. "I'm standing in front of you with my butt and breasts out and all you can do is think of a sermon?"

"There's no call for lying and trickery, Nola." He moved her hands away. "I was scared to death thinking you were dying or something."

"I *am* dying." She leaned her butt against the white dresser with pearl accents. "Dying for some attention and some affection. I'm tired of coming in second, third, fourth and fifth to whatever you got going on."

"We're having this discussion again?" His face twisted until his eyebrows met in the center of his forehead.

"You darn right we are." She laid her hand on the dresser. "You haven't been handling your business."

He stood, laughing. "Come again?"

"In church you're always telling people what they need but you don't have a clue what your own wife needs. I'm lonely, Reuben."

"How can you be lonely when you got charities, events, and church issues to deal with?"

"I'm lonely for *you*." She clamped her lips together. "You were supposed to see me and run to the bed, take me in your arms and make love to me like two horny teenagers who just discovered sex but all you did was talk about your sermon." She dropped her head, covering her eyes before the tears began. "Are you still attracted to me?"

He groaned. "Come on, Nola."

"Seriously." She caressed her pear-shaped hips and parked her hands on her loose breasts. "I know I'm sagging more than I used to and anything I eat goes straight to these hips but just be honest with me."

"I love your hips, boobs, legs, everything." He snickered. "Stop talking silly. I don't care if we're eighteen or a hundred. You will always be the most beautiful woman I've ever seen, and I'll never want anyone else."

"That's good to hear because my next question was gonna be if you were having an affair."

He grimaced, huffing. "How could you think something so ridiculous?"

"Then why don't you want me?"

"I *do*. Where is this coming from?"

She pulled at the back of the negligee. "What do you see when you look at me?"

"I see my wife, my partner, a devout Christian, a kind soul, a mother—"

"Do you see a woman?" She leaned forward. "That's the problem, Reuben. I'm tired of only being your wife, the first lady or Ginger's mother. I want to be a woman again." A tear fell. "I want you to see me and treat me like a woman."

"I'm completely confused." He shook his head, eyes rolling. "You mean the world to me. There's nothing I wouldn't do for you or Ginger. You're my rock, Nola. Are you saying I don't appreciate you?"

"I'm not—"

"Because I don't break my back doing sermons and all this other stuff for my health. I do it because it's my duty and because I want to give you the life you deserve."

"Money doesn't mean a thing to me."

"Yeah, now that we have it." He held out his arms. "I doubt you'd wanna give it up."

"Yes, I would." She stuck her finger in his face. "I'd give up this house, those cars, the trips, and the status, everything to get some time alone with you. To get you to see that I need you even more than others do. I'm supposed to come first, Reuben."

"I'm sorry." He lifted her chin and bent down almost half his body size to reach her 5'5 height. "I'll do better."

"That's what you said the last ten times we had this discussion."

"All I want is to make love to you." He kissed her, caressing her hair. "And, we'll do it more often I promise."

"You still don't get it." She pulled away from him. "I don't want you to do it out of duty or because I tell you to. I want you to want me, Rueben." She wiped a tear from her chin.

His eyebrows lowered. "I want you more than anything, Nola."

"How come it doesn't feel like it?" She slumped to the doorway.

"Honey, wait."

She waved him off and left the room.

****

The Following Evening

"Ow." LJ slapped another mosquito off his arm. "How do you guys do it?" He pulled at his sleeveless white tank that was plastered to his body due to the afternoon humidity. "I'm getting eaten alive out here."

"Try this." Shirtless in red, denim shorts and flip-flops, Rocco tossed LJ a bottle of bug repellant.

"You had repellant all this time while the mosquitos have me for a buffet?" He sprayed it on his arms. "So much for always having my back, cuz."

Rocco jumped up and down, howling at his friends who wrestled in the three hundred acre lake surrounded by the woods.

"Ha, ha!" Beau Midnight put Isaac in a headlock and held him in the water.

"Hey, watch it." Isaac bobbed, swinging his skinny, mocha-brown arms. "You can't be throwing a brother in the water like that." He patted his drenched, uneven fro. "You crazy?"

Rocco and Rafael laughed.

Beau splashed water on Rafael. "What you laughing at?"

"Wait; watch my hair too, man." He patted his Bruno Mars pompadour. "I gotta meet my girl later."

Beau and Isaac guffawed.

"What girl?" Rocco sat beside LJ in the rickety lawn chair. "Your momma?"

They laughed, including LJ.

"Yeah man, you pathetic." Isaac pulled his green shorts over his crack. "Don't never have no woman."

"Here." LJ passed Rocco the repellant.

"Having fun?" Rocco straightened his shades. "Glad you came out with us."

"Thanks for inviting me."

"I'm shocked you came, LJ," Rafael said. "Rocco bet us ten dollars each you wouldn't."

"Yeah." Beau ran out the water, his toned pecs glistening as he got a beer out the cooler. "What made you join us today?"

"I got tired of Rocco teasing me about not going anywhere." LJ slapped Rocco's thigh. "Besides, guess a little male bonding wouldn't hurt."

"Be careful though." Isaac got out the water followed by Rafael. "Hanging around these fools can lower your IQ." He laughed.

"What?" Beau wrapped his arm around Isaac's neck and bent him over. "Say that again."

"Get off." Isaac pushed him off, playfully bucking up to him.

"I'm glad you came too, LJ." Rafael sat on the blanket in the grass. "Rocco presented us with a mission for you tonight."

"Excuse me?" LJ shook his feet.

Beau and Isaac grinned.

"Okay, come clean." LJ lifted his shades to his forehead. "What you got up your sleeves?"

"Your cousin said you've been a little lonely." Beau snickered, sipping from the beer can. "The four of us are kinda known as the hook-up squad."

Rocco removed his cap, scratching his head.

"Oh no." LJ glared at him. "You tell these guys to fix me up?"

"He told us to get you laid in no certain terms." Isaac guffawed. "Don't be mad at the brotha. He's concerned. It ain't healthy for you to be worried about them cars all the time."

"That's right." Beau sat Indian-style in the grass, his fluffy bleach-blond hair blowing in the fresh-water breeze. "The hood of a car ain't the only hood you can be tinkering with if you know what I'm saying."

Rocco, Rafael, and Isaac cackled.

"I appreciate the gesture, fellas." LJ waved. "But, I don't need help in the woman department."

"Then why haven't you gotten laid since you been here?" Beau flexed his tanned arm.

"Who says I haven't gotten laid?"

Rocco reclined in the chair. "The only movement you make is from the house to the junkyard."

"How do you know?" LJ threw his head back. "You're just as bad as I am, at the bait shop all the time."

"Yeah, but I'm getting a paycheck to be there." Rocco wiggled his toes. "It's not healthy for you to not see any women. People are starting to talk."

"Let them." LJ gripped the arms of the chair. "What I do is my business and you guys don't know what I do."

"I know you like ice cream." Rafael giggled.

"What?" Beau grimaced, holding his beer can in the air.

"LJ likes ice cream." Rafael hit LJ's leg. "Don't you?"

LJ sunk into the chair, awaiting the teasing. "Damn I hate small towns."

"What?" Isaac looked back and forth at LJ and Rafael. "Is 'ice cream' a code name for pussy?"

The guys laughed.

"Let's just say I saw someone's Silverado truck at the Icebox yesterday at about nine-twenty." Rafael tucked his chin. "And, it and a Mazda Miata was the only two cars in the parking lot."

Beau extended his neck. "You were with Ginger?"

"Whoa, ho, ho!" Isaac bounced on his knees. "Don't tell me you hitting *that*?"

"No." LJ grimaced. "But, if I were it's not your business."

"Ooh," the guys said.

"Seriously?" Rocco nudged his cousin. "Did you get some of that?"

"No."

"You couldn't handle it no way," Beau whispered, snickering.

Rafael and Isaac slammed their hands over their mouths, hiding grins.

"What's that supposed to mean?" LJ ripped his shades off, staring Beau in the eyes.

"Ginger used to be Beau's girl when we was in school." Isaac pinched Beau's earlobe. "Ain't that, right?"

"Yep." He watched LJ, veins jutting from his neck. "I tore that ass up too."

"Oh, snap." Isaac lay over, kicking. "Beau."

Beau smacked his lips after drinking. "She's a lying bitch so I'd be careful if I were you."

LJ scooted to the edge of the chair. "Believe me; I can take care of myself."

"Tough man, huh? Let me guess." Beau's mouth rose in one corner. "She listened to your

heartfelt story of you being in prison and your mom dying."

LJ's blood bubbled through his veins.

"Gave you that cute smile and acted like she understood you better than anyone. Bet she even said she liked you because you were different." Beau leaned forward, amusement vanishing from his face. "Did she offer to buy you an ice cream cone too?"

LJ huffed and puffed, squeezing his shades in his hand.

"Join the club," Beau said. "She's run them same lines on almost every dude under twenty-five." He stuck out his chest. "She ran them on me, but I was too much for her apparently."

"Beau just salty as hell." Isaac hit him on the back of the head. "Don't listen to him, LJ. I can't blame you for trying to get with that. Ginger fine as a motherfucker." He nudged Beau, grinning. "Shit, if Beau wasn't my homey I'd be up in that ass too."

Rocco fixed his cap. "Like Ginger would want your broke ass."

"I'm telling the truth, man." Isaac sucked his lip, grabbing his crotch. "I go to church just to see what she got on." He cackled. "Her sexy, apple-bottom ass. Ooh. Don't no preacher's daughter got no business with an ass like that."

"She's an alley cat." Beau balled a fist. "Best fuck I ever had and you can ask several guys and they'll say the same."

"Beau," Rocco said. "Chill, okay?"

"I'm just trying to save your cousin for falling into the trap I did. Shit, I thought Ginger cared about me but she doesn't care about anyone but herself. She's a user and only after LJ because he's the new dick in town."

LJ looked at the others.

"Ginger will use you up and spit you out." Beau crumpled the beer can in one hand. "All she knows is running game on men. It's a hobby for her. Why do you think she's with Da'Kuan? Fucking him for free weed." He tossed the can. "What? Think you're special?"

"Nothing's going on between me and Ginger."

"Bull." Beau propped his arms on his knees. "I can see by your face you like her already. You think you and her can have true love?" He laughed and then spit in the grass. "How can she love someone else when she doesn't love herself?"

CHAPTER EIGHT

"Okay, um." Reuben sat on Ginger's living room floor, struggling with the artificial tree branch. "This should be color coded." He pushed up his reading glasses and got the manual. "This is ridiculous."

Ginger stood by the coffee table with her thumb between her lips, snickering.

"It's a shame this has become so complicated." He glanced at her, his long legs curled Indian-style. "The tree we got at the house only takes twenty minutes to put up if that." His glasses slid off his sweaty nose. "These branches aren't fitting the holes." He got another branch and examined it.

"We'll figure it out."

"Daddy, you didn't have to do this." She slid the *Oprah Magazine* to the side and sat on the coffee table. "I didn't need a tree."

"Nonsense." He assembled another branch into the stand. "How can the preacher's daughter not have a Christmas tree? Your momma and I had ours up before Thanksgiving."

She smiled; knowing him bringing the tree was his way of apologizing for hitting her.

"You're sweating like a drunk on New Year's Eve." She touched his slick brow. "Gross, Daddy."

"You'd be sweating too if you were struggling with this tree. Why don't you help instead of making fun?"

She grinned. "I'll start by doing what we should've done first and read the manual." She opened it to the first page. "Did you get Momma's Christmas gift yet?"

"Course I did." He maneuvered another branch into the stand. "And, I'm not telling you because you can't keep your trap shut to save your life."

She laughed. "Since when?"

"Ginger." He glared at her over his glasses. "How many times have you spilled the beans about birthday gifts and Christmas presents for your mother? Too many to count."

"I didn't mean to tell her." She grinned. "Momma has a way of sweating things out of you. Anyway, whatever you get, she'll love."

"I hope so," he mumbled. "I can't afford to make her more upset with me."

"What are you talking about?"

He sighed, setting a branch in his lap. "What do you think of our marriage?"

She froze. "Huh?"

"Do you think I'm a good husband?"

"Dad, this is a little weird. Why are you asking me this?"

"Keep this between us. The last thing I need is Beluga gossiping about me and your mother and blowing things out of proportion."

"Are you and Momma having problems?"

"Darn leg's falling asleep." He stretched out his right one. "The problem is I thought everything was great until about two months ago. She thinks I don't pay attention to her. I know I'm not as attentive as I used to be, but I'm so busy."

"This isn't the first time she's felt this way." Ginger flinched. "Before I moved out, she said she was lonely and that you do nothing outside the church with her anymore."

"I'm blindsided." He stroked the nape of his neck. "Why didn't you tell me?"

"Mom asked me not to." She turned a page of the manual. "If it's getting worse, you have to fix it."

"I'd spend all the time in the world with your mother if I could but that's not possible."

"She doesn't want all your time, just *some* time."

He exhaled with his hand over his mouth. "I got an idea." He smiled. "She's working at the soup kitchen tonight. I'll have her favorite meal cooked and waiting for her when she gets back."

"That sounds great."

"It's almost six-thirty and she'll be done by eight." He stood, checking his watch. "I need to go to the grocery store so I can have dinner ready." He stepped over branches. "Uh—"

"Don't worry about the tree." She chuckled. "I can do it myself."

He stepped over the box of decorations. "You sure?"

"Yeah."

"Okay, sweetie." He kissed and hugged her and afterwards touched the cheek where he'd hit her. "I love you, Ginger."

She sniffed his strong, spicy cologne from his wrist. "I love you too."

****

At the Love and Hope Center, Quinn washed and dried the last bowl and put it in the cabinet with the others. "Woo." He slumped against the sink, apron loose at the waist. "I've never seen so many dishes in my life."

"Me either." Nola sprayed cleaner on the stainless steel table and wiped it. "I've been in charge of more church events than I can count with hundreds of people and still never saw so many dishes before."

"Jesus." He took off the apron.

"You use God's name in vain a lot, don't you?" She peeked at him over her shoulder.

"What?" He stuck a cigarette in his mouth and lit it. "Gonna lecture me about religion? I'm more religious than anybody. Catholic." He winked. "Sorry if me using God's name offends you."

"It doesn't bother me." She cleaned the other end of the table. "But, there are other ways to express yourself."

He snickered, smoking flowing from his lips. "Lady, you don't wanna know how I like to express *myself*." He got another bottle of cleaner, a rag and wiped the other table. "How you like working here?"

"Have so many emotions. The serving is the hardest for me. On one hand it feels good to help people, but it's so sad to see so many in need."

"Hm-mm." He brushed his butt against hers when he passed, and she got another odd tingle. "Sorry."

She straightened her apron, feeling flushed. "That's okay."

"Are you afraid of me, Nola?"

She turned as he stood on the other side of the next table. "I was at first, but I realized I shouldn't be that way."

"Afraid of me because I was in prison?" He took the cigarette out his mouth. "I'm glad you were honest. That's something I can appreciate."

She rolled the rag in her hands.

"Something you want to ask me?"

She moved to his table. "Why were you in prison?"

The light vanished from his passionate eyes. "At the risk of sounding stereotypical, guess you can consider my family a subset of the mafia." He raised his hands. "But, not me anymore at least. My family comes from Vegas and we own a chain of casinos. I headed up the casino in Atlanta for over twenty years and let's say the way I did business didn't follow the guidelines of the IRS." He rubbed his eyes. "It was money laundering and fraud."

"Wow." She rubbed the table. "You were in federal prison then."

"I was a multi-millionaire." He twirled the rag. "Now I don't have a pot to piss in. The little money I have comes from money my uncle gave me. It's enough to rent out the place I'm staying in and pay for food and stuff, but I need a job." He scoffed. "Isn't it funny how the world works? Ever since I was a kid, life was easy for me. My family always had money and took care of me, but the minute I got caught; they acted like they didn't know me."

Nola shook her head.

"My daughter..." He gulped as if his breath caught in his throat. "Hates me."

"You have a daughter?"

He exhaled, his shoulders rising. "She turned twenty-three last week."

"My daughter's twenty-two."

"She's disappointed in what I did." His knuckles turned white. "Nothing feels worse than your kid being disappointed in you, Nola. Prison don't even come close." He struggled to swallow. "Man. Why did I bring this up?"

"I'm sorry for what you're going through, Quinn."

He put on a smile but she knew it wasn't genuine. "You got another layer of me now. What do you think?"

"I hope things work out with your daughter." She stood beside him. "You can't give up on her. Family is all we have."

"Maybe I'll take a page out of your book and pray on it sometime."

"Do you go to church?"

"There aren't any Catholic churches in Beluga." He sucked the cigarette. "Kinda got out the habit, anyway."

"Praising the Lord is praising the Lord no matter the denomination. Ever been to a Baptist church?"

"Is that an invitation?" He held a half-smirk.

"Yes." She wiggled her neck. "I'm inviting you to come to Beluga Baptist Church and see my husband preach if you want to." She got the rag. "The invitation stands for eternity."

"I might. Though the church might burst into flames if I walked in there."

They laughed.

"Shit, what time is it?" He checked his watch. "Man, my bus probably left." He scrambled to the back cabinet and got his satchel. "Oh, man."

Nola heard a loud motor and looked out the window. "Uh-oh."

"What?" Quinn joined her.

The dingy, white bus flew past the center.

"Damn it!" He threw down his bag. "It'll be eleven until the next bus. I'll have to wait here three hours."

"Do you have anyone you can call to pick you up?"

"No." He crossed his arms, cheeks turning red. "What the hell am I gonna do now?"

Nola shifted her eyes left and right. "Where do you stay?"

"On Bell Row."

"Oh, the houses by the old railroad track." She nodded, folding the rag. "I'll take you home if you want."

"Are you sure? I wouldn't want to cause you any trouble."

"It's no trouble." She fidgeted, afraid of being alone in a car with him. "Let's finish these tables and we can go."

He rocked, gaping at her. "Thanks, Nola."

She gave a tight smile. "It's no problem."

CHAPTER NINE

"Here we go." Nola parked in the driveway of Quinn's brown, one-story, European-style dwelling. "I've always loved the houses over here."

"Yeah, it's a peaceful spot." Quinn got his satchel and opened the passenger door. "Thanks again."

"You're welcome." She smiled, tapping her fingers against the steering wheel. "See you at the center."

"Yeah." He got out but stuck his head back in before closing the door. "Would you like to come in?"

Is he crazy?

"Oh, no." She chuckled, breathless. "I have to get home. Hubby's probably wondering what's taking me so long."

"It's just that..." He widened the door. "There's something I want to show you. Wait." He laughed. "That's not what it sounds like."

She fidgeted, faking a chuckle. "Thankfully."

"There's something I'm working on and I could use an outside opinion." He flinched. "Kind of embarrassed but you'd be helping me a lot."

"I don't think that's a good idea."

"You are scared of me."

"No." She sighed, avoiding eye contact.

"Yes, you are. I got an idea." He closed the door. "Don't leave all right? I'll be right back." He went inside.

A second later the porch light flicked on and he returned holding a black bottle. "Take this and you can come inside and feel safe."

"Pepper spray?" She grimaced. "What in the world?"

"Are you coming in now? I need your opinion with this venture."

"It's not illegal, is it?"

"I'll give you a hint." He smiled, his gold necklace glimmering under the streetlight. "It's something very sweet."

She shook her head, flustered. "What?"

"Come on." He laughed, closing the passenger door.

Nola did a quick prayer and followed him inside the house.

"So?" He stood in the bright foyer, holding his arms out. "What do you think?"

Yellow lightening lengthened the space while the beige walls and wooden panes enveloped Nola in country coziness.

"It's nice." She nodded her approval. "Love this." She touched the wooden bench decorated with brown and beige pillows. "What did you want to show me?"

Sweat beaded around his greasy hairline. "It's in the kitchen."

They walked through the checkered, brown tile floor and into a modern-style kitchen.

The room glowed with stainless steel countertops and subdued, yellow overhead lights. Stained cherry-wood gave the cabinets a chic pop, and the granite countertops enhanced the otherwise discreet island.

He hopped in front of the two-door refrigerator, rubbing his hands. "I'm more nervous than when I went to prison."

She laughed, sitting at the curvilinear island. "What is it?"

"I got this hobby of mine I picked up in prison." He cleared his throat. "Turns out I'm great at it. You said you loved sweets, right?"

She nodded.

"Here's my secret." He opened the refrigerator and Nola's eyes rested upon the cakes, pies, and muffins on the second shelf. "I bake." Quinn winced. "Eh, yeah."

"You bake?" Nola touched her chest, finding that adorable. "I never would've guessed that."

"It's nothing I go shouting from the rooftops." Sweat drizzled off the side of his face. "Paula told me you were a super baker, so

I wanted you to taste them." He took the treats out one by one. "People in prison said my desserts gave them chills they were so good but the inmates are lucky to get anything sweet in there so I wasn't sure if I really have skills."

Nola walked to the table, examining the mouthwatering desserts he'd decorated with a fascinating eye.

"That's better than sex cake." He gestured to the square cake with the white frosting and sprinkles. "I crushed chocolate candy and pecans on top of it." He pointed to the skinny, rectangular yellow cake. "This is lemon."

"Oh, I love lemon cake."

"I make mine kinda like a coffee cake. The drizzle is just a regular confectioners' sugar glaze."

"Mm." Nola salivated. "What kind of muffins are these?"

"Banana-cinnamon."

Nola sniffed them, the banana scent clogging her nostrils. "It smells heavenly, Quinn."

"And this right here is a strawberry cheesecake." He gestured to the creamy concoction in the glass container. "And that is a regular peach cobbler or pie. Whatever you wanna call it."

"Wait a minute now." She touched his arm. "You making a peach cobbler in Georgia you got to come on with it. Hand me a fork."

"Yes, Ma'am." He got a fork and a knife out the drawer by the dishwasher. He cut her pieces of each dessert and put them on a plate. "Now, be honest. Don't hold nothing back."

"Well, you've come to the right place if you want an opinion on sweets." Nola sat on the stool. "I've judged and won so many dessert contests, I bleed peach cobbler."

He put his hands together and held them to his mouth. "Be honest and if you got tips, I'd love to hear them."

Nola sampled each one, her taste buds jolted by exuberant flavors and rich textures. "Whoa." She swallowed a mouth full of lemon cake. "Quinn." She licked glaze from her lips. "This is unbelievable."

He dropped his arms. "For real?"

She continued eating, her body awakening as if she'd pumped it with a drug. "Excuse my choice of words but hell yes."

He laughed, touching his chest. "That's a load off."

Nola chomped the tangy peach cobbler. "Your behind needs to be baking in a five-star restaurant somewhere."

"I put in an application at Bethany's Bakery." He sat on the stool beside her.

"Bethany is one of my closest friends. She's been a member of the church since Reuben started preaching. When did you put in the application?"

"About a week ago." He squinted. "I was hoping to hear back by now. There's no way in hell I expect to walk into her shop and become one of her bakers but figured if I can clean or do something around there I'll work my way up if my food's good enough."

"Oh, you're good enough." Nola licked cake from her fork. "Why not try for a baker position?"

"Nola." He tilted his head forward. "Bethany has prize-winning, trained bakers who've won Food Network contests. No way I could lick their shoes let alone become one of them at this point."

"I've been eating Bethany's desserts for years and your baking is right up there with her bakers. Trust me." She bit into the muffin, eyes rolling back into her head. "It's addicting it's so good. You didn't bake before prison?"

He shook his head. "They let me work in the kitchen and I started experimenting with the baking ingredients and the inmates went crazy." He patted his head. "It comes straight out my head. I don't use recipes just a list of ingredients."

She grabbed his wrist. "You can't be serious."

He nodded.

"Quinn, you have a gift here." She set down the plate. "You can't let it go to waste. I'm serious when I say you need to be in a kitchen making money off this."

"Easier said than done when you're an ex-con. What if Bethany isn't interested in a felon?"

"Bethany's isn't the only place in Beluga where you can bake."

"But her bakery is one of the most successful in the south. If I want to make a second career out of this, I need to get in with Bethany."

"She hasn't said no, right? Maybe I can put in a good word for you."

"No." He held his pudgy waist. "I can't put this on you and I don't want handouts."

"I'm sure in the casino business you dealt with contacts, right? That's all this would be. It's about who you know, Quinn."

"I can't ask you to do that for me, Nola."

"You didn't." She smiled. "I offered."

CHAPTER TEN

"Well, look what the cat dragged in." Reuben sit at the kitchen table, sipping grape juice. "Glad you decided to join me, Nola."

"What's this?" The absorbing aroma of mushroom gravy and buttery cornbread swarmed the kitchen. "Did you cook?" She set her purse on the table.

"Your favorite." He gestured to his plate of half-eaten food. "Salisbury steak, macaroni and cheese, cornbread and green beans."

"Mm." She touched her stomach. "What's the occasion?"

"It's almost eleven, Nola." His expression remained stiff. "Where have you been?"

"Is it?" She faked a chuckle as she glanced at her watch, knowing she was late. "I gave one of the volunteers at the soup kitchen a ride home. He missed his bus."

"He?" He crinkled his nose. "Who?"

"I doubt you know him." She got a plate out the cabinet and filled it with food. "This looks wonderful, honey. Thanks so much." She covered the food and heated it in the microwave.

Reuben rose from his seat, grunting. "Nola, who was this man?"

"He works with me at the soup kitchen like I said." She rolled her eyes, laying the plate on the cabinet. "He missed his bus, and I gave him a ride. That's the Christian thing to do, isn't it?"

"Is that all you gave him?"

She gasped. "Reuben Ryder."

"Don't play with me." He moved from around the table. "This is the last time I ask who this man is."

"Quinn Moretti."

His nose twisted. "Who?"

"He's from Atlanta and recently moved to Beluga for a fresh start."

"He's Italian?"

"Does that matter?"

He crossed his huge arms. "He needs a fresh start from what?"

"He wants to change his life, that's all." She cut up the steaming ground beef.

"Is he a young man?"

She tasted the gravy. "He's around our age."

He stood at the stove, eyebrows furrowing. "What time did you drop him off at his house?"

She stirred the macaroni and cheese on the way to the table. "I'd really like to eat—"

"Tough." He blocked her. "What time did you take him home?"

"About eight when we finished cleaning at the center."

"Eight?" He chuckled in his hand. "I know you didn't just say eight, and it's eleven. That means you've been with him all this time." He clamped his lips together. "Doesn't it?"

"Are you questioning my honor?"

"I'm question your actions."

"Why are you acting like this? Normally you wouldn't even notice if I were home." She slammed the plate on the table and sat. "I'm a good woman and don't like what you're insinuating."

"Don't pull that innocent mess." He stood beside her. "What am I supposed to think when you come in hours late after being with another man? After all that whining you been doing about attention and I take the time to make your favorite meal and your behind can't even come home?"

"How dare you?" She stood, pushing the plate away. "I've never even looked at another man since being married to you. Never given you a reason not to trust me."

"Until now."

She exhaled. "I was late one time and you flip? Yet you stay out hours upon hours?"

"Working."

"I was working too." She snatched her purse on her way out the room. "Forget this. You wasted your time cooking because you've ruined my appetite."

"Nola, get back here." He stood in the doorway. "I'm still talking to you."

"You can keep talking." She continued through the hall. "I won't be listening."

****

"Hi, Mrs. McCormick." Ginger ran up the brick steps and onto the panel deck of the McCormicks' white, two-story the next morning.

"Ginger." Felicity hung out the screen door with a smile stretching across her round face. "What a lovely surprise."

"Sorry I stopped by without calling." A soothing breeze swept through, blowing Ginger's flimsy, red and white summer dress. "You been okay?"

"Yeah, just running late for work as usual." Felicity straightened her navy blue blazer. "I can't never get out of here on time. Please, come in."

Ginger entered the large, southern-style beige living room flattered with crisp white linens and floral patterns. "Smells great in here."

"We had my famous blueberry waffles and maple syrup." Felicity straightened the clamp on her blonde hair she'd swept into a whimsical updo. "Between Judson, Rocco and LJ it's a wonder I get any food."

Ginger laughed.

"There's still a couple waffles left if you want some." Felicity got her purse off the wicker chair and searched it. "Go to the kitchen." She pointed toward the hall. "Help yourself."

"Thanks. I already ate." Ginger stepped on the side of her white flip-flops. "Is LJ busy? I see the truck outside or did he walk to the junkyard?"

"LJ's not feeling well." Felicity checked her makeup in her compact mirror. "Says he has a headache, so he went back to bed after breakfast. Rocco and Judson left for work." She fluffed out her pleaded skirt, rushing to the door. "Lord have mercy." She examined her black, stilettos. "Should've been at the bank fifteen minutes ago."

Ginger smiled, holding her hands behind her back.

"Go on up to LJ's room." Felicity opened the door and backed out of it. "It's the second bedroom upstairs. Have a nice day and Merry Christmas."

"Yeah, you too..."

Felicity shut the door.

"*Okay.*" Ginger walked up the traditional, carpeted staircase, reaching the beige hallway. She knocked on the door to the second bedroom. "LJ?"

No answer.

She twisted the doorknob and peeked inside the bright, white room with shiplap walls that sloped inward beside the brown, panel bed.

LJ lay inside white, linen sheets, shirtless with his back to the door and his arm under his head.

Ginger approached the bed.

A sour whiff of sweaty feet came from LJ's sneakers and dirty socks he'd strewn on the beige carpet.

"Gross." Ginger passed the window, brushing up against the white, lace curtains. "LJ?" She knelt in the bed, tapping his back. "LJ?"

"Huh?" He jerked, sitting up on his elbows. "Ginger?" He swept his hand across his crinkled face. "What the hell are you doing in my room?"

She snuck a peek of his blue boxers. "Wanted to see if you were okay."

"What the hell you talking about?" He rubbed his eye, yawning. "I had a headache, so I was resting. What do you want?"

"Are you mad at me or something?" She sat straight. "I haven't seen you since we had ice cream at the shop."

"So?" He squinted as if to adjust his eyes.

"We exchanged numbers, remember? I told you to call me and you never did."

He groaned, laying his head on the wooden headboard.

"I called you three times." She poked his arm. "Left messages and even texted so don't say you didn't get them."

"I got them," he barked. "Now what?"

She fidgeted at his aggressive behavior. "Did I do something wrong?"

"Maybe I should've made this clear but I'm not a fool. You've been playing me."

"What the hell are you talking about?"

He propped his legs up underneath the sheet. "Let's talk about your reputation with guys."

"Wait, a minute—"

"I hear you use them and spit them out and the only reason you're interested in me is because I'm the new dick in town."

"You asshole." She hit his arm. "Don't talk to me like this."

"Then get the hell off my bed." He pushed her.

"Hey." She stumbled but caught her balance. "Don't push me."

"I can do whatever I want." He ripped the covers off and stood, giving her a chance to check out those amazing abs. "Whatever you had planned, it's not going down okay? Stay the hell away from me, Ginger."

"Hold up." She marched to the other side of the bed, sticking out her chest. "What is this about?"

"It's about this game you play." He pulled up his shorts. "Stop acting innocent. I'm from Chicago, baby. You think I've never met girls like you before? I knew I should've stayed away from your ass but I was stupid." He walked around her. "I'm doing the best I can to stay sane and on the right track and the last thing I need is you screwing everything up."

"LJ—"

"Don't say nothing just leave me the hell alone." He got his T-shirt off the closet door. "Get out because I need to get dressed."

"No you wait just a minute here." She got in his face, pointing. "You can't just throw accusations and not let me explain myself."

"I don't care." He plopped on the bed, yawning.

"That's a lie because if you didn't care about me you wouldn't be so mad. Who've you been talking to?"

"Does it have to be anyone specific? Haven't you been with half the town?"

"Fuck you. You don't know shit about me. Yes, I flirt and have fun but the rest is just lies."

He grinned. "Right."

"Has Beau Midnight gotten to you?" She scoffed, shaking her head. "I figured that was coming."

LJ looked at her, lips tight.

"You're definitely listening to the wrong person."

He rolled his eyes. "Am I?"

"Yes," she snapped, sitting beside him. "Let me tell you about Beau."

"Oh, he told me." He chuckled. "Yeah, he hit it and you quit it. Just threw him away like you do all the guys when you're tired of them. Beau and I talked for a long time. He said you were only after him because of his football scholarship to Ohio State then when he lost it, you dumped him."

"That's not true."

"Not surprised you'd deny it."

"Why would you choose to believe Beau over me? Come on, LJ. Beau just doesn't want me with you. He doesn't want me with anyone he thinks I can actually like."

His expression relaxed.

"He doesn't care that I hang around Da'Kuan because he knows I don't have feelings for him."

"Yeah." He scratched his arm. "You're just with him for the weed, right?"

"I smoke weed." She shrugged. "I drink beer too. So what? I'm twenty-two and I can do whatever the hell I want. Look, I dumped Beau but not because he lost his scholarship. That's a lie."

"He says all you've ever wanted was to leave this town, and you used his chance to play football as your ticket out of here."

"Bullshit." She swung her arm. "I don't need Beau to leave this town. I'm saving my money and I'll leave, regardless."

"Why haven't you then?"

"I'm not ready to leave yet." She wiggled her neck. "But, if and when I do, it will have nothing to do with Beau or any man."

"Makes me wonder if you're playing up to me so I can take you to Chicago or something."

"I wouldn't go to Chicago any damn way." She grimaced. "Trust me, if I did I wouldn't need *you* to take me. Beau and I dated in high school for two years. He lost his scholarship because he was caught at a party with cocaine."

LJ squinted.

"Beau had a major coke habit, and he treated me like shit because of it. I loved Beau, and he was my first lover."

LJ twisted his body toward her.

"I broke up with him because he was possessive and abusive. When he was high, it was like he was a whole different person, not even human. While he was telling you stuff about me did he say how my parents had him arrested for beating me up?"

"He beat you up?"

She exhaled, holding in tears. "When I broke it off, he beat the shit out of me. He busted my lip, nearly broke my jaw and I had a concussion. My dad almost killed him but it was the grace of God that he didn't." She looked away. "After that, Beau's parents put him in rehab. He's clean now, but I haven't said one word to Beau Midnight since."

CHAPTER ELEVEN

LJ looked confused as if to process the information. "His ass should be in jail."

"His dad's the deputy sheriff." Ginger sighed. "He begged and pleaded for my parents to have mercy on Beau. Mom and Dad made a deal with Beau and his parents that he stay away from me and go to rehab and we wouldn't press charges."

"That son of a bitch." LJ held his breath. "He left out a lot, didn't he?"

"Beau still wants me and he'll try to sabotage any relationship I have. LJ, I'm a flirt but I'm not a slut. I've only been with three people and Beau was one of them. The other was Da'Kuan and a dude who doesn't even live in Beluga anymore. A guy I dated a few times after Beau. Just because I like to have fun it doesn't mean I sleep around and I take issue with anyone who says I do."

"Beau hit you?" He froze with his eyes wide. "If he ever touches you again, I'll kill him."

She smiled. "That means a lot."

"I'm sorry, Ginger." He put his arm around her. "I believed what I wanted to believe, and it wasn't fair to you."

"I really like you, LJ." She stuck her fingers in between his. "That's why I flirt with you. It's not for any other reason."

"But, what's so special about me?"

She stared into his eyes, seeing heaven. "Your eyes. When I look at them, I see everything I've always wanted to experience and to be. I see hope." She touched his rugged cheek. "And proof that there's more to me than being the preacher's daughter."

"You are more than that." He grabbed the back of her head and plunged his lips on hers, her nipples and crotch throbbing for more of his touch.

She cut the kiss short despite wanting to continue. "Why did you do that?"

He smirked. "I've been wanting to since I first saw you. Now I got an excuse." He kissed her again, and she touched his thigh. "I'm sorry, Ginger."

"Wanna make it up to me?" She pinched his nipple.

"Ow." He snatched her hand, wincing and grinning. "Hands off the merchandise."

"I want us to go out on a date." She tingled. "My friend Tisha's invited me to have dinner with her and her folks Saturday."

He removed his arm from her shoulder. "Uh—"

"Don't feel weird. I want Tisha to meet you and it'll be fun." She pulled his earlobe. "In relationships, you got to sacrifice, LJ."

"Relationships, huh?" He caressed her hair. "Is that what this is?"

"It can be." She put her arm around his waist. "If you play your cards right. You wanna get closer to me?"

"Oh, yeah."

She snickered. "Then do we have a date for Saturday?" She stood, fixing her dress.

He stared at her thighs. "Definitely."

****

Saturday

"I swear I can't take it anymore." Nola and Paula carried the lemonade and glasses to the Ryders' veranda, its curved roof giving a relaxed yet elegant aura. "If Reuben doesn't get his act together I might be filing papers soon."

"*Nola*." Paula set the glasses on the table in front of the wicker sectional upholstered in white fabric. "Bite your tongue."

"It's the truth." She poured lemonade into the glasses, making sure both got at least one lemon wedge. "How much is one woman supposed to take, Paula?" She sat, crossing her legs in the purple, kimono robe. "He's been sulking for the last two days because I came home late."

"You were with another man." Paula sipped, smirking.

"Quinn missed his bus and needed a ride."

"Flip it and understand how this looks to your husband." Paula bit into one of Nola's homemade oatmeal raisin cookies. "How would you feel if you had a romantic meal waiting for Reuben and he'd been late because he took a woman home?"

"And, how is that different from what he usually does?" Nola snatched a cookie out the bowl, swatting a fly. "I'm always waiting on his behind to come home."

Paula watched her out the corners of her eyes. "You skipped over the woman part."

"I'd expect Reuben to take a woman home if she's stranded." Nola chomped the cookie. "He's a pastor after all."

"Nola." Paula put her elbow on the table. "Don't play me for a fool. You'd be jealous and upset too."

"What I don't get is why Reuben is jealous? It's not like he pays me any attention, anyway. So, I got to give a man a ride home for him to be jealous?"

Paula shrugged one shoulder.

"Men. How dare Reuben give me the silent treatment when he's the one in the wrong? Besides, nothing happened between Quinn and me, anyway."

"That doesn't matter to your husband." Paula moaned, sticking out her lips. "All he knows is you were late and with another man. No telling what thoughts ran into his head."

"If that's what it takes for him to pay me some attention than so be it." Nola nibbled on a raisin.

"Since we are talking about Quinn..." Paula raised an eyebrow. "I understand why Reuben would be suspicious because I see how you two are at the center. Just be giggling and laughing." She gave a suggestive look. "Saw you and him getting down to 'This Christmas' the other evening."

"So we had Christmas music on the radio." Nola stretched, looking away. "Blame the holiday spirit."

"I haven't seen you smile like that in a long time, Nola."

"Paula, this is insane. Nothing is going on between Quinn and me. After all you're the one who told me to be nice to him."

She nodded. "I did."

"I'm treating Quinn like I would anyone."

"Whatever you say." Paula chuckled. "Where is Reuben anyway?"

"Where he always is." Nola sat back. "Working on his sermon with Pastor Marroquin for tomorrow's service."

"I saw Pastor Marroquin preach in Augusta and she throws it down. I can't wait to see her in person."

Nola grumbled as she took another bite of the cookie.

Paula leaned forward as tires screeched. "Who is this flying like a fool?"

An army green Ford pickup make a sharp turn, sped up the Ryders' driveway and parked behind Nola's car.

"Quinn?" Nola stood, clutching the opening of her robe.

He jumped out the truck, with his forehead glistening from the gunk in his hair.

"What's that stuff he puts in his hair?" Paula whispered. "Man's greasier than a fried pork chop."

"Stop." Nola swatted at her, trying not to laugh.

"Hello, ladies." Quinn marched up, whistling. "There she is." He held his hands out to Nola. "The beautiful woman I wanted to see."

"You're bright-eyed and bushy-tailed."

"And you're wonderful." He skipped up the steps and hugged her. "Thank you so much."

Nola caught Paula's teasing stare. "I'm confused."

Quinn kissed her hands. "I got the job with Bethany's bakery." He danced in place. "Isn't that great?"

"Oh, Quinn." Nola threw her arms around his shoulders not caring what Paula thought. "I'm so happy for you." She let him go, patting his thick chest. "Now you got a job and everything will fall into place. You're baking then?"

"No, she's gonna train me to decorate cakes, but she told me to bring in a sample of my desserts and she'll see about making me an apprentice. If it hadn't been for you, she probably wouldn't have thought twice about my application."

"Congratulations, Quinn."

"Thanks, Paula."

"Does that explain the truck?" Paula asked.

"Oh, that's my neighbor's. He's letting me borrow it for the day." His gold chain nearly blinded Nola. "Which brings me here, Nola. I want to show my appreciation. What you did means the world to me."

"No need to thank me." She sat. "I'm glad it worked out and once she tastes your sweets she might make you head baker."

He laughed. "Are you busy? Got plans for the day?"

"No." She smiled. "Why?"

"I was on my way to the farmers market outside town to get some berries." He glanced at Paula. "It's for a pie I wanna make Bethany."

"You mean Aimes Farmers Market?" Nola asked. "Gosh, I haven't been there in a while. I love looking at the fresh fruit and veggies."

Paula grinned and Nola did her best to ignore her.

"Someone told me they got the best berries and nothing's too good for Bethany," Quinn said. "Figured you'd like to come along."

Paula glared at her friend.

"I'd love to go but not sure I should." Nola crossed her legs.

"I could really use your help around the place since it's new to me and all." He put his hands in his pockets. "Whatever you pick out is on me." He tapped his chest. "My way of thanking you."

Nola looked at Paula.

"What?" Paula shrugged.

"Come on, girl." Quinn teased Nola with playful squinting. "You know you want to go."

Paula snickered, biting a cookie.

She rolled her eyes at Paula and then smiled at Quinn. "Okay, give me a few minutes to change."

CHAPTER TWELVE

"I've never seen so much food in one place and I'm Italian." Quinn laughed with a basket full of berries and fruit. "Feel like a kid in a candy store."

"I love berries." Nola walked with him under the mile-long tent that shielded the people and food from the scolding sun. "My grandfather was a berry farmer."

"Really?" Quinn picked up a giant strawberry and sniffed it. "These smell so good you can taste them." He grabbed a bagful. "Tell me more about your grandfather."

"He had his own orchid in Blue Ridge for years." Nola pushed a curl behind her ear. "Me and my cousins would go there every summer until it was time to go back to school."

Quinn smiled.

"We'd pick the berries and help Pawpaw sort them." She laughed. "And cause a ruckus in the meantime."

"Pawpaw?" Quinn chuckled.

"That's what we called my granddaddy."

"He sounds like a great guy." Quinn's eyes popped as he caught sight of the fat tomatoes at the front of the tent. "Look at those big tomatoes." He held one up to her, and she sniffed it.

"Uh-huh." She exhaled the fresh, earthy scent and put some in her hand basket. "Can't wait to put these babies in a salad."

"Go on." Sweat slithered underneath Quinn's gold chain. "You were talking about your Pawpaw."

"Those summers were so much fun." She closed her eyes, imagining being back on that field of berries. "His strawberries were ten times bigger than these. Some big as your head."

"Is his orchid still around?"

"He sold it not long before he died because he was too old to run it." She sighed. "Pawpaw was my daddy's father and he wanted to keep the orchard in the family but Daddy didn't wanna deal with it."

Quinn glanced at her between searching through tomatoes. "Seems like that bothered you."

She shrugged. "Not that Daddy would've cared what I thought."

"What do you mean by that?"

"Never mind."

They passed a smiling Hispanic family as they headed toward the peaches.

"Can't make killer peach cobbler without Georgia peaches." Quinn grabbed the large, furry balls. "Everything smells so fresh."

A breeze swept through the tent, lifting Nola's spaghetti-strapped summer dress. "Used to come here all the time when I was young."

"You're still young."

She rolled her eyes, grinning. "Remind this body for me then."

"It doesn't need reminding." Quinn ogled her as if no other woman existed. "Surely your husband tells you that."

She scoffed.

"I like your hair." He put peaches into a bag. "You combed it different."

She touched it. "Excuse me?"

"You usually comb the bangs to the right." He swatted a gnat. "Combed them to the left today."

She gaped. "You notice how I do my bangs?"

"Yeah." He shrugged a shoulder. "Why wouldn't I?"

"Reuben wouldn't notice if I shaved my head." She laughed. "In fact, many men wouldn't notice what side a woman combs her bangs on."

"I did." He winked.

A rush of warmth penetrated her and she took a deep breath.

"Besides, you gotta be exaggerating about your husband." He straightened the basket on his arm and examined a huge lemon.

"On the outside we look perfect." She crossed her arms. "But, we have problems like other couples do."

"If he's dropping the ball don't make excuses for him." His brows rose. "Not good when your husband ignores you."

"I shouldn't have told you that." She stuffed lemons in a sack and laid them in her basket. "Please, don't tell anyone what I said."

"Nola." He touched her hand, sending an electric shock through her veins. "Anything you tell me is between us. I'm great at keeping secrets."

"I'd better make sure *I* am." She adjusted the basket on her wrist. "Because if Reuben knew I was with you he'd have a fit. He's been mad I gave you a ride home."

"Why?"

"He was jealous, but should know I'd never cheat on him."

"Are you saying that to convince me..." He brushed up against her to get to the next section of food. "Or yourself?"

"What?"

He smirked, continuing toward the legumes.

****

"I don't get it though." Rocco stood beside LJ scoping out the black Camaro in the junkyard. "Why do you wanna fix this up now?"

"It's a classic, man." LJ ran his fingers along the smooth yet dusty interior. "Camaros never go out of style."

"Nah, gotta be more to it than that." Rocco wiped sweat from underneath his cap. "When I told you to fix it up you said you weren't interested."

"I am now." LJ held his waist, rocking. "Besides, Ginger likes it."

Rocco guffawed. "I should've known."

"She has a point." LJ looked at the Silverado. "I love the truck but what's wrong with having two rides?"

"This thing's in worst shape than the truck." Rocco kicked the front tire. "It'll take you months to fix it."

"What else have I got to do?"

Rocco leaned back on the car. "What's up with you and Ginger?"

"I like her." LJ fidgeted, staring into the sun. "She makes me feel good when I'm with her. Something awakens in me."

Rocco huffed.

"Is there a problem? Ever since I got here, you wanted me to meet women. Well, I met one."

"It puts me in a tough spot, man. You're my cousin and Beau's my boy."

"Yeah well your boy Beau is a lying scumbag." LJ walked to the other side of the car and checked out the black, leather interior. "Ginger told me he abused her, and he was on drugs too. Why didn't you tell me?"

"For what?" Rocco grimaced. "I wasn't aware Beau's personal business had anything to do with you. He had a coke habit but he's clean now."

LJ rose. "How can you be sure?"

"Because he went to rehab and I trust him too."

"It doesn't bother you he's a woman beater?"

"Beau's better now. He had a lot of stress after losing his scholarship. His whole world turned upside down."

"He lost it because he was doing drugs." LJ got into the passenger's seat, getting a feel for the car. "It's no one's fault but his own."

"He regrets his mistakes."

LJ rubbed the dashboard. "Once a druggie, always one."

"Oh yeah?" Rocco propped his arm on the passenger door and leaned into LJ's face. "Some folks would say the same thing about an ex-con. Out of all the people who would judge Beau, I'd think you'd be more understanding."

"He had no right putting his hands on a woman." LJ got out the car. "Maybe you can forgive that but I can't. You forgot how many abusive bastard boyfriends my mother had?"

Rocco sighed, turning away.

"How many black eyes and bruises she had to cover up?" LJ slammed the car door.

"Beau's changed, and he's my friend."

"I'm not saying you can't be his friend." LJ walked to the trunk and opened it. "Just don't expect me to be. He thinks I'm stupid. He was trying to persuade me not to see Ginger. That's why he talked that shit about her."

"You really like her, don't you?"

"I'm going with her to her friend Tisha's to have dinner tonight." LJ slammed the trunk closed. "What does that tell you?"

CHAPTER THIRTEEN

"You're going to the Easons' for dinner?" Rocco chuckled under his hand. "You know Tisha's father is the deacon of the church?"

"Ah, shit." LJ raised his head. "You serious? Ginger conveniently left that out."

"That's gonna be one hell of a dinner." Rocco leaned over, laughing. "Wish I could see it. You and Deacon Eason will spend the whole night arguing about Jesus."

LJ covered his eyes. "Hell."

His cell phone rang.

He got it from his jeans and checked the ID. "Shit."

"What?"

"Rockford Corrections."

Rocco took off his cap and wiped sweat off his face. "Your daddy's prison?"

The phone rang in LJ's shaking hand. "What do I do?"

"Answer it."

"You answer it." He held the phone to Rocco.

"I ain't never talked to your daddy and I don't wanna start now." Rocco pushed the phone away. "If he's calling it's a good reason."

LJ hesitated.

"If you're gonna do it you better hurry. The man's in prison and I doubt they'll let him sit on the phone all day."

"Fuck." LJ answered, listened to the little automatic message and accepted the call.

"Hello?" Columbus Beatty's scratchy voice sounded from the other end. "Luther, you there?"

LJ held his breath. "Yeah, I'm here, Dad."

"Son." Columbus exhaled, chuckling. "It's great to hear your voice. How you doing?"

"All right." LJ squinted at Rocco.

"Was hoping you'd call me or email when you got out. You're in Beluga with Judson and Felicity, right?"

"Uh-huh." LJ exhaled with impatience.

"Must be quite the change from a big city like Chicago to that rabbit hole." Columbus cackled.

"No harder than adjusting being out of prison after two years."

Rocco motioned to LJ. "I'm gonna go," he whispered. "Gotta run errands for Momma."

LJ nodded, ignoring Columbus' rambling.

Rocco ran to his truck and left.

LJ interrupted Columbus' hollow conversation, "Something you wanted, Dad? I got things to do."

"Just wanted to shoot the breeze since I never hear from you. I call you all the time but you never answer. Surprised you did today, but I get it." Columbus groaned. "You're a young man with your own life. I'll cut to the chase." He coughed. "I'm sick."

LJ scratched his nose. "Got a cold or something?"

"I wish." Columbus snickered. "I've had this nagging cough for a while and uh, last week they took me to the hospital because when I was lifting weights at rec, my chest tightened up and I was struggling to breathe."

"You all right?"

"I'd been losing weight and hadn't been that hungry. I thought I had pneumonia."

"Dad, just tell me what's going on. I'm shaking all over here."

"Want the good news or the bad news first?"

"The bad news."

He paused for a minute and then continued, "I got first stage lung cancer."

LJ fell back on the car as if someone let the air out of him.

"Want the good news?" Columbus grinned. "It ain't pneumonia," he joked.

LJ's breathing quickened. "Are they...are they sure?"

"Yep." Columbus' jolly nature subsided. "I struggled with telling you this since your mother had the same—"

"God." LJ's stomach tightened.

"Did you say 'God'?"

"How's the prognosis though? Did the doctor say if you'll make it?"

"Shit, I hope I do." Columbus laughed. "I'm just taking it one day at time but at least it's early. Beyond that, I know little myself."

"Damn it." LJ gripped his head.

"I don't want you to worry, son."

"You have lung cancer, Dad. Am I supposed to ignore that?" His stomach twisted. "It's always something. Every time I turn around someone's sick or dying." He pressed his palm on the car and leaned over. "This might sound crappy but I wish you hadn't told me this."

"I wish I didn't have lung cancer."

"Are you scared?"

"It's my fault. I've been smoking since I was ten."

The automated message warned them they had a few minutes left to talk.

"That's not the only reason I called."

"I can't take much else." LJ rubbed his face.

"I need to see you, son. That's all I'm gonna say. Please, think about it and let me know if that's possible."

The thought of visiting his dad scared him more than the horrible news.

"I love you, Luther." Columbus breathed into the phone. "With all my heart."

****

"Hey." LJ slumped into the McCormick kitchen with his hands in his pockets.

"Hi there." Felicity laid beef cutlets in a bowl of milk. "What's up?"

"What are you doing?" LJ got a can of soda out the fridge.

"Marinating these cutlets in buttermilk so I can make chicken fried steak tonight." She licked her lips. "Yum."

"Sounds good." LJ sipped the cherry soda. "Too bad I got plans but can you save me some?"

She watched him under her lashes as she put the bowl of meat in the refrigerator. "With Judson and Rocco you're lucky to get a piece if you were here."

LJ chuckled, sitting at the table.

"I'll save you one." She rinsed off her hands and dabbed them with a dishtowel. "You okay?"

He wiggled his legs. "Dad called me earlier."

"Wow." She held her narrow hip. "Bet that was a surprise."

"Not as much as what he told me." He sat back, stretching his legs. "He's got first stage lung cancer."

"What?" She touched her cheek, green pupils expanding.

"Just like Momma."

"LJ." She hugged him and kissed his forehead. "I'm so sorry, sweetheart."

"Yeah." He sniffed her peachy scent. "Nothing we can do about it so no need in getting upset."

She sat beside him, caressing his hand. "When did he find out?"

"Last week." He drank. "He doesn't know when they'll start treatment. They still have more tests to do."

"At least they're catching it early."

"Aunt Felicity." He moaned, laying his forehead against the table. "I gotta go through this again?"

"Sh." She rubbed his arm. "Look, doctors or not, they don't decide Columbus' future. Only God can do that."

"Please." He let go of her hand. "I don't want to hear that."

"It's the truth." She relaxed her arm on the table. "I'm going to pray for your daddy, and we're here for you, LJ. We always will be."

"He wants me to go see him."

She sat erect. "Will you?"

"Think I should?"

"Honey, it's your decision." She touched his cheek. "You're the one who'll have to live with the choice. Whatever you decide we'll support you and don't worry about money." She smiled. "Judson and I will pay for it if you go."

"I couldn't ask you to do that. You're already doing so much for me."

"Yeah, well we're family." She got up and hugged him. "That's what families do."

CHAPTER FOURTEEN

Mrs. Judith Eason took another bite of the duck breast, smiling at LJ from across the table as if it took the strength of a hundred men to do so. "How's the duck, LJ?"

He glanced to his right at Ginger who winked as she chewed.

"It's amazing, Ma'am." He coughed into his hand. "Thanks for allowing me to join you tonight."

"We wish we'd had more of a heads up though." Deacon Tim Eason sucked his teeth as waves of red undertones glowed underneath his bright, yellow skin.

"Daddy." Tisha glared at him with her braids tied up with a ribbon. "LJ is our guest."

Tim chewed hard, wincing. "If you say so."

LJ cleared his throat. "Your home is beautiful." He tapped the gold and red tablecloth. "I love this."

"Do you?" Kinky, black curls surrounded the sides of Tim's bald, round head.

"Does that surprise you?" LJ sensed the wrath approaching.

"This is a Christmas table cloth." Tim's bifocals sat lopsided on his long nose. "Since you don't believe in Christmas, why would you like the cloth?"

"Deacon, that's not fair." Ginger ate potatoes. "LJ would just like people to respect his beliefs as he does others."

"Does he respect others' beliefs?" Judith chewed, a mix of snobbery and disdain covered her toasted-brown face. "If so, then why would he come here tonight?"

Ginger grimaced. "Excuse me?"

"Ginger." LJ patted her arm. "It's okay."

"No, it's not. Mrs. Eason you have no right to talk to LJ like this."

"I'll remind you to stay in your place, young lady," Tim said. "Does your father know you're out with this—"

"This what?" LJ asked. "See, this is why God isn't real. You're supposed to be Christians but you only act like it when it suits you."

"How dare you, young man?" Judith stuck her hand in the air, quoting a scripture about respecting elders. "I don't know what you're accustomed to LJ, but we don't allow Tisha to speak to us any kind of way and we sure won't allow you to do it either."

"This is ridiculous." Ginger threw her fork on the plate. "LJ's been nothing but kind, which is a lot more than you deserve seeing how you've been treating him."

"See, Judy?" Tim asked. "Look how Ginger's talking after hanging out with this God hater."

Ginger gasped.

"Ginger, you know better," Judith said. "You're the first daughter. How can you condone being with someone who disrespects the Lord?"

"Who I'm with is none of your damn business."

The Easons gasped while Tisha covered her face.

"We're not gonna take this crap." Ginger stood, throwing the Christmas napkin on the table. "We appreciate the invitation Tisha, but if your folks don't want us here, then we'll leave." She grabbed LJ's hand. "And, if you're Christians then I'm embarrassed to be one."

"Oh." Judith gyrated, her high cheeks expanding with air. "Ginger, you've lost your mind."

"Reuben will snatch a hole the size of a baseball field out your behind when I tell him how you spoke to us." Tim pointed. "This happens when you hang around with criminals."

LJ set his eyes on Tim's face.

"Yeah, I said it." He nodded. "You need to know the truth. That's God's way. I've heard you had a hard life and I'm sorry, LJ. But, did you ever wonder if that's because you don't believe in God?"

Tisha covered her eyes. "Daddy, stop it."

"I'm trying to help him." Tim stood from the table, sweating. "You need Jesus in your life, son. That's the only way you'll get rid of the sin."

"How dare you?"

"Cool it, Ginger." LJ stood, holding his hand in front of her. "This is nothing I haven't gotten before." He looked at the Easons. "Like I said, Christianity seems to be convenient around here. It's fine to be Christian and help out the homeless but you wanna boycott my uncle's shop if he hires me."

The Easons dropped their heads.

"No, I don't believe in God but I believe in treating others with kindness and respect if they show you the same." He straightened the chair. "There's more I could say but I won't disrespect you in your home. I suggest the next time you try to scold someone on Christianity you do a little brushing up on it yourselves."

Tisha glared at Ginger.

"It was nice meeting you, Tisha." LJ took Ginger's hand and walked out the kitchen.

"I'm sorry." Ginger got her purse off the hook by the front door. "What was I thinking?"

"Don't worry about it."

They exited the house and walked down the porch steps.

"When you hear that stuff so much it doesn't even bother you."

"They had no right to treat you that way." She stopped him before they got to her car. "I thought they'd at least be nice."

"I'm glad they didn't hide their dislike." He half-smiled. "I'd rather someone be honest than not." He pointed at the Easons' beige and brown brick house. "Tisha looked like she was having a stroke."

They laughed.

LJ kissed Ginger's cheek. "Sorry if I ruined the evening."

She twirled in the navy blue jersey dress. "I was bored anyway and that duck was tough as my shoe."

He laughed, brushing lint from his relaxed jeans. "Did I tell you how nice you look in that dress?"

"Yes." She gripped her curves. "But, you can tell me again."

He placed his hand on the back of her neck and guided his mouth to hers, tasting the salt from her tender lips. "You smell so good."

"The night's still young." She got the car remote from her purse. "You want to hang out?"

He sauntered behind her to the car. "In Beluga?"

"No." She unlocked the car. "Out of town."

He opened the passenger door. "Where?"

"Can you roller skate?" She smirked, tilting her head.

"That's an odd question." He rubbed his hair, chuckling. "Haven't done it since I was a kid. Why?"

"Heard of the Capricorn? It's a skating rink and pizza place outside town. Tisha and I go there all the time."

"Oh, yeah. Rocco was telling me about it."

"It's a way to have fun and escape all the busybodies in Beluga. How about it?" She swerved her gorgeous body. "I can show you more of my moves on skates. You can show me yours too."

His stomach flip-flopped as a prickling sensation cruised through his spine. "I'd love to."

****

"Come on." Quinn pulled Nola through the crowded parking lot and into the double doors of the Capricorn.

"I can't believe you talked me into coming here." She jumped in behind Quinn as rowdy teenagers flew past. "I need to go home."

"Why?" They walked to the front counter to order pizza. "Your husband's off getting ready for his sermon tomorrow. You'd just be at home bored and wallowing." He took out his wallet as they waited in the long line. "Life's too short so you shouldn't waste a minute of it, Nola."

"This isn't me." She hugged herself, checking out the red and white striped walls. "What if someone from Beluga sees us?"

Quinn turned to the side to speak to her. "I don't think going to a skating rink and having pizza is a sin."

"But being with another man who isn't my husband is."

He looked at her, heavy eyebrows falling. "We're doing nothing wrong."

She inched up as the line moved. "Then how come I feel so guilty?"

"Nola, you can't complain about things then don't change them. One minute you're upset about your husband ignoring you but then you don't want to have fun. Which is it?"

The aroma of pepperoni and fresh-baked crust engulfed her. "I'm first lady and there's a certain type of fun I'm supposed to have."

"You wanna leave?" He got out of line. "I'll take you home then."

"Wait." She touched his arm, and he got back in place. "We drove all this way. Having pizza won't hurt."

"You're not getting off that easy." He clicked his jaw. "We're skating too."

She laughed. "I haven't skated since before I got married."

"Well, get ready for a ride down memory lane." Quinn stepped to the waiter at the counter. "Because we're not leaving until you skate with me."

She sighed.

CHAPTER FIFTEEN

"Ha, ha, ha!" Nola covered her mouth as she chewed the thick, gooey pepperoni and sausage pizza. "You're kidding me."

"No, I ain't." Quinn laughed, holding his arms out across the table. "I peed on myself right there on the rollercoaster."

Nola laughed, grabbing her soda. "Then what did you do?"

"What could I do?" He sipped from his straw. "All the people at the carnival could see it. I was so embarrassed." His face turned red. "There I was my senior year of high school and I was with the girl of my dreams and I piss myself."

"Wow." Nola fanned, eyes watering. "That's worse than when I was cheerleading in high school. One time I did a flip during the biggest football game of the year and my panties slid off."

Quinn leaned forward, choking from pizza and laughter.

"Yep, I gave them a halftime show to remember. I tell you that."

"Damn." Quinn picked a mushroom off his pizza slice and ate it. "Isn't it funny how when you're a kid these things seem so big but then you look back on them years later and you wonder what the big deal was."

"Hm-mm." She chewed cheese and crust.

The lights dimmed over the rink and couples gravitated to the hardwood platform holding hands.

"Ah, it's couples skate." Quinn dabbed his mouth. "Remember that?"

"Reuben couldn't skate." She balled up her napkin. "So he'd always sit and watch me with other guys."

"How did you and Reuben meet?"

"Like most in Beluga, we grew up together." She patted her cheek. "People kid and said we have an arrange marriage." She giggled. "Both our dads were preachers and my dad wanted me to marry a preacher and Reuben was being pruned to take his father's place at Beluga Baptist." She rocked, smiling. "Daddy loved him some Reuben Ryder. I'm an only child and Reuben was like the son Daddy always wanted."

Couples skated around the rink, holding each other close.

"Reuben was the man of my dreams. Made me feel wanted and protected in a way I never have."

"But your parents picked Reuben, not you."

She looked at him. "I fell in love with him."

He nodded with a skeptical glow in his eyes. "You'd have gone out with Reuben if your parents hadn't insisted?"

"I was lucky Reuben would even look at me. Every daddy in the town wanted their daughter with him because everyone knew he'd be preacher one day. In Beluga, preacher is king."

He wiped pizza grease from the corner of his mouth. "You have no regrets?"

"Of being with Reuben? We've had twenty-five years of marriage, live in a
beautiful home, have money and a wonderful daughter. What more could I ask for?"

He moved his mouth left and right. "Attention?"

"What about you and your ex-wife?"

"Similar to you and Reuben." He propped his arm on the back of the chair. "We grew up together in Vegas. Not sure we were that much in love but comfortable with each other." He looked at the leftover pizza crusts on his plate. "I was more concerned with the business and she liked being along for the ride."

"What's her name?"

"Angelina."

"That's a pretty name. Is she Italian?"

He nodded with a distant stare.

"I bet she's beautiful." Nola sipped soda. "Italian women are always so pretty."

"She was all right." He scratched his shoulder. "When times got rough, she wasn't around." He shrugged. "If not for my daughter the relationship would've been a waste."

"You still haven't heard from your daughter?"

He sniffled, shaking his head.

"I'll continue praying."

"Okay enough of this sad and sappy talk." He rubbed his eyes. "We came here to have fun." He stood, holding out his hand. "Come on."

"What?"

"We had a deal." He helped her out the chair. "We're supposed to skate."

"Couples skate?" She hesitated. "I don't think that's a good idea."

"I'll keep my hands to myself." He winked, leading her to the counter. "Unless you don't want me to."

She glared at him.

****

"Now this is what I'm talking about." Ginger and LJ entered the Capricorn, bypassing the loud children who played at the front doors. "I love this place."

LJ took Ginger's hand, and she welcomed the courteous gesture. "Guess this is our first date, huh?"

She tingled. "Guess so and I'm gonna whip your butt on the rink."

He stuck out his chest. "Care to wager on that?"

"Hm." She moved to the opposite side of him. "What do I get if I win?"

"You get a pizza on me." He looked at her through his lashes. "Now, what do I get?"

She turned her shoulder to him. "You'll find out if you win."

"Okay." He laughed, bumping her with his elbow. "You wanna play like that, huh?"

"Look, LJ." She pointed to the rink. "It's couples skate. It's so romantic." They walked up to the railing that separated the rink from the eating tables.

He smiled. "What are we waiting for?"

They went to the booth, got skates and returned to the skating area.

LJ kissed Ginger's hand. "May I have this skate?"

"Yes, you may."

He helped her onto the platform and put his arm around her waist. "Hold on."

They swayed to the music, feet and bodies in synch.

"You're good." LJ winked, the pink and green lights flickering across his face. "How often you come here?"

"As much as I can. It's relaxing, huh?"

"Yeah." He wrapped his arm tighter around her. "Thanks, Ginger."

"For what?"

"For being so nice." His face stiffened. "Besides Rocco, you're my only friend around here. I still feel bad for the Beau stuff."

"Please, forget Beau." She tangled her fingers in his. "I have. So, are you ever going to tell me about the woman in your past?"

He wiggled his nose.

"Fine thing like you I know you've had someone special."

"I don't want to talk about her." He swerved Ginger in front of him, holding her shoulders. "Let's enjoy this moment between *us*." He lowered his lips to her neck and kissed it.

She shivered. "That tickles."

"I'm getting hooked on you," he whispered into her ear. "You're the first person who's made me wanna stay here."

"Don't stay, LJ." She closed her eyes. "You're too good for Beluga."

"I was thinking the same thing about you." He turned her head toward him and kissed her as they skated to the blasé music.

Ginger released his lips in time to see a woman skating in a canary-yellow summer dress, hanging onto a stocky guy with slick hair and a hawk tattoo.

The woman did a quick turn, facing Ginger.

Ginger gaped, staring right into her mother's face. "What the hell?"

"What?" LJ looked in the direction she did. "Wait, is that your—"

"Momma!" Ginger shouted so loud everyone on the rink stopped.

Nola and the stranger looked Ginger's way, and Nola's face dropped.

"Momma." Ginger zoomed past couples and skidded to a stop in front of Nola. "What the heck are you doing here?"

"Ginger." Nola tossed her head. "What are you doing here?"

LJ rode up beside Ginger and held her waist.

"I asked you first, Momma." Ginger pointed to the guy who bounced from left to right. "Who is this man?"

"I'm Quinn Moretti." He held his hand out to Ginger.

She smacked her lips and crossed her arms.

"Quinn works at the soup kitchen with me." Nola clasped her hands in front of her. "We ran errands and came here to relax." She gave Ginger a condescending glance. "No more no less."

"Mom, you are the first lady of a church." Ginger raised her hand. "You're a married woman. Where in your world is it proper to be out fornicating with a strange man?"

"You better watch your mouth, young lady," Nola said. "No one is fornicating. We're skating that's all."

Ginger gave Quinn the stank eye. "He had his hands all over you."

"Excuse me, Quinn." Nola smiled at him and snatched Ginger's arm. "I need to talk to my daughter in private."

CHAPTER SIXTEEN

"Let go of me." Ginger tussled as Nola pulled her out the Capricorn. "Momma, what's going on? Whoa." Her skates slid on the pavement. "How can you do something like this? What would Daddy think—"

"Hush, girl." Nola stuck her finger in Ginger's face. "Now listen and stop jumping to conclusions. Quinn and I had pizza and skated. That's it. I don't have to explain myself to you."

"Do you realize what would happen if someone from Beluga saw you with that man? Your reputation would be ruined."

She laughed. "You're lecturing me about my reputation when you run all around town car surfing and doing whatever crazy thing jumps into your head?"

Ginger took a deep breath. "This isn't about me."

"That's right it's not." Nola patted her bosom. "What's so wrong about me having fun, Ginger? Every day of my life, I give to someone else. Every decision I make benefits someone else. Can't I have one moment for me where I can have fun and not have to worry about the whole world?"

"Momma, that man was looking at you in a way that no man is ever supposed to look at a married woman."

"You're insane."

"It's not you I don't trust. It's that guy."

"Well, it's not your place to trust him. Quinn and I are friends and it's none of your business." Nola wobbled in the skates, jerking to catch herself from falling. "This conversation is over."

"Are you attracted to that man?"

"No."

Ginger scoffed. "What about Dad? He won't be happy when he finds out—"

"He's not going to find out." Nola bared her teeth. "Because if you say anything to your dad about me and Quinn, he'll get an earful about you and LJ. Trust me, he won't like that either."

Ginger batted her eyes. "Are you blackmailing me?"

"I'm telling you to leave it alone. Nothing is going on between Quinn and I and it makes no sense for you to turn this into some big deal when it's not."

"Momma—"

"I'm done." She went inside.

"Shit." Ginger kicked at air and almost fell on her butt. "Ooh."

LJ rushed out and grabbed her. "What happened?"

"My mother's acting like someone's stolen her brain." She leaned on him for leverage. "Can you believe her?"

LJ floated around her as if born on skates. "What's the big deal?"

"LJ, she is married and the frigging first lady of the church. She can't be going out on dates."

"Do you trust your mother?"

"I don't trust that greasy guy she's with." She shook a fist. "Did you see how he was looking at her? Like he wanted to rip her clothes off right in front of us."

LJ tucked in a grin. "I didn't see all that, but he seems to like her."

"Jesus." Ginger leaned back, rubbing her forehead. "Is this really my life right now?"

"Why are you so upset? You act like they were fucking."

"If anyone from Beluga hears about this, they might as well be." She sat on the pavement and untied her skates. "Take these back in there so we can go."

"What?" He took her skates, sliding backward. "We just got here."

"I can't go back in there and see my mother with that man."

"Ginger."

"You can stay if you want but I'm leaving." She hobbled on the gritty parking lot in the socks from Capricorn. "Hurry up and don't forget my shoes." She unlocked the car with her remote. "I can't stay here another minute or I'm gonna hurl."

****

"Ginger, slow down."

"There's no one out here." She sped through the highway, strangling the steering wheel.

"Doesn't mean you need to be driving like this."

"I'm mad, LJ." She maneuvered the steering wheel.

"It's not just because you're worried for your mother's reputation, is it?"

She kept her eyes on the road.

"You're mad because you're scared."

She turned on her signal and switched lanes.

"You're scared your parents might break up."

"I've never seen my mother act like that before." She leaned against the door, driving with one hand. "It's made me wonder how much I know her."

"Because she was skating and having pizza? I might not be the best to comment on this church stuff, but is it that big a deal?"

"In Beluga, yes." Fear crossed her face. "If this gets out, it could be a huge scandal and my mother doesn't deserve that."

"I'm sure your mother can take care of herself. Anyway, some could say this is payback. Don't you think your mother gets scared at the way you act sometimes?"

She nibbled her thumb. "Whose side are you on?"

"No one's." He stuck his head in the air. "I'm the voice of reason."

"I want to know what the hell she's thinking." Ginger passed the sign that said they'd be in Beluga within a few miles. "She seemed drunk too."

"She was happy, not drunk." He laid his head back on the rest. "Wanna go somewhere else?"

"Nah." She rubbed her pristine French roll. "Not in the mood to do nothing but go to bed."

"Hey." He snickered. "Sounds good."

"You wish." She snickered. "You're in a good mood, huh?"

"Tonight took my mind off things, and I needed that."

"What things?"

"My dad called me today." He adjusted the seat belt. "He has lung cancer. First stage."

"LJ." Her mouth fell open. "I'm sorry. That's what your mother had too, right?"

He shrugged, pulling on his navy blue T-shirt.

"I'm sorry."

"What's pitiful is that wasn't even the scariest part." He sunk in the seat. "He asked me to visit him."

"Are you going to go?"

He cut his gaze to her. "Should I?"

"I can't make that decision for you." She turned off the highway. "You're the one who'll have to live with it. Do you want to see him or not?"

LJ rocked with the motion of the car, scanning the thick trees in the darkness. "Not sure I could make it with the guilt if I let him die or something and we don't resolve things."

"I'll pray for you and your dad. Is that okay?"

"Suit yourself."

"What's his name?"

"Columbus."

She nodded.

"If I go, the flight will take a little over an hour at the most. My aunt and uncle will give me the money."

"When are you going?" She wiggled in the seat. "I mean, if you decide to?"

"Next week probably." He rubbed his knee. "Judson said he'd go with me but I'd rather go alone."

"Why?"

"I'm not a baby. Besides, I don't plan to spend more than a night in Illinois and I wouldn't want him to close the shop just for that. He needs to work."

"You shouldn't go alone. How about I go with you?"

He sprung up in the seat.

"Would you be okay with that?"

"Ginger—"

"You need someone to be there for you." She sat erect, swaying her shoulders. "It's no problem for someone to cover for me at work. It'll just be a day, right?"

"Or two at the most." He squinted. "Ginger, this is too much. I can't ask you to do this."

"I offered." Her face relaxed into a serene smile. "Unless, you don't want me to come. If so, I'll understand."

"I'd love it if you came."

They exchanged drawn out glances.

"But, won't this cause trouble with your folks? Your dad will be super pissed, I'm sure. The last thing he'd want is his precious little girl running off to an Illinois prison with the God-hating, ex-con."

"My dad doesn't have to know. Besides, I'm a grown woman. Is it a deal?"

"Yeah." He smiled, warmth filling his body. "I'll let you know when we'll leave. Why are you doing this when you barely know me?"

"You're a good person, LJ." She touched his thigh. "I don't have to know you for years to realize that."

He touched her hand.

CHAPTER SEVENTEEN

"Nola, it's okay." Quinn turned into Nola's neighborhood. "We did nothing wrong."

"Ginger was right to be upset with me. I had no business skating with you."

"It's my fault."

"You didn't make me do anything I didn't want to." She touched his arm, he looked at her hand and she let him go. "Quinn, we can't do this anymore."

He exhaled, wincing. "Do what?"

"Hang out outside the soup kitchen." She clasped her hands in her lap. "I have to think about Reuben and all he's worked for."

"What about yourself and what you want?" He turned onto Nola's block, passing upscale, three story homes that resembled Nola and Reuben's place. "You deserve a life full of fun and excitement." He made eye contact. "You're miserable."

"I never said I was miserable." She straightened her dress. "I enjoyed the day but we can't do this anymore."

"Bullshit if you expect me to believe this is because of your husband or your reputation." He rocked. "You're afraid that if you keep seeing me something might happen."

"Quinn." She closed her eyes. "Stop, okay?"

"Pretending doesn't make it go away." He wrapped his long fingers around the wheel. "You're attracted to me, Nola. Newsflash, I'm attracted to you too and think about you all the time."

"Stop it."

"You bet your sweet ass I think about you." He straightened his body, looking ahead. "I can't control it and don't want to."

"Ginger was right?" She huffed. "You've been seducing me?"

"Don't put this on me. You have feelings for me too."

"Nonsense."

"Deny it all you want but it doesn't mean it's not true." He turned into the Ryders' driveway and parked behind Reuben's car.

"Shit, Reuben's here." She put her hand over her mouth. "Look at me. Cursing. I'm sinning all over the place." She tore off her seatbelt and grabbed the paper sacks of fruit and vegetables from the backseat. "I'll see you at the center."

He touched her arm. "Let me finish what I'm trying to say—"

"Just leave before Reuben sees you."

"I'm coming to church tomorrow."

"Are you crazy?" She got out the truck.

"You invited me."

"I'm uninviting you." She slammed the door.

"Too late." Quinn drove away before she could reply.

Nola did a quick, selfish prayer before going in the house. She carried the sacks through the foyer and stopped at the modern-style living room.

Reuben sat on the maroon sofa jotting in his notebook with practice sermons strewn around him.

"Hi, sweetheart." Nola stood in the doorway, jiggling the sacks. "Got fruit and vegetables from the farmers market. I can make a nice, soothing salad. Would you like that?"

"I already ate."

She held her breath at his unyielding tone. "I don't mind making you a salad."

"Nola." He took off his reading glasses, lines bursting from his forehead. "Where the hell have you been?"

Her shoulders dropped. "Is that any way to speak?"

"I'll ask you once more." He closed the notebook and slid it from his lap. "Where have you been all day?"

She lifted the sacks. "I said I went to the farmers market."

"What time?"

"Does it matter?"

He tilted his head.

"Around noon."

"Aimes closes at six and it's nine-fifty." He stretched his arms on the back of the sofa. "Where have you been?"

"I was at Capricorn."

He raised an eyebrow. "That skating place?"

"Yes." She pretended the bags were heavy. "I got to get these to the kitchen." She rushed out the room.

"Nola?"

She darted to the kitchen and set the bags on the table.

Reuben rushed in. "Who were you with?"

She jerked fruit out the bag. "Huh?"

He stood beside her. "Were you with Paula?"

"As a matter of fact—"

"Don't bother lying." He held two fingers in her face. "I called her so I know you weren't with her. She said you were out with a friend. One of the church ladies."

Nola exhaled at Paula having her back but hated she'd lied.

"Which one?" Reuben pulled up his pants.

"Reuben." She did a nervous chuckle, snatching potatoes out the bag. "Feels like I'm being integrated here." She loaded the food into the refrigerator. "Used to be when I said something it was enough."

"That was before you started being sneaky."

"Sneaky?" She whirled around with her arms full of tomatoes. "I hope you're not implying I'm lying."

"You weren't with a church lady. I called every one of them!" He breathed hard, nostrils spreading. "Now you tell me the truth. Who were you with?"

She flounced around him to get to the refrigerator. "Why are you checking up on me, anyway?" The tomatoes slipped from her shaking hands. "Shoot." She snatched the rolling fruit off the floor. "I told you where I was and won't repeat myself." She put the tomatoes in the fridge, waltzed back to the table and snatched the sack of strawberries.

Reuben grabbed her, turning her in his direction. "Who were you with?" He shook her. "Answer me."

"Let go of me." She clawed at his solid arms but it didn't faze him. "What's wrong with you?"

"I'm not playing with you." He held her to his huge body. "Were you with that guy? Quinn."

"Let go of me, Reuben."

"Not until you tell me—"

"Let go!" She slapped him.

"Ah." He jerked back, rubbing his cheek.

"What's wrong with you?" She fixed the strap of her dress. "Don't ever put your hands on me like that."

"I have every right." He pointed to the floor. "You're my wife and you've been running around with another man."

"Who told you that?"

"No one has to tell me." He punched his chest. "I'm plugged into you like no one else."

She huffed, folding her arms.

"Are you having an affair?"

"I won't dignify that with a response." She turned around and got more vegetables.

"Woman, you ain't gonna be coming up in here with this lying and sneaking around. Answer my question."

"Move." She bumped into him on her way to the refrigerator.

"Put this stuff down." He grabbed the food and threw it on the floor.

"Reuben."

"Are you sleeping with someone else?"

"One day I'm not sitting up in this house and I'm cheating?" She nodded. "I do something for me and I got to be wrong?"

"Answer me." He huffed and puffed, sweating.

"Isn't this a switch? I could have sex with a man right in front of you and you wouldn't notice."

"You're being secretive and going off for hours not telling people where you are. Not answering my calls—"

"You do the same thing." She stabbed her finger at him. "How many hours, days, Reuben have I sat in this house waiting on you?"

"But, you knew where I was always." His lip trembled. "When I'm out this house, I'm working."

"Well, I was working too." She grabbed her hips, rolling her neck. "I was working on doing something for me, for once. I'm tired of sitting in this house all the time. Church shouldn't be the only thing I look forward to."

He turned around, rubbing his nose.

"We don't go out anymore. We haven't had a date since Easter and it's almost Christmas." She swung her arm. "We used to go to the movies, to the park, we used to dance and have fun. Since Ginger moved out, you pay me less attention than when she was here." She sucked in tears as he turned back around. "Your congregation and sermons aren't the only things that need you. When some church member, organization or charity calls, you drop everything and go running. I want you to do the same for me. I'm your wife. What is that the bible says about how you should treat your wife?" She said a scripture. "Have you forgotten that, Reuben?"

"Know what I don't get, Nola?" He stood against the stove. "How come everything is my fault? If I'm late for dinner or don't spend time with you, it's my fault. When you go out all day long, don't call, lie, it's my fault."

She rolled her eyes.

"If I'm such a bad husband, maybe it's because you're not that great of a wife."

She gasped.

"Nola, when things go wrong for me I don't go shifting the blame. I realize I might be doing something wrong and there's something I should change. You need to look within yourself for happiness." He got close to her. "It's not my responsibility to make you happy. That's on you."

"Excuse me?" Her voice cracked.

"Nothing I do is enough for you." He held out his arms. "If I'd have stayed with you today, you'd have something to say."

"I've never felt more alone than I do right now."

His forehead wrinkled as if he'd realized how much he'd hurt her.

She left the kitchen with tears streaming down her face.

CHAPTER EIGHTEEN

Sunday morning, Ginger looked away from the flat screen TV in her parents' living room when Nola pranced inside.

"Well?" Nola stuck her arms in the air and twirled in the slim-fitting dress with three-quarter, ruffle sleeves. "How do I look?" The salmon-pink glowed against her delicate, brown tone.

"Wow." Ginger stood from the sofa in her pink and white floral chiffon blouse, which tied at the waist and a neon-pink pencil skirt. "You'll be the best-looking thing in church as usual." She checked out Nola's leather, peach heels with the white toe. "Like you stepped off a movie, Momma."

"Thank you, sweetie." She tilted her wide brim peach hat with the embellished bow. "Gotta have the hat now."

"First lady." Ginger did thumbs-up. "No one's hat can be bigger than yours, right?"

They grinned, Ginger knowing her mother found their pleasantries as fake as she did due to the awkwardness last night.

"How come you didn't invite LJ?"

Ginger put the pillows on the couch back in place. "Momma, you know LJ isn't coming to church."

"He's so mysterious and antisocial. How long you been seeing him?"

"Not long." Ginger shot her mother a warning glance. "I didn't appreciate you threatening to tell Daddy about us."

"Just said your father would be surprised if he knew you were out with him last night."

Ginger scoffed. "I doubt that would be the only thing about last night that surprised him."

Nola pursed her lips. "Your dad already knows I was with Quinn."

Ginger gaped. "You told him?"

"Yes so drop it."

"You told him everything?" Ginger gave her mother a onceover. "That you were skating with Quinn and he had his hands all over you looking like he wanted to sop you up with a biscuit? You told him all that?"

"I told him enough." Nola clenched her teeth. "Now forget what you saw."

"I can't." Ginger shivered, disgusted. "That's the problem."

Reuben swaggered into the room in a double-breasted, indigo pinstriped suit with pleated pants.

The women whistled.

"*Daddy.*" Ginger danced toward him. "They should take the word 'sharp' out the dictionary and replace it with your photo." She kissed his cheek. "You look amazing."

A breeze of his Armani cologne swept through when he fixed his sleeves. "Let me get my case and we can go." He turned on his heels and left the room.

Nola blew a big breath.

"Ooh." Ginger sucked her teeth. "He's pissed."

"Once he gets to the church, he'll be all right." Nola flicked her hand.

"Never seen Daddy like this."

"He's fine." Nola jumped to attention when Reuben reentered with his briefcase in one hand and fat bible in the other.

"Ready?"

"Don't you like my outfit, Reuben?" Nola did another twirl. "First lady's got to be dressed to kill, right?"

"You going to fit in the car with that hat on?"

Ginger turned her head, grinning.

"We better get going." Reuben's tone remained curt.

"Honey." Nola stroked the blazer of his suit. "Give me a few minutes to talk to Ginger."

"Hurry up. You know how Beluga traffic is on church Sunday, and I can't afford to be late fooling with y'all. Not today." He stomped out the living room and a second later the front door slammed.

"Whoa." Ginger recognized the sadness on her mother's face. "He's not mad, he's hurt."

"We had an awful fight last night." Nola's shoulders dropped. "Both said things we shouldn't have said."

"I hope it doesn't affect his sermon."

"He'll be fine." Nola wiggled her fingers, nails the same color as her dress. "That man gets behind the pulpit and he's like Michael Jackson on a stage."

"We'd better get going before he gets more upset."

"Ginger." Nola grabbed her arm. "I'm sorry for last night. You were only looking out for me and you had a right to worry."

"It was weird and all." She straightened her feet in the pink, patent high-heel sandals with the ankle straps. "Seeing you acting like that with another man. That's how you should be with Daddy."

"I don't want you worrying about us, okay." Nola gripped Ginger's shoulders. "Everything will be all right."

"Are you going to see that man again?"

"Not outside the center, no."

Ginger smiled, relieved.

"I wanted to make sure you and I were okay." Nola touched Ginger's cheeks. "I love your father and I love you too."

"I love you too."

They hugged as Reuben honked the car horn.

Ginger jumped back. "Let's get going."

"Right, before he blows a gasket."

The women dashed out the living room.

****

Nola and Ginger gathered under the arch of the church while Reuben did his usual ritual of speaking with church members after the day's service.

"You all right?" Ginger asked. "Breathe Momma, breathe."

Nola sipped lemonade from the plastic cup, doing her best not to lock eyes with the man in the white shirt and cream slacks. "I can't believe this."

Quinn walked around the courtyard, chatting with the usual members of the congregation.

"Is he trying to give me a heart attack?" Nola shrieked. "How could he show up like this?"

"You invited him."

"That was before these fights started between your dad and I." Nola lifted the cup to her mouth but didn't sip. "Look at Reuben."

Reuben stood in the crowd as people clamored to get time with their beloved minister.

"He keeps looking at Quinn," Nola said. "Like he wants to kill him or something."

"It's not every day your wife's boy toy waltzes into the middle of your sermon so I'm sure Daddy's a little shocked."

"That's not funny." Nola tilted her hat to block the sun from her eyes. "As if things weren't tense enough? Is Quinn trying to ruin my marriage?"

Ginger watched Nola from the corners of her eyes. "That's what I'd like to know."

"Sh." Nola fixed her posture. "Here comes Quinn."

"Play it off." Ginger pushed her shoulders back, sticking out her bosom. "Keeping up appearances is what we do."

Nola sighed as Quinn approached.

"First lady." He bowed to both the women. "Ginger."

"Mr. Moretti." She wore a stiff smile. "Surprised to see you here."

"I could tell by your expressions when I walked into the church."
He grinned, forehead glistening from that gunk in his hair. "I didn't
mean to cause problems, Nola."

"Then why are you here?"

"You invited me."

"That was before Reuben found out about me hanging out with
you. Do you realize what you've done? I'm walking on egg shells at
home as it is."

Quinn smiled at Ginger. "May I speak to your mother alone?"

"You think that's wise?" Nola caught Reuben glancing their way.
"It's taken the power of God for Reuben not to pound you. Plus, I
don't need the church people gossiping."

"Too late." Ginger tipped her chin at the gang of old
churchwomen who stared at Quinn, whispering in a tight circle.

Nola swiveled her shoulders. "Darn it, Quinn."

He stepped closer to her, his gold chain catching the sun. "Can
we please talk?"

"It looks more suspicious if you don't," Ginger said. "Then they'll
really think something's going on." She kissed Nola's cheek. "I'm
gonna go talk to the McCormicks."

Ginger joined Judson, Felicity, and Rocco at the refreshment
table.

"Your husband was amazing," Quinn said. "His sermon was the
most moving one I've heard. It's easy to see why he touches so many
people."

"How dare you come here?"

"I wanted to prove a point."

"Mission accomplished."

He moved beside her. "I didn't come to hurt you."

"You're not a fool." Nola snapped her head in his direction. "You
had to know this is a bad idea."

"I'm confused about us the same as you are."

She sipped lemonade. "I'm not confused."

He smirked. "I came for guidance."

"You came to size up Reuben and be nosy."

He sighed, rubbing his black tie. "That was an interesting topic he chose for his sermon."

She scoffed. "I'm sure Reuben doing a sermon on trust and secrets wasn't a coincidence."

"I apologize for how I acted last night in the truck. When I said I had feelings for you."

"Don't." She lifted her head, watching him under her hat. "Please."

"You look beautiful." His cheeks tightened. "Just like a little brown, porcelain doll."

She sighed, struggling to focus on the crowd.

"I definitely had to pray during service. Pray to stop looking at you."

"Stop it, Quinn."

"Your husband just finished a sermon about being honest. Well, that's what I'm doing. I need to tell you how I feel."

"I don't want to hear it and you need to repent. I'm a married woman."

"You're still a woman." He tried to touch her hand, but she moved. "Nola, this won't go away just because we ignore it."

"Why are you doing this? Why make this so hard for me knowing what I'm up against?"

"You deserve happiness."

"I'm the first lady of this church." She shook her hand. "People worship me. Do you realize what would happen to my reputation if this got out of hand?"

"If you're thinking of sinning, you're already sinning."

She dropped her head as Reuben walked up to them.

Quinn smiled, bouncing. "Pastor Ryder."

Reuben squinted with his face hard as stone. "Mr. Moretti."

"I was telling your wife your service blew me away. You and Pastor Marroquin are a match made in heaven."

"I appreciate that." Reuben rocked on his heels. "Nola, would you mind giving Mr. Moretti and I a moment?"

Nola blew out her cheeks. "Sure."

CHAPTER NINETEEN

"Pastor," Quinn said. "Let me make things clear. Nothing is going on between Nola and I." He chuckled. "She's a lovely woman, and I've enjoyed working with her."

"Seems to me you enjoy it too much." Reuben glanced toward the thinning crowd. "I'm speaking to you now as a man and not an instrument of the Lord."

Quinn raised his head. "Okay."

"Stay away from my wife."

Quinn took a deep breath. "Pastor—"

"I don't need to hear anything from you." Reuben held a close-lipped smile. "This isn't a suggestion. This is a rule and if you break it even God can't save you from my wrath."

"You threatening me?" Quinn peeked at Nola. "On the Lord's day in front of the Lord's house?"

"You disrupt my marriage and now my sermon and I'm supposed to just sit back? I'm a pastor, not a saint."

"And, how many times do I say you're wrong about me and Nola?"

"Have you or have you not been seeing her outside the soup kitchen?" He crossed his long arms. "Whether you're religious or not, is that ever proper behavior?"

"Married women can have male friends."

"I'm talking about *my* wife." Reuben leaned forward. "My wife can't be friends with men who take advantage of her for either money or flesh."

"You got the wrong idea of me."

"You're out of your league, son." Reuben patted Quinn's shoulders. "Nola's just acting out, anyway. You seriously think she'd be interested in you?" He closed his blazer. "I appreciate you checking out the service but find somewhere else to worship from now on."

Quinn jeered. "I'm not allowed to come to your church?"

"You're not allowed to come near anything that's mine. We got that?"

Quinn squinted as Reuben left.

Nola click clacked on the pavement in her heels. "What happened, Quinn?"

"Nothing." He loosened his tie. "Except being talked down to by your husband."

"What? Reuben wouldn't do that."

"Would he threaten someone?" He rolled his eyes. "Because he did that too but I don't care, Nola. He can't control what's going on." He brushed against her as he passed. "Not even you and I can."

"Where are you going?"

"Where I go to think." He continued walking. "The lake."

****

Nola walked toward Quinn, her heels sinking into the soggy grass.

"What are you doing here?" He sat with his knees up, staring into the peaceful lake.

"I followed you." She debated whether to continue standing or sit and mess up her dress.

"I don't get you." He tore off blades of grass. "You tell me we can't see each other outside the center but now you're here?"

She nodded, sucking her lip. "I'm as confused as you are."

He looked up at her, his focus taking special interest of her legs. "You gonna sit down or hover over me the whole time?"

She sat beside him as soft as possible, hoping not to get grass stains on her dress.

"What are you going to tell Reuben when he asks where you were?"

"I won't lie." Her mind drifted with the crystal waves of the water. "I'm a grown woman."

He laughed. "You are?"

"Don't be condescending it doesn't flatter you." She struggled to position her legs in the tight dress. "I haven't been here in months." She laid her hand in the grass, slanting her body. "Can you swim?"

He nodded. "Learned when I was ten. You?"

"Yeah, but not without something on my head." She patted it, grinning. "Want to know a secret?" She dusted her hands. "I hate dressing up."

He raised an eyebrow.

"I hate this hat." She snatched it off and tossed it in the lake.

He laughed. "What the hell?"

"I hate these pearls." She threw her earrings in the lake one by one. "I hate this bracelet." She flung it in the water.

"Jesus." His mouth drew up in the corners while a seductive smirk tugged at his lips. "You hate that dress too?"

She caught his flirtation and chuckled. "No."

"Damn." He winked. "I was hoping so."

"I'm sorry for whatever my husband said to you. He has no right to treat you bad just because of me."

"I can't blame him." He tossed grass and tore off more. "He sees what's happening and we do too."

"I'm just being a friend, Quinn." She wiggled her feet. "Not sure what you've been seeing."

"I'm seeing what you show me every time we're together. Let me finish what I wanted to say last night."

She caught the intense glow in his eyes and rose. "I should go."

He grabbed her hand, forcing her back down in the grass. "I want you."

"Quinn."

"I've wanted you since the first day we met. You're one of the sexiest women I've ever met, Nola."

"*Quinn.*"

"When your face lit up when we talked about Eldorados, something clicked inside me." He stared at her chest, panting. "I wanted to kiss you then. I always want to kiss you."

"Don't do this." Her body relaxed as if something bigger than Jesus commanded it. "We have to leave this alone."

"Whatever happens after this moment, it's your call." He wrapped his arm around her trembling waist. "But, you got to give me this one chance."

"Wait, a minute—"

"You don't know how this tortures me to spend time with you and then you go home to a husband who doesn't appreciate you. It's like dangling meat in front of a shark, Nola." His breathing intensified. "I can't have you and it's killing me." He pressed her harder to him, squeezing her bosom against his chest.

"What..." She laid her hands on his shirt. "What are you doing?"

"I'm kissing you." He licked his lips. "I have to get it out my system, Nola. I have to have just this one moment and then I'll leave you alone."

"We can't do this." She pushed his chest as he grabbed the back of her head. "Quinn..."

His fleshy mouth took hers, and Nola's apprehension disappeared. She clung to him, desperate to capture that wondrous, hypnotic feeling only he provided.

"Mm." Quinn let her go with his mouth stained from her pink lipstick.

Nola savored the taste of his lips despite the impending guilt. "What have we done?"

"Not near as much as we should." He caressed her lap and reached for her again but this time commonsense rescued her. "You want this, Nola. Just as much as I do."

She covered her quivering lips and stood. "God, what have we done?" Tears tore at her eyelids. "What have I done?" She ran toward her car, stumbling in the heels.

"Nola, wait." Quinn remained sitting with his arms in the air. "You can't keep running!"

CHAPTER TWENTY

Four Days Later

(Rockford, Illinois)

A female prison guard from the Rockford Corrections facility directed Ginger and LJ inside a large cafeteria-like room full of square gray tables and plain white walls.

"Please wait here," the guard said. "The inmates will be in, in a minute."

Ginger and LJ sat at the first table surrounded by tables of others waiting to see loved ones and friends.

As soon as Ginger settled into her seat, LJ grabbed her hand.

"You're doing fine." She smiled, catching the glance of an obese white woman with slimy-looking blonde hair. "Don't be nervous."

"How can I not be?" LJ shook his leg. "It's been so long since I've seen him. He sent me a picture right after Momma died."

"Did you send him one?"

He shook his head, face flushed. "I'm scared, you know? What if he looks all sick and stuff?"

"Don't think like that."

A middle-aged man and woman entered the room hand in hand and sat at the table beside LJ and Ginger.

"He said he's been losing weight." LJ propped his elbows on the table and clasped his hands. "With lung cancer you can go to later stages quick. My mom looked like a skeleton by the time she—"

"LJ." She grabbed his hand. "You're making yourself crazy and the man hasn't even come out here yet. Everything's gonna be fine."

His eyes reclaimed their shine. "I don't know what I'd do if you hadn't come with me."

"Glad I could help."

He kissed her hand, and she'd never felt something so tender. "You're sweet, you know that?"

She grinned. "Sweet isn't exactly the word people use to describe me."

A super-tall, bulky officer with a bald head announced the inmates' arrival as the room filled with orange jumpsuits.

Ginger tensed up, looking away when the inmates shot her curious glances.

LJ rose from the chair as a tall white man with blondish-gray hair slicked back into a long ponytail strutted to their table with a male guard.

"Sit down." The guard pushed the man in the seat across from LJ and Ginger. "I'll be watching you, Beatty."

Columbus clicked his jaw as the guard walked to the corner of the room.

"What's going on, Dad?" LJ grimaced. "Been causing trouble?"

"Nah." He stroked his gray mustache which curved downward. "Just got anxious to get here so was a little mouthy." He wore his sleeves rolled up, his forearms littered with black, homemade tattoos. "It's great to see you, son."

Ginger squinted, trying to find a resemblance to LJ underneath Columbus' rough expression and jagged features.

"God." Columbus put a fist to his mouth. "It's been so long. Can't be crying in here though." He sniffed. "But, I'm so happy to see you."

LJ nodded, stiff-faced. "This is my friend Ginger."

"Nice to meet you, Ginger." Wrinkles jutted from around Columbus' apple-green eyes making it appear as though he were smiling even when he wasn't. "You sure are pretty."

She tingled at the breathless remark. "Thank you."

"Sorry for staring." He squinted. "It's been a long time since I saw a beautiful young lady like you." His breath smelled of stale coffee. "Son, you're a lucky man."

"Well, I'm here." LJ cleared his throat. "You surprised?"

"Yeah." Columbus stroked his chin. "Been what, since you was little I last saw you in person. Your Momma sent me some pictures a while back." He smiled. "You wasn't this big though."

"I'm a man now."

"Yeah." Columbus sighed with a dulled expression. "No thanks to me."

"We don't have to get into the past. Leave all that where it is."

"I can't," Columbus whispered. "Luther, it kills me every day I wasn't a better man for you. That I had the chance to be your father and just pissed it away and for what?" He held up his palms. "Twenty-eight years in prison? It's hurtful to think about those wasted years."

"We can't change the past," LJ said.

"Don't give me this 'grown man' shit, Luther." Columbus rocked, rubbing his fist. "You're hurting just like me. Stop trying to be tough."

LJ's throat rippled when he swallowed.

"Luther, I'm dying but not from no cancer. Fuck cancer. It's because I've lost the life, I could've had. I love you." Columbus gripped the front of his jumpsuit. "If I could turn back time and erase that stupid decision I made, I would. We're both in this prison stuck behind these walls together. Always have been. I gotta make it right."

"You're years too late, Daddy." LJ's jaws pulsated. "The pain you felt, I felt it ten times worse because I needed you more than you could ever need me."

"That's where you're wrong."

"I can't tell you how many times I cried because I couldn't be with you," LJ said. "I didn't have a man to look up to or to tell me everything would be all right."

Columbus' eyes watered and he dropped his head.

"Daddy, when you robbed that place, you robbed us of the life we could've had. I needed you." LJ sobbed. "I've gone through so much alone. I lost you at an early age, you might as well be dead you been gone so long."

Columbus coughed, struggling not to cry.

"I lost my baby sister." LJ's voice muffled from sobbing. "I lost my mother, and she was all I had." He closed his eyes. "I let myself get weak and go to that dark place Momma always warned me about."

Columbus lifted his head. "I'm so sorry."

"You wanted to give me something, Daddy?" LJ leaned forward. "Huh? You did. See, I turned out just like you. I did everything not to, and I still did. I ended up stealing and going to prison just as you did. All because you weren't there and I'll never forgive you for that."

Columbus nodded. "You shouldn't and I don't want you to. I don't deserve a damn thing from you."

"What hurts the most is I still love you." LJ sat back, scoffing. "I'd still do anything for you, and I still want to be your son."

Columbus squeezed his hands into fists.

"I'm here to forget the past because we might not have much time left. I didn't want you to die not knowing I loved you."

Ginger cried, covering her mouth.

"That no matter how much I said I hated you, I never did." LJ licked tears from his lips. "I couldn't live with myself if something happened to you and you didn't know I care."

"That's all I ever wanted." Columbus snatched LJ's hands. "I'm so proud of you and of the man you've become. Your Momma did a hell of a job raising you. That's one reason I could survive in here all these years without going crazy. I knew you were in good hands."

LJ wiped his eyes.

"All I ever wanted was a chance to make things right." Columbus cocked his head to one side. "A new beginning before it's too late."

"I'm here, aren't I?" He put his arm on Ginger's chair. "I'm sick of being angry because it hasn't done me no good. When I get angry, I get stupid and I can't afford to end up back in prison—"

"You won't," Columbus said. "Don't let nobody tell you different." He swept his face clean of tears. "Got me in here crying. The boys gonna tear me up when I get back to GP."

LJ grinned.

"What's GP?" Ginger asked.

"General population," LJ said. "How is your health?"

"Fine for now." Columbus smiled. "I'll start chemo soon."

LJ rubbed his thighs, exhaling. "That's good."

"I talked to Judson last week."

"He didn't tell me that."

"You never call or answer my calls half the time and I needed to know how you were doing. He said he wanted to hire you but those church bastards in Beluga threatened to boycott his shop."

"Yeah."

"Just so happens there's a friend of mine who used to be in here. He's an auto mechanic. Got a degree and everything."

LJ leaned on the table. "Yeah?"

"I called him the other day and told him you was coming to see me. I'd already told him about you loving cars and learning the trade in prison." Columbus rubbed his hands. "He said he might can hook you up at his shop."

"What?"

"His father passed a year ago and left him some money. He opened a repair shop in Palo Alto, California. Since he's an ex-con he makes it his mission to give cons a shot if they prove worthy of the chance."

LJ laughed. "Are you serious?"

"Ain't saying you got a job or nothing yet. He'll wanna talk to you and stuff but it might be something." Columbus looked around. "I wasn't allowed to bring any paper or anything. Gotta get the guard." He called over the bald guard. "Do me a favor and write something down for my son?"

With his eyebrow raised, the guard took out a pen and a tiny notepad.

Columbus recited his friend's name, number and name of the man's shop.

The guard wrote the info on the pad and handed it to LJ.

"Wow." He read it.

"Now you can Google and read about the shop online," Columbus said. "Call him or email. He's on Facebook too. I said you'd probably be contacting him."

"I don't believe this." LJ stared at the paper as if it were gold. "Ginger, isn't this great? I could work at a shop for real."

She smiled though it killed her to think of him leaving.

"Thank you, Dad." LJ reached over the table and hugged him.

"Come on now." Columbus patted LJ's back. "Just take it as an apology for being such a shitty father."

LJ let him go and then put the paper in his pocket.

A guard announced the end of visitation.

"Let's go." The guard pulled Columbus from the table.

"Can I get another hug?" Columbus asked LJ.

LJ rushed to him, wrapping his arms around him. "I love you, Dad."

Columbus squinted as if trying not to cry again. "I love you too."

"Okay, until next time." The guard ushered Columbus to get in line behind the other inmates.

"Dad?" LJ waved. "Merry Christmas."

Columbus guffawed. "Now I didn't expect *that*." He blew LJ a kiss as he followed the others out the room.

"Merry Christmas?" Ginger stood. "What was that about?"

"Like you said..." LJ did a half-smile, staring at the door. "You have to sacrifice for the ones you love. If me wishing him a Merry Christmas will make him happy, what harm would it do me, huh?"

"LJ." She kissed his cheek, snickering. "You're something else."

CHAPTER TWENTY-ONE

That night, a knock on her motel door interrupted Ginger washing her hair.

"Just a minute." She snatched the towel off the bathroom sink and wrapped it around her head. "Coming." Barefoot in only the baby-blue shorts and tank top she planned to sleep in, she opened the door to LJ smiling at her. "Hi there." She leaned against the doorframe. "You all right?"

"Yeah, just wanted to talk." He walked into the room, beaming with a newfound pep in his step. "You took a shower?"

"Nah, washing my hair." She closed the door. "They have these shampoo samples at the front counter and there was nothing else to do so what the hell?"

He smiled, sitting on the edge of the full-sized bed with lime-green sheets. "Sorry we couldn't make more of a trip out of this."

"It's fine." She waved. "This was about you, not me. What's up?" She sat beside him, resting her hands between her thighs. "You seem happy."

His smile got even bigger. "Talked to that guy my dad told me about on the phone. Albert. It went well. He asked me my skill level and what goals and expectations I have for my career."

"That's wonderful. So he likes you?"

"He seems to. Now, he didn't offer me the job yet. He wants to consult with me more and make sure I'm serious and honorable."

She plastered on a phony smile. "You're taking the job if he offers?"

"You nuts?" He cackled. "I'd be a fool not to. Being able to work on cars is my dream, Ginger. It'll be cool being in California. I was always curious about it."

She nodded, sucking her lip. "That's good."

"Hey." He put his finger underneath her chin and turned her face toward him. "Are you sad?"

"I'm happy for you." She tried to smile but couldn't. "I want things to work out, but I don't want you to go." She stared at the delicate, blue walls.

"I don't want to leave you either when we're just seeing where things will lead." He sighed, clutching her hand. "You're a gift I never thought I'd find. But, if I get the job I gotta take it."

"It's just that what we got going just started and I got a feeling it could be special." She looked into his eyes. "I don't want things to go back to before we met. I was so empty."

"Ginger, what you did for me today is the sweetest thing anyone's ever done." He laid his forehead against hers. "I'll never forget it and I'll never forget *you*."

She closed her eyes, stroking his cheek. "I'm in love with you, LJ."

He gave her wrist a soft kiss. "I'm not worthy of your love."

"Bullshit." She snapped her head back. "I want to be with you."

"Here, it's easy to get lost in each other." He leaned forward, gazing at the neutral carpet. "But, our lives in Beluga are real and there is no way your parents would ever allow you to be with me."

"I'm a grown woman."

"No disrespect but you say that a lot yet they run your life." He tilted his body toward her. "Ginger, you can't have it both ways. You can't be independent of your parents then have them footing the bill for you. Don't you see that them paying for your house and car and everything else is how they keep a hold on you?"

"When I turned nineteen, I was dying to get out the house, and I didn't have the money to do it on my own."

"I understand that, but you send your parents mixed signals. Your dad treats you like a baby because in ways you still act like one."

"What?" She scowled.

"I don't mean it as a dig."

"How can that not be a dig?"

"Your folks will continue to run your life unless you cut them off."

"Everyone's not like you, Luther-James. I can't just ditch my family and act like they don't exist."

"Who have I ditched?"

"You turned your back on your dad and isn't that the same thing you accuse him of doing to *you*?"

He puffed out his chest.

"We've both made mistakes in how we've handled our families, LJ. You're the last one to give advice."

"I'm trying to help you because you deserve more than being stuck in Beluga."

"You don't think I know that?"

"Then why are you there?"

She crossed her arms and rocked. "Guess I'm a little scared to break out on my own."

He exhaled.

"Excuse me for being just a small time country girl." She rolled her eyes. "I haven't been exposed to the things you have in Chicago. You know how to survive."

"Ginger." He chuckled. "There is nothing small time about you. I knew girls in Chicago who weren't as worldly as you are. Nothing wrong with being scared of living. You don't think I get scared?"

"I never pictured you scared of anything."

"I am." He widened his legs. "Prison didn't change that."

"Are you in love with me?" A pain pulled at her gut at the possibility of him not feeling the same.

"Yes."

She fought the urge to giggle. "Can we talk about the elephant in the room?"

He leaned back on his elbows. "What's that?"

She laid on her side, facing him. "How did you end up in prison for theft?"

"I always had an attraction to being bad." He pulled at the sheet. "It was exciting and made me feel powerful. Since I was fourteen, I'd been into petty theft and other misdemeanors. I had a group of friends who weren't the best role models in the world."

"They led you down the wrong path?"

"I can't blame them." He turned on his side, propped up his arm and rested his hand under his cheek. "Momma did all she could to raise me well, and I never wanted for nothing so it's not like I had to steal."

"Why did you?"

He looked toward the ceiling. "Naomi Sells." He leaned his head back. "The first time I saw her it was like a thunderbolt zapped me upside my head."

Ginger smiled despite being jealous.

"She was gorgeous. Had long, thick red hair and the greenest eyes you'd ever see. You know who Ann-Margret is?"

She nodded.

"Back in the day, Ann-Margret was the shit." He laughed. "Least Uncle Judson always said so. Naomi looked like her. She was stylish and man she was just different."

"You were head over heels?"

"Never believed in love at first sight until her. Wasn't anything I wouldn't have done for Naomi. I was an idiot."

"What do you mean?" Ginger lay flat on her back with her hands under her head.

"Naomi made it more than clear that if I wanted to keep being her man, I'd better keep cash in my pocket. One day I found out she was hanging around this other dude and I got scared she would dump me." He sat up. "I was dealing with Momma having cancer and couldn't imagine losing Naomi. She and Momma were all I had."

"What did you do?"

"Me and my buddies decided to rob the neighborhood liquor store." He poked out his lips, shaking his head. "Got caught the next damn week. So, there I was, arrested and going through this while Momma was on her deathbed. Since it was a Class Three felony, we got two years each. Momma died right after they sentenced me."

"I'm sorry."

"You think that was the last memory I wanted my mom to leave this earth with? Knowing her screw-up son got two years in prison? I can live a hundred years and won't live that down." He hit her thigh. "That's my story."

"You went to prison for a girl?" She rose. "Ah, so that's why you wanted nothing to do with me at first. Thought I'd steer you down the wrong path too?"

"I knew you could." He brushed his nose against hers. "Because that thunderbolt that hit me when I first saw you was ten times stronger than the one that hit me when I saw Naomi."

She put her arms around his shoulders, trembling as she gave him a kiss she hoped removed any doubt he had about her. "What happened to Naomi?"

"I don't know." He pulled Ginger into his arms. "And, I couldn't care less."

They kissed.

CHAPTER TWENTY-TWO

Quinn got his satchel from the cabinet in the back of the room. "I guess I'll be leaving now."

"Okay." Nola wrestled with the dishes in the sink.

"Nola." He walked toward her, making every hair on her arms rise. "How long are you gonna ignore me?"

"I'm not ignoring you." She scrubbed a pan. "It's just been busy around here with Christmas coming up and all. A shame a place as small as Beluga has so many in need."

"I'm not talking about the center." He grabbed her hand out the water. "You've been avoiding me since the lake and I can't take it anymore."

"Don't you have a bus to catch?" She slammed a pot into the soapy water. "I told you we can't see each other anymore outside the center."

"But, do you want to?"

She shifted her weight to the other foot. "I don't want to talk about this every day, Quinn. If you can't respect my wishes then I'll find something else to do with my time."

"Meaning?"

"Meaning I won't come back to the center if you keep bothering me."

"I want you to talk to me." He grabbed her. "We have feelings for each other and we can't act like they aren't real."

"Let me go."

"No. We need to talk about this."

Paula walked in, clearing her throat. "Is there a problem here?"

"No." Nola plunged her hands into the water and dug for silverware. "Quinn was leaving for the day." She glared at him. "Goodnight, Quinn."

He turned toward Paula, hesitating.

"Maybe you should go before you miss your bus," she said.

He gave Nola a long glance and left the room in a huff.

"Okay, enough of this." Paula stood by the table. "What in the world's going on? For days, you've been snapping at Quinn and when you aren't snapping at him you're avoiding him."

"Drop it, Paula."

"No way." Paula marched to the sink. "You're not leaving until we talk. You have feelings for Quinn."

Nola dropped a fork in the water. "You know?"

"What am I, blind?" Paula grimaced. "Heck, you went white as a sheet when he showed up at the church, and since you're black, that's hard to do."

Nola managed a laugh. "This isn't a joking matter, Paula."

"Sit." She patted a chair at the table and sat in the next one. "Leave those dishes alone."

Nola dried her hands and joined Paula. "It's difficult to put into words."

"Just be honest with me and yourself."

"I'm considering cheating on my husband."

Paula's mouth hung open.

"Goodness." Nola exhaled. "Feels like a thousand pound weight's been lifted. Aren't you gonna something?"

"Let me get my lip off the table first." Paula fanned her face. "Ooh, child. You're thinking of cheating on Reuben?"

"I feel horrible, but Quinn makes me feel like a woman, and Reuben hasn't in a very long time. What do I do?"

Paula turned her head to the side and laid her hand on her cheek. "Shoot, who you asking?"

"Quinn and I have fun. He's spontaneous and when he wants to do something, he just does it. There's no rule book or guideline like with Reuben. With Quinn, I can be free." Nola hooked her hands together. "Like going skating. Oh, Paula it was so amazing. My body

came alive in a way it hadn't in years. And the way he touched me."
She closed her eyes. "He put his arm around me and pulled me close
without permission. Just held onto me like I was his and I knew
he wanted me." She opened her eyes. "It's been so long since I felt
desired. I love Reuben but even that doesn't outweigh how my heart
pounds when I see Quinn."

"Pounds?"

"Paula, my hands shake and get sweaty just from thinking about
him. My knees knock and I feel like a teenage girl with her first crush.
With Quinn, I have the fun I missed. What I've longed for." She
clutched her apron. "He kissed me at the lake Sunday."

"What?"

"I pushed him away." Nola's eyes narrowed. "But, I didn't want
to. I wanted him to keep going, Paula. The only thing that stopped
me was thinking of Reuben and Ginger. If it hadn't been for them..."

Paula rubbed her mouth, gaping.

"That kiss made me...wet."

"Jesus." Paula gripped the table. "You need to talk to Reuben and
air things out before it's too late."

"I've talked to Reuben about this and it goes nowhere. He
doesn't even try to do better. I wonder if he still loves me."

"Course he does." Paula took Nola's hand. "He worships you."

"It'll be Christmas soon and we haven't made love since the day
before Halloween and Reuben doesn't seem to care. It's like he's
found things to replace what I meant to him."

"Wait, a minute." Paula batted her eyes. "Did you say it's been
over a month since you had sex?"

"Oh, girl we've gone longer than that before." Nola pouted. "The
only thing that's been inside me lately is a tampon."

"Maybe he's going through some health issues and can't
perform."

"Please, he's focusing on everyone else in town except me that's the problem. He has obligations to more than the community and he needs to remember that."

"I'm not as young as I used to be but I couldn't go two *weeks* without riding the donkey let alone a month." Paula stroked the diamond on her wedding ring. "Heck, I'd be divorcing Jamell if it came to that."

"I want my man back and my relationship full of passion and excitement like it used to be. I'm not asking him for the world just some attention. Reuben's gotten so routine it's ridiculous. You can set a watch by what he's going to do. I'm sick of begging him for attention that Quinn gives without hesitation."

"Don't be too quick to give Quinn credit. It's easy for a man to treat you well when you're not his wife." Paula raised her eyebrows, lips stuck out. "Quinn doesn't have to make a relationship work so his job is easy. He shows up, gives you some compliments and an ear to listen. Reuben's the one who has the hard job trying to figure out how to make you happy and the same for you. As for Quinn, how do you know he isn't just trying to hit it?"

"We've talked and shared. He wouldn't have taken time to do that if he only wanted sex. He could get a single woman for that. The way he looks at me proves he cares."

"How does he look at you?"

Nola steadied her gaze on Paula's face. "Like he's *hungry*."

"Whoa." Paula shivered. "What are you gonna do?"

"Finish these dishes." Nola returned to the sink.

"I mean about Quinn, girl."

Nola got a pan out the water. "Your guess is as good as mine."

CHAPTER TWENTY-THREE

Three Days Later

"Sure is a beautiful day." Tim sipped ice tea from a can as he and Reuben relaxed in the wicker chairs on the Easons' front porch. "It's good to enjoy peace and quiet, isn't it?"

Reuben widened his legs in the chair, embarrassed to have to relinquish authority to get advice from his old friend. "Can we talk?"

Tim shifted his dark-brown eyes Reuben's way, his high-yellow skin appearing paler than usual in the sun. "You never have to ask that."

"I mean us talking as old friends and men, not as the pastor and the deacon."

"Okay, we're talking as old homeboys." Tim sucked his top lip. "What is it?"

"Keep this between us."

"Reuben." Tim pushed up his glasses. "You never have to tell me that. We've been friends since babies. Have I ever given you a reason not to trust me?"

"My marriage is falling apart." Reuben leaned to the side, rubbing his chin. "And, I don't have a clue how to fix it."

"This can't be real." Tim lifted his can, chuckling. "You and Nola are the perfect couple. What problems could y'all be having?"

"She claims I've been ignoring her."

"Ah." Tim scratched behind his ear. "Seems familiar."

"Huh?" Reuben swatted a gnat out his face.

"Judy was whining about the same thing a few years go. Nola will get over it."

"Did Judith ever step out with another man?"

Tim coughed, dribbling tea. "Reuben, what in God's name is wrong with you?" He stuck his head in the air. "Judy wouldn't cheat on me."

Reuben looked away, sighing. "I thought the same thing about Nola until recently."

"Nola is cheating on you?" Tim's brow bone protruded.

"It's that Italian guy who was at the church, Quinn Moretti."

"The one she works at the center with? They seemed to be just friends."

"You weren't looking hard enough." Reuben rubbed his hands. "Besides, I'm her husband and a husband knows. Plus, she's been hanging around with him outside the center and lying about it. If that's not a guilty woman than what is?"

"I'm sorry, man." Tim hit Reuben's back. "I can't believe this. You and Nola's marriage is what everyone strives for theirs to be."

"How did we get in this position?"

Tim quoted a scripture on marriage. "Put your foot down and remind her who's boss." He did a quick nod. "If she's running around with this man, that's complete disrespect and she knows better. This could ruin both your reputations."

"You're right." Reuben punched his palm. "Nola's my woman, and I'm not letting any man take her away from me."

****

"Mm." LJ finished his meatloaf and set the empty plate on Ginger's coffee table that night. "That was the best meatloaf I've ever eaten."

Ginger chewed the crisp potatoes she'd roasted on the side. "Stop lying."

"I'm serious." He sunk his back into the couch pillows. "The more we're around each other, the more you impress me."

She became anxious from the allusive glint in his eyes.

"You threw me for a loop when we first met." He put his arm on the back of the couch. "Had me guessing because I couldn't figure you out."

"Seems like you did a good job though." She set her plate on the table and got her cup of orange juice. "It's good for someone to see the real me. No one's ever taken the time to."

"Not even Beau?"

She took a long sip of the juice, catching pits.

"Sorry again you had to go through that."

"Beau's history." She hooked her leg underneath her, concentrating on the Martha Stewart rerun on TV.

"Rocco brought him by the junkyard today. I wanted to kill him for how he treated you, but I managed my cool."

She slipped her fingers in his. "I'm glad you came by tonight."

His cheeks lifted as his brow lowered. "I'm glad you invited me."

"Does it bother you?" She glanced at her shimmering Christmas tree in the corner. "The tree?"

He stroked her thigh over her warm-up pants. "I don't care about anything in this room but you."

She closed her eyes and prepared for another fascinating kiss when a car drove up outside blasting gospel music. "Oh, no."

"What?" LJ stroked her hair.

She dashed to the window and peeked out the curtains.

Reuben climbed his gigantic body out his shiny, onyx Mercedes Benz, talking on his phone.

"Shit." Ginger jumped from the window. "It's my dad."

"So?" LJ propped his foot on the table, wiggling his shoulders.

"He can't see you here. He'll turn this whole house upside down."

"Aren't you grown? Isn't that what you keep saying?"

"This is the last thing I need." She pressed her cheeks on her flushed face. "Hide."

"I'm not hiding like some teenager you snuck into the house." He groaned. "Anyway, I'm sure he sees my truck outside. Deal with it, Ginger."

"But—"

"Come here." He stood and grabbed her hand. "If we're gonna take a crack at this relationship, then we gotta be honest." He kissed her. "He might not even care."

"That I'm seeing an ex-con who happens to be an atheist?" She crossed her arms. "If you believe that I got a farm to sell you."

Reuben beat on the door. "Ginger?"

"Fuck." She slammed her eyes shut as LJ meandered back to the couch with a sly grin. "This isn't funny."

He moved a pillow aside and sat. "Yes, it is."

"Ginger?"

"Coming, Daddy." She rushed to the door, struggled to compose herself and opened it. "Hey." Her knees shook. "Isn't this a pleasant surprise—"

"We need to talk." He busted in the room and glared at LJ. "Ginger, this is unacceptable."

"Now, Daddy..." She closed the door. "This is my home, remember? I appreciate you and Momma helping me out with finances but that doesn't mean you own me."

Rueben towered over her. "What?"

"Listen." She held her palms out to him. "I love you, but we can't keep going on like this. I'm a grown woman."

"Ginger—"

"I'm seeing LJ." She pointed at him and he smiled back at her. "You don't agree with him being an atheist or having a record and I don't care. This is my life and I'm living it the way I want."

"Girl, I don't care nothing 'bout no LJ." Reuben flapped his big hand. "I'm here about your momma."

"What?"

"Where is your mother?" He held his waist.

"What?"

"She's disappeared." Reuben paced, looking at the peach carpet. "I've been looking everywhere and I've been calling everyone I can think of and no one's seen her."

"Okay, calm down. I'm sure there's an explanation."

"Oh yeah there is." He nodded. "Yeah, she's off gallivanting with that ex-con."

Ginger gaped. "Who are you talking about?"

"Quinn's an ex-con." Reuben huffed. "I Googled his behind."

LJ scooted to the edge of the couch.

"Can you believe your mother's been running around with a man who's been in prison? He's from Vegas and served time for racketeering and tax evasion. He's probably in the mob. Has Nola lost her mind?"

"This is outrageous." Ginger clenched her hands. "I didn't know he was an ex-con. We can't let her be with someone like that."

LJ cleared his throat.

Ginger locked eyes on him as his shot fire bolts through her. "Shit."

"Girl, watch your mouth."

"I'm sorry, Daddy. LJ, I didn't mean that. You're not like Quinn."

"I'm not?"

"No. Anyway, this isn't about you."

He rolled his eyes.

"You sure you're not covering for her, Ginger?" Reuben asked. "You guys cover for each other when you don't want me to know stuff."

"Daddy, I wouldn't do that to you."

"Mm-hm." He tapped his foot. "Has she said anything about Quinn?"

She shrugged. "Like what?"

Reuben glanced at LJ. "Did she say if she's having an affair with him?"

LJ's face turned flour-white.

"No," Ginger squealed. "Don't be ridiculous. Momma wouldn't cheat on you."

"Then where the hell is she?"

"I haven't even seen Mom since I got back from Illinois." She slammed her eyes shut. "Damn."

"Illinois?" Reuben jumped back. "When did you go to Illinois?"

She bit her lip. "Recently."

He slapped his forehead. "Does anyone in this family tell me anything anymore?"

"I went with LJ to see his father in prison."

"Oh, this just gets better and better. What else you hiding?"

"Let's get back to Momma. Did you try Paula?"

"I tried her first and called every church member I could think of. Ooh." Reuben's cheeks filled with air. "I swear on everything holy that if Quinn puts his hand on your momma, they'll need to resurrect *him*."

LJ grinned.

"Daddy?"

"I gotta go." He stomped to the door.

"Wait." Ginger reached for him. "I want to make sure everything is clear with you about LJ. I'm gonna be with who I want to be with."

"Ginger, I don't care if you date Charles Manson right now." Reuben flung the door open. "I have to find your momma."

"But, Daddy—"

"Bye!" He slammed the door in her face.

CHAPTER TWENTY-FOUR

"Well." LJ rubbed his hair from the back to the front. "That was an interesting revelation."

"I'm sorry." Ginger jumped beside him on the couch. "I didn't mean to offend you with what I said about Quinn."

He nodded with tight lips. "I thought you were the one person in this town who saw me for more than an ex-con."

"It had nothing to do with you."

He moved his hand when she tried to grab it. "The first thing that came out your mouth when your father said Quinn had a record was that you were worried about your mother."

"LJ, this dude was in prison for some serious charges. Ten times worse than what you did."

"No, it's not." His top lip curled. "Be honest. You think about me being an ex-con, don't you?"

"No."

"You wonder if you can be with someone like me for the long term." His shoulders slumped. "Aren't I right?"

"You're a good man, LJ." She touched his white T-shirt. "You were raised well and I know in my heart you'd never hurt me on purpose. I trust you." She kissed him, making a smacking noise at the end. "I'm sorry for saying what I said, but I'm worried about my mother. Come on. Would I be alone with you in my home if I saw you as nothing but an ex-con?"

A smirk tore at his lips.

"What's that?" She pinched his cheek. "Is that a smile? Yeah, it looks like it. You forgive me?"

He burst into full laughter.

"What in the world?" She chuckled. "What's so funny?"

"Your dad." He pointed to the door, laughing. "He said you could date Charles Manson and he wouldn't care. Isn't that a switch?"

"Shouldn't be laughing though. What if my parents break up?"

"They're not breaking up." LJ rocked his foot against the table. "Did you see the look in your dad's eyes? He loves that woman with everything he's got. He won't give up on her."

She lay on him, inhaling his musky odor. "I want things to work out for them."

"I need to thank Quinn for keeping your parents out our business."

They laughed.

"Everything will be okay." He wrapped her in his arms.

"Have you heard from that man in California again?"

"As a matter of fact we talked today." He removed his arms from around her. "He's going to get back to me in a few days about the job."

"That's great." Her voice cracked as she lowered her head. "I'll miss you."

He pressed his nose against her cheek. "You won't have to miss me."

"What are you saying?"

"I want you to come with me." He kissed her.

"What?" She turned left and right, touching her cheek. "Are you serious?"

He kissed her again. "Does that answer your question?"

"Whoa." She grabbed the top of her head. "Fuckin' whoa."

"California, Ginger. You've wanted to get outta this town forever. It would be perfect. I'd have a job and we can get an apartment and I'd take care of you—"

She batted her eyes. "We'd live in sin?"

He chuckled. "Eh, I'm not trying to be an asshole but you're playing the preacher's daughter card now?"

"Yes. I've done things that's not appropriate, but I promised my parents I'd get married before living with a man."

"Okay." He frowned, pulling at his ear. "Can we take one thing at a time? Say we don't live together in California but you come with me?"

"That means you don't want to marry me?" She turned her body away from him and faced the television.

"Ginger." He laughed. "We haven't even known each other a year yet. Isn't it too fast?"

"If you expect me to move out of the state and away from my family then don't I deserve to know it will last?"

"Just because we got married doesn't mean it will last."

She parted her lips. "LJ."

"It's the truth."

"Not when you're Christian." She plopped her back to the couch, arms crossed. "If I'm willing to take that step then you should be too."

"Ginger, we haven't even had sex yet."

"Oh? That's what this is about, sex?"

"Time out." He did the referee signal with his hands. "When we first started this, you came onto me like gangbusters and now you're the perfect little choir girl?"

"That's before I knew you. Now we're together, and I want it to last. I need reassurance."

"Ginger, this is the real world." He pushed his finger into the couch cushions. "We can't just throw caution to the wind and get married with no plans. This isn't Romeo and Juliet. With marriage you need a foundation and we don't have that right now."

"Are you going to California for sure?"

"If I get this job, yes."

"Then where does that leave me?" She sobbed. "Here stuck in this place like I've always been."

"You sound like the only reason you're with me is to get out of town." He squinted. "Was Beau right?"

"I risked my father being upset to be with you." Tears fell over her lips. "Would I've done that if I didn't care?" She cried into her hands. "Just go."

"Ginger." He sighed, pulling her close. "I'm sorry."

"I care about you because you're the only person who doesn't expect something from me. You like being around me no matter how I act or what I do. I've always dreamt of a man to love me like that." Her heart pounded. "I'm scared of losing you and scared of leaving without assurance you'll be there."

"Look at me." He took her hands. "I wouldn't leave you, okay? Even if things didn't work out; I'll never turn my back on you."

She batted her eyes, slow.

"I wouldn't let you uproot yourself and abandon the only world you've ever known. Let's be honest. You're just afraid to leave and you're looking for excuses not to."

"LJ—"

"Sh." He touched her lips. "You'll be in Beluga forever unless you get the courage to move and it has nothing to do with anyone else but you. You have to live your own life." He sighed. "I'm scared too. I've never been to California."

"But, you're from the big city."

"So? We'll be together." He lifted her hands. "If that doesn't erase your fear, what will? What are you afraid of?"

"Being alone," she whispered. "Of failing and not having anyone there for me if I do."

"I'll be there." He wrapped his arms around her waist and kissed her, sending shock waves from her nipples to her knees.

She sucked his neck, tasting his salty skin. "I've wanted this since I first saw you."

"Yeah?" He gave her another kiss while lifting her blouse over her head. "What if I said I loved you?" His intense, begging eyes looked into hers. "Would you believe it?"

"Right now?" She grabbed his face and pushed his soft lips onto hers. "I'd believe anything you said. I just want the escape of being in your arms."

"If we do this..." He slid off her white bra strap, his lips replacing its position on her shoulder. "It means we're committed now and forever."

She shivered, the tingle between her legs turning into an incurable throbbing.

"Are you ready for that, Ginger?" He sunk his tongue deep into her mouth, his hot breath holding the flavor of paprika from the meatloaf. "Ready to start a new life with an ex-con who's an atheist?"

She took his shirt off him and tossed it to the floor. "I'm ready for anything as long as you promise me you'll always be there."

He lay her over, pushing his rough hand up her skirt.

"I don't wanna lose you and go back to how things were before you got here." She widened her legs as he settled between them. "I want a new life, LJ. Can you give me that?"

"I love you, Ginger." He kissed her.

She tore her lips away. "Why?" She crawled her fingers into his silky hair. "Why do you love me?"

"Because, you see the real me." He pulled down her panties as a tiny pant escaped Ginger without warning. "And, no one's ever done that before. No one's wanted to."

"Mm." She reached up, locking her lips onto his. "I love you, LJ." Her crotch pulsated, begging him to be inside of her.

"Then show me." He licked her lips with his sticky tongue. "And, I promise you won't have to be afraid of anything again."

She wrapped her arms and legs around him, trembling for what was to come.

CHAPTER TWENTY-FIVE

Reuben sat in the rocking chair on the porch, swaying with the porch light blaring on him. "She thinks I'm a fool." He checked his watch again. "Well, you'll see what fool I am, Nola." He gripped his thighs. "Trust me, you'll see."

The headlights of Nola's Cadillac turned into the driveway.

Reuben let out a sharp chuckle cloaked in anger.

Nola got out the car humming and clacked toward the house in nude, stiletto heels. "Reuben." She stomped up the steps.

"Uh-uh." He jumped out the chair and blocked the door. "Oh, no, no, no, no. You got it wrong Miss Thang if you think you're walking up in here when you been gone all day. You're not getting in this house."

"Move, Reuben." She stuffed her car keys in her purse. "I wanna take a bath and go to sleep."

"It's nine-fifteen, Nola." He poked the face of his watch. "This stops now! You're not making a fool out of me anymore. Now tell me where you were."

"Move or I'll scream and embarrass your behind in front of all these neighbors." She shoved his much bigger body out the way and entered the house.

He stomped in behind her. "I'm not playing with you, Nola."

"Close the door before you let every cockroach in the county come in here." She kicked her shoes off in the middle of the floor. "The only time you notice me is when I'm *not* here. Isn't that ironic?"

"Did you know Ginger went to Illinois with that boy?"

"LJ?"

"No, Elvis. Of course LJ."

"Yeah." She shrugged.

"And didn't tell me?"

"She's grown." She twisted toward the kitchen.

He slammed the door, following her. "I'm sick of being kept in the dark by this family."

She got a glass from the cabinet and opened the fridge.

"I'm sick of this!" He hit the table. "You've shamed yourself, me, and our marriage and it stops tonight."

She poured orange juice into the glass. "You better cool this yelling."

"Don't tell me not to yell, woman." He walked from the table. "I've been driving up and down this whole damn town looking for you." He pointed at the floor. "You were with Quinn and it's never happening again."

"Reuben—"

He flung his hand at her. "Shut up."

She gasped. "Excuse me?"

"I'm the man of this house and see my foot, Nola?" He stomped it. "See it? It's down, Nola. I'm putting my foot down and you staying out all hours with that ex-con is over."

"You know Quinn has a record?"

"I Googled his butt." He grimaced. "I never thought I'd see the day when my wife *and* daughter hooked up with ex-cons."

"I'm not hooking up with Quinn." She slammed her glass on the counter. "I was at Mrs. Snow's house all day."

He stood back, squinting. "Mrs. Snow?"

"She's in charge of the Christmas festival this year and needed me to help with an issue she's been having with some of the vendors. I didn't expect to be gone that long, but it took all darn day." She got her cell phone from the pocket of her dress. "Call her."

He grumbled, looking at the phone. "How come you weren't answering your phone then?"

"I turned it off by mistake."

He snickered. "A convenient excuse."

"Call Mrs. Snow then. Go on. Since you don't trust me."

"What do you expect when you been running around with another man and lying?"

"Where's my apology?" She set her phone on the cabinet.

"Ha! I'm the one who deserves an apology, Nola. Your behavior is unacceptable, and it's not happening anymore. You're grounded."

She stuck her neck out and batted her eyes. "Grounded?"

"Did I stutter?" He did the George Jefferson walk. "I'm the man and the head of the house and you gonna do what I say. You're not leaving this house unless I approve of where you're going."

She grinned.

"You can laugh all you want, missy. And you're not working at that center anymore."

"You're forbidding me to feed the homeless, Reuben?"

"With that Italian stallion of yours? You damn right." He nodded. "I've spoken, those are the rules, and that's it."

"Ooh, Jesus." She took off her earrings. "Let me go get into the tub before I catch whatever has crawled into your head and eaten your brain. Let me tell you something, *Pastor*." She wiggled her neck. "You can shout and rant all you want but you don't tell me what to do. I can go anywhere I want and do anything I want and if you don't like it you know what you can kiss."

He gasped. "Nola. And no you can't do anything you want. Have you forgotten you are a married woman?"

"I've done nothing wrong."

"Bull, Nola." He bent over her, shouting. "Straight bull!"

"You better get out my face, Reuben." She walked around him. "Carrying on like a lunatic."

"What do you expect? Me to just let my wife go here there and everywhere with another man?"

"I've not seen Quinn outside the center since he came to church." She gripped her hip. "I'm sick of being accused every time I walk into this house. Either you believe me or you don't." She left the kitchen. "I'm not explaining myself to you."

"Nola." He chased her to the stairs. "Nola!"

She stomped up the winding, white staircase.

"Nola, get your butt back here!"

She kept walking.

"Nola." He hopped up the stairs, stumbling. "I'm still talking to you."

"You can keep talking." She stood in the doorway of the master bedroom. "And, while you're at it, here." She got the blanket and a pillow off the bed and tossed them at him. "Have a good night, Reuben."

"What is this?" He picked up the blanket. "You're kicking me out the bedroom?"

"You answered your own question." She walked into the master bathroom and ran the bathtub. "Bye." She flounced out, unbuttoning her dress.

"We're not doing this, Nola." He threw the blanket on the floor. "You're always twisting stuff to make it look I'm in the wrong but this is about you. I'm not sleeping on the couch."

"That's fine." She wiggled her neck. "We got five guest bedrooms or you can sleep in the hallway. I don't care."

"I'm sleeping in our bed."

"Not with me you ain't." She shoved him out the door.

"Nola, what the..."

She kicked the blanket and pillow in the hall. "Sweet dreams."

"Nola?"

She closed the door and locked it.

"I know she didn't just lock this door." He twisted the knob. "Nola, open this door." He banged on it. "Woman don't you ignore me. Nola!" He yanked on the doorknob and when she didn't answer, grabbed the blanket and pillow. "This don't make no damn sense."

He glanced back at the door as he continued down the hall. "She stays out all the time and *I'm* kicked out the room?"

CHAPTER TWENTY-SIX

Two days later, Nola leaned on the hood of her Cadillac waiting for Quinn to show up at the lake.

"What's wrong with you, Nola?" She dabbed her sweaty brow with a handkerchief. "Got no business being here." Just as she'd made her mind up to leave, Quinn cruised through the grass in a shiny, yellow Eldorado convertible. "My goodness." Nola stooped over, laughing. "Quinn, what the heck?"

"This is my new baby." He honked the horn. "Isn't she a beauty?"

"It's amazing." She ran to the car as he parked. "Isn't this like the one you drove when you were a kid?"

"Yep. Nineteen-eighty-five." He hung his arm out and patted the side of the door. "Bought it with the money I've made from working at Bethany's. You like it?"

"I love it." Nola hopped in place, checking out the authentic beauty. "It brings back so many memories."

"Look at this interior." He whistled, stroking the leather. "They don't make them like this anymore."

"Where did you get it?" Nola checked out the back.

"That used car place down by McCormick's Auto Shop." Quinn turned around in the driver's seat to face Nola. "What are you waiting for, girl?" He honked the horn. "Get in."

"What? Oh, no I can't."

"Why not?" His gold bracelet dangled from his big wrist. "Come on, Nola. It'll be just like old times."

She walked back to the driver's side. "Quinn—"

"Just for a minute."

"Reuben would kill me. I'm having enough issues already."

"He won't know."

"I don't want to hide things from my husband, Quinn."

"All right." He got a cassette out his pocket. "'Rhythm of the Night.'"

She laughed, snatching it. "Where the heck did you get this thing?"

"I still got cassettes from back in the day. Told you it was my favorite song."

"Me and my friends played music every Saturday afternoon and this would be the first thing

in the boom box." She giggled. "We would be on the porch jump roping and playing jacks. Ooh." She held the tape to her chest. "Go roller skating at the rink and drinking malts while this played. Seems like a lifetime ago."

"You wanna go the rest of your life without one more dip into memory lane?" He revved the motor. "Come on."

She rolled her eyes skyward, gyrating. "Okay but only for a few minutes."

Squeaking, she jumped in the passenger side.

****

"Girl, I'm serious," Mrs. Moore said to Judith over the phone. "It was Nola. Saw her riding around with that Italian man from the soup kitchen. What was his name?"

"Quinn Moretti?" Judith stood at the stove, stirring the stewed strawberries for her pie. "Are you sure?"

"Yes. I saw her for myself. They were riding around and Nola was sitting on top of the seat on the passenger side, dancing and singing to El Debarge."

"El Debarge?" Judith grimaced.

"Yeah, 'Rhythm of the Night'. And I'm not the only one who saw them. Eleanor saw them pass the beauty shop. Flora saw them passing the bank. Others saw them too. I've been getting calls ten minutes straight."

The line beeped.

"See?" Mrs. Moore huffed. "That's another call now."

Judith tasted the hot strawberry sauce and added more sugar to the tart concoction. "I can't believe Nola would jeopardize her reputation like this. Maybe we should have an intervention."

"She needs prayer." Mrs. Moore moaned her disapproval. "I could tell something was going on between her and that guy when he came to church. Lord knows I didn't want to have those sinful thoughts about our first lady but they've been confirmed."

"Sh. Don't say stuff like that. You trying to say she's sleeping with that man?" Judith lowered her voice, peeking out the kitchen hallway. "That's a terrible accusation, Glenda."

"If you saw how she was gyrating in front of him and carrying on you'd think the same thing too. And, girl Quinn works at Bethany's Bakery with Eunice's little nephew. The one with the pimples."

"Pimple-face Edgar?"

"Yeah, and Eunice said Edgar said Quinn's got a record. Girl, he done been to prison."

"Insane." Judith rubbed her forehead. "Has Nola lost her mind?"

"I called Paula to get dirt, but she pretended she knew nothing but she does."

"Course Paula knows." Judith stuck her nose in the air. "She and Nola are closer than ice and water. Shoot, Paula knows if Nola farted before Nola does."

Glenda cackled. "Girl, you crazy."

Tim walked in. "Hey Pudding Pop." He kissed Judith's cheek.

She faked a smile at him. "Glenda, I'll call you back."

"We're all going to the Ryders' later because this has to stop," Glenda said. "It's for the good of the church. Nola can't be acting like this."

"All right, all right." Judith exhaled. "I'll call you in a few minutes." She hung up the phone. "Lord, help us."

"What's the matter?" Tim sampled the strawberry sauce. "Needs more sugar."

"I already put a cup in." She poured more from the bag. "Forget the sauce, Glenda just told me something horrible."

"What, babe?" He pulled her to him by her waist.

"She said Nola was riding around with that Quinn guy."

"What?"

"Yeah in a Cadillac Eldorado singing 'Rhythm of the Night.'"

"That song brings back memories." He licked his lips. "Popped my cherry to that song."

"Tim." She swatted his chest. "You should be ashamed of yourself having those wicked thoughts."

"Oh, baby we all had fun back then." He kissed her.

"I'm talking about Nola." She pushed him away. "We gotta save her before she makes a big mistake." She took off her apron. "I hope it's not too late. Some of us church ladies will talk to Reuben. The entire community could be at stake."

"Why can't you leave it alone, Judy?"

"Nola and Reuben are our friends." She twisted to the doorway. "If we don't help then who will?"

****

"Whoa." Ginger held on to LJ for dear life as he flung her around on the Capricorn skating rink. "Stop!"

He laughed, grabbing her by the waist. "Isn't this fun?"

"Ah!" She stumbled, flinging her arms while he swayed her from side to side. "Stop, LJ. You're going to make me fall."

He slid beside her and took her hand. "Just having fun."

"What's gotten into you?"

"I'm happy," he howled. "I landed my dream job and on my way to California to start a new life."

Ginger swayed, watching her red and white skates gliding on the hardwood.

He pulled her in front of him and kissed the back of her neck while a slow song began. "Look." He turned her around where she faced him and secured her in his strong arms. "It's couples skate."

She gave him a loud, sloppy kiss that made her lips vibrate afterwards. "Glad you're having fun." She put her head on his shoulder and they skated between other swooning couples.

"How's things going with your parents?" The scent of the pepperoni pizza they'd eaten lingered on his breath.

"Hectic." She sighed, lifting her head from his shoulder. "I was hoping this would blow over, but it's more serious than I thought. What if my mother really cares for Quinn?"

"She might." He slid his hands to her denim shorts. "People can't help how they feel."

"But, it's wrong, LJ."

"Is it?" He had a dazed look in his eye. "If a feeling is real then can it ever be wrong?"

"That's silly." She snapped her eyes away. "Momma belongs with Daddy."

"Your mother's a grown woman who has to make that decision for herself. This isn't your fight, Ginger."

"My parents' marriage is my world. It gives me hope. If they don't work out then would we?"

"We're not your parents." He kissed her, clamping her bottom lip in his mouth. "We're the rulers of our own destiny."

She laid her head back on his shoulder. "You meant what you said about us being serious?"

He tightened his hold on her. "What does this tell you?"

"Then there's something you got to do."

He held his breath. "What?"

She raised her head and looked him in the eyes. "You have to ask my dad permission to court me."

"Court you?" He laughed. "What's this? Nineteen thirty-five?"

"We're a traditional, southern, Baptist family even if I don't always act like it. It's a Ryder tradition that the man has to ask the father if he wants to be with his daughter."

He wobbled his head. "Ginger—"

"It's not about religion but respect. Beau did it."

LJ's face coiled. "You two must've been more serious than I thought."

"I've only asked two guys to do this, you and Beau. My dad needs to know you're special."

"Mr. Ryder said he didn't care if you dated Charles Manson."

"He didn't mean it," she said in an even tone. "Will you do it?"

He glanced at another couple and licked his lips. "I'd do anything for you, Ginger."

She smiled as he kissed her.

"Does this mean you're coming to California with me?"

"What do you think?"

"For real?" He picked her up and swung her around with the other couples gawking. "Yes!"

Ginger laughed, kicking.

CHAPTER TWENTY-SEVEN

Beau froze when he entered Capricorn and saw LJ and Ginger skating to the slow song under the romantic lights.

"What do we have here?" Isaac moved from behind Beau, playing with the red pick in his afro. "Is that who I think it is?" He reached up and slapped Beau's shoulder. "Looks like your girl's in love."

Ginger held onto LJ, smiling with that twinkle in her eye she used to have with Beau.

"No big thing." Beau held his breath, curling his large hands into fists. "She's dated other guys since me."

Isaac plucked his fro, grinning. "Nah, this is different."

"Ginger doesn't know how to love anyone."

They got in line at the counter to order pizza.

"Thought she loved *you*." Isaac bobbed beside Beau, laughing.

"He's a fucking ex-con." Beau snatched his wallet out his pocket. "Has Ginger lost her mind? First she's hanging with that dope dealer Da'Kuan and now LJ?"

"He's a cool guy. He's Rocco's cousin, remember?"

"Rocco's my boy." Beau got out pizza coupons. "But I don't trust LJ as far as I can throw him."

"You were fine with him until he started seeing Ginger." Isaac snickered. "Your attempt to sabotage at the lake was a big fail. Admit it, Beau. You still want Ginger and you always will."

Ginger walked into the secluded areas where the bathrooms were.

"Here, order the pizzas." Beau passed Isaac the money. "I need to go to the bathroom."

****

"Oh." Ginger jumped when she came out the women's bathroom.

Beau blocked the walkway, leaning to the side with his hand against the wall, smelling of gasoline. "Merry Christmas."

She tried to pass, but he switched his 6'3 frame to the left, blocking the little space she had. "Move, Beau."

"I can't even get a decent greeting from you nowadays? You too good for that?"

"You're not supposed to talk to me, remember?"

"It's a free country."

She gave up trying to leave and stood against the wall. "I'm not in the mood."

"For what? Me?"

She looked away, remembering how she loved stroking his fluffy hair and the way his steely, Irish-green eyes made her feel when they dated.

He shifted from left to right wearing a faded, opened denim shirt with a dingy, white T-shirt underneath it.

"With LJ now, huh?" His chiseled facial features glowed underneath his even tan.

"What do you think?"

He moved his tongue around in his jaw. "You sleeping with him?"

"What business is that of yours, Beau?"

"What happened to Da'Kuan? Sure move fast, Ginger."

"Da'Kuan and I weren't ever a couple."

"Oh, right." He lifted his hand, the long, denim sleeve flopping at the end. "You don't need him anymore and moved on to your next victim."

"Get out of my way."

He remained in place. "You were just using Da'Kuan for the free weed. What I can't figure out is what you're using LJ for."

"I'm not using LJ."

He held a close-lip smile. "You use everyone, Ginger." He poked her arm. "That's your MO."

"Don't touch me."

He pulled his hand back, the semi-smile flat lining. "You used to beg for me to touch you." He moved closer.

"*Get* away from me." She backed up, bumping into the old pay phone.

"You ever think about me?" His gaze fell to her shorts. "About us?"

"Only when I have nightmares."

"I think about you all the time and what we could've had if things hadn't gotten so screwed up."

"I should kick your ass for what you did."

"What are you talking about?"

"Those lies you told LJ. Keep my name out your mouth."

"I didn't lie."

"All that crap about me being with a bunch of guys and using you. I'm sick of you spreading rumors about me. Let it go."

"You didn't use me?" He thrust his large chest at her. "That's not how I see it."

"I'm so sick of you whining about your life. Get over it."

"I lost my scholarship, my future, and my girl."

"Whose fault is that?"

"You weren't there when I needed you the most." His face tore with pain. "Ginger, I was on my way to Ohio State. I'd have made pro for sure. One of the top five college linebackers in the country."

She nodded. "Yes, you were."

"I worked my ass off for years to get to that."

"And threw it away."

"I wanted to give you the good life, but I got stuck working at the damn gas station." He punched the wall, knocking the calendar off its hook. "The fuckin' gas station?"

"You're young and you have plenty of time to find another career."

"Football wasn't just a career; it was my life." He waved his hands. "I should be in a mansion making millions and married to you not pumping gas at some rundown station."

"Your life turned out this way because of your own actions." She stuck her finger in his face. "You got hooked on coke. You made stupid decisions, and you lost your scholarship. Then you beat the hell out of me."

"I didn't—"

"I still have scars on my body from the things you did." She hit his chest. "I loved you, you big asshole, and you tore me down to nothing. After being with you my confidence was shit, and it took a long time to get over that."

He dropped his head.

"You ask if I think about what we had?" Her voice cracked. "I do sometimes and a part of me wishes I could change how things turned out."

He pinched his nose, sniffling.

"Beau, you were my first love. I gave my virginity to you." A tear fell on her cheek. "I thought we'd be together forever. Remember, you took me to the tree at the lake and promised me we'd be together always."

"I meant it."

"I gave you everything, and you turned on me. You treated me worse than anyone and I didn't deserve that, Beau."

He lifted his head, eyes penetrating her.

"Stop blaming me for your life being fucked up because the only person you have to blame is yourself."

"I never stopped loving you." He grabbed her. "I swear."

"Beau." She pressed her hands to his chest. "Let me go."

"You still feel something for me, Ginger." He held her to him, the gasoline stench making her gag.

"Get away from me."

"Ginger." He tried to kiss her. "Let me remind you what we used to be. Remind you of the good times—"

"Beau, stop it!" She shoved him. "It's over."

"It'll never be over for me. Now you're here with LJ?" He pointed toward the doorway. "Rocco told me LJ got a job, and he's leaving for California. Is that why you're with him?"

"Beau—"

"Everyone knows you'd sell your baby to get out of Beluga but you don't have the guts to leave on your own."

"Maybe I would have the guts if you hadn't taken all my confidence. I'm done with this conversation and with you. Now get out of my way."

"Or what?"

"Or I'll scream."

"How can you build a life with a felon? What if that job in California doesn't work out? Then where would you be?" He grabbed his shirt. "Even if I lost my job I can get another one. LJ can't." He reached for her hand but she moved. "Come on. I'll take care of you better than he ever could—"

"Whatever happens with me it's none of your damn business anymore."

She pushed him as she walked away.

CHAPTER TWENTY-EIGHT

Ginger returned to LJ who waited by the skating platform. "Ready to go?"

"Hell no." He kissed her. "It's still couples skate."

"Not in the mood anymore." She looked toward the bathrooms as Beau exited with his hands in his pockets.

LJ tilted his nose in the air. "What the hell is he doing here?"

"Hey, it's a free country, right?" Ginger sat on the bench and undid her skates. "He has every right to be here but we don't have to."

"We're not leaving because of him." LJ glared at Beau who returned the gesture on the way to a table. "We were here first."

"Who cares?" Ginger took off her second skate and threw it on the floor. "Can you get our shoes, please? I want to leave."

LJ squinted at Beau. "I'm not ready to go yet."

"Would you stop looking at him?" Ginger pulled LJ down on the bench. "Ignore him."

Beau took out his cellphone, leering at them. "You got a problem, LJ?"

"No," he snapped. "Do you?"

Beau chuckled, tinkering with his phone. "You don't wanna mess with me, lil' boy."

"No?" LJ stood. "Like to bet on that?"

"LJ." Ginger grabbed his hand. "Stop."

"You think I'm scared of you or something, Beau?"

"No." He got up and slumped toward them. "But you're insane if you're trying to step up to me."

"Should I be scared?" LJ got nose-to-nose to Beau. "I'm a man and from what I hear you're more interested in hitting women."

Beau lunged at him.

"Stop." Ginger squeezed between them. "Beau, go sit down."

"No, it's your ex-con, limp dick boyfriend that needs to sit down before he gets knocked the fuck out."

"By you?" LJ laughed. "Come on then." He closed his eyes and stuck out his face. "Or should I put lipstick on to encourage you?"

"Motherfucker." Beau locked his hands around LJ's throat.

"Get the fuck off me." LJ kneed Beau in the stomach.

Beau howled and stumbled backward.

"Stop it," Ginger screamed as the other customers took notice of the scene.

"You want some of this, boy?" LJ delivered a monstrous right hook to Beau's jaw. "That's what you get when you step up to a man."

"Ah!" Beau charged LJ, grabbed him by the waist and slammed him.

Ginger hopped, flapping her arms. "Stop it!"

LJ and Beau rolled around on the floor, exchanging punches while knocking over a table.

"Help," Ginger shouted. "Security!"

"Beau!" Isaac ran through the crowd of people who documented the fight with their cell phones. "What the hell you doing?" He set the pizzas on the table and pulled Beau off LJ. "Settle down, bruh."

"Step off, Isaac." Beau threw punches in the air while Isaac held onto him. "Let me kick his ass. Give him my personal Beluga, Georgia ass whipping."

"Come on!" LJ jumped up and charged Beau, his eyes red and a purple bruise forming on his chin. "Son of a bitch."

"Fuck you, man." Beau spit at him, his eye swelling shut. "You think you're something, but you ain't shit! You're a felon and that's all your ass will ever be."

"Yeah? This coming from the cokehead loser who beats on women?"

"Stop it." Ginger leapt in front of LJ, pushing him back. "You're better than this, LJ. Don't go down to his level."

"My level?" Beau huffed and puffed. "When did you get so damn high and mighty, Ginger? With the shit you do?" He chuckled, looking at Isaac. "You'd swear this bitch was Mother Teresa."

"Who you calling a bitch?" LJ pushed Ginger aside. "Huh?"

"LJ, it's okay." She tried to grab his hand, but he swatted hers away.

"He needs his ass kicked." He pointed at Beau. "Any man who'd hit a woman doesn't deserve to live."

"I didn't do shit." Beau tussled in Isaac's hold. "You believe anything she tells you."

"You know it's true, Beau," Ginger retorted. "Don't make it worse by lying."

"You stupid slut." He spit at her.

"I'm gonna kill you." LJ grabbed Beau and punched him, sending him flying to the floor. "Who you think you are spitting on her?" He stood over Beau and socked him again. "Motherfucker! You have no respect for women at all."

"Hey!" A security guard rushed through the crowd. "Break it up!"

"Settle down." Another one ran up waving his baton and grabbed LJ. "That's enough, fellas."

"Out!" The first guard pulled Beau from the floor and held his hands behind his back. "You're both leaving."

"It was him." Ginger pointed at Beau. "He started it."

"It was him." Isaac got his pick off the floor and pointed at LJ. "He pushed up on Beau."

"That's a lie." Ginger got in Isaac's face. "You weren't even here when they started fighting."

"You better get out my face, girl."

"Enough!" The second guard swung LJ away from the table. "We don't care who started it but we're finishing it. Now, either you guys leave like you got sense or you can go to jail."

"The decision is yours," the first guard said. "What will it be?"

"Get off me then." Beau snatched his arms away from the first guard. "Come on, Isaac." He fixed his shirt. "This place sucks anyway."

Isaac grimaced at Ginger, snatching the pizzas off the table. "All this trouble because of yo' ho ass."

LJ blocked Ginger, shaking his head. "Say it again, Isaac."

"You better back up, white boy." Isaac followed Beau. "I'll send your ass back to Chi-town in a body bag."

LJ nodded. "Yeah, we'll see about that."

Beau and Isaac left.

"Okay, go back to what you were doing," the second guard told the crowd. "Nothing left to see here."

"And, in case anyone else get ideas about fighting..." The first guard put his hands on his waist. "We'll call the cops next time."

The people dispersed, a few groaning while others gave LJ thumbs up.

The second guard motioned to LJ. "Hurry up, get your skates off, and get out of here." He left behind the other guard, eyeing LJ over his shoulder.

Ginger sat on the bench, ogling LJ.

"Don't look at me like that." He sat and untied his skate. "He spit at you, Ginger. The ultimate disrespect. I should've killed his ass."

"I'm done with letting Beau's actions control me." She took his hand. "It's you I'm worried about. "LJ, one assault charge and you'll be back in trouble. You're on the right track. Don't let an idiot like Beau ruin that." She kissed his cheek. "He's not worth you messing up what you're working for." She hugged him. "I wouldn't ever want you to do that."

"I hear you." He put his arms around her. "I'll be more mindful next time."

She let him go, squinting. "Promise?"

He took off his other skate. "If Beau stays out my face."

CHAPTER TWENTY-NINE

"Wee!" Nola twirled into Quinn's den, the brown and tan color palette relaxing her even more. "That was so much fun, Quinn."

He stood in the doorway, face alive with a sensual expression. "I'm glad you think so."

She dropped her gaze and checked her watch. "Uh-oh."

"What's wrong?"

"It's almost seven. We've been out for hours."

"Uh-huh." He walked to her. "It's easy to forget the time when you're having fun." He gave her that sexy glare with his head tilted and eyes looking up at her. "Don't you think?"

Her tight nipples puckered within her satin bra. "Quinn."

He glided his index finger on her arm. "It sure is hot today, isn't it?"

She swallowed, glancing at the thick, curly hairs underneath his white tank. "It's always hot." She gave a slight chuckle. "It's Georgia, remember?"

"It's easy to forget it's even winter." He drew his lips into a tight, teasing smile. "I have to keep reminding myself it's almost Christmas."

"That's fitting seeing how I have to keep reminding myself I shouldn't be here."

"Why shouldn't you?" His oak cologne penetrated her senses. "You belong here, Nola." He clamped his huge hands on her waist. "With me." He pursed his lips for a kiss.

"Quinn." She touched his chest, feeling his flesh ripple. "We can't do this."

"We've *been* doing this. It might not have been physical until now..." He grabbed her ass and a whimper escaped her lips. "But, we've been making love." He held her to him, swallowing her in his body heat. "We've made love with our conversations and with the way we look at each other." He snatched the clamp out her hair, releasing her thick reddish-brown tresses. "I stopped kissing you at the lake." He pushed his hand up her dress. "But, I'm not stopping tonight."

"Quinn." Her breath caught in her throat. "Don't."

"Don't what?" His gaze told her he wouldn't let go if his life depended on it. "You want this as much as I do."

"I can't." Nola grew hot between the legs as Quinn's burly hands rubbed the outside of her panties. "No, no." She shook her head. "We can't do this."

"Don't you want to?" His eyes turned into slits.

"I'm married." She panted, massaging the material of his shirt. "I'm the first lady of the church—"

"What happens in these walls, stays in these walls." He scooped her in his arms.

"Quinn." She slapped her forehead as he carried her to the tan and red striped couch. "What are you doing?"

He smashed his lips onto hers; sinking his tongue so deep in her mouth she couldn't breathe.

She ripped her lips away, desperate for air. "No."

He laid her on the couch. "You want to leave?" He grabbed her head, pushing those meaty lips to hers once again. "Say so."

She cursed herself as he sat beside her. "I can't."

"Good." He gave her another restricting kiss and slipped one strap off her shoulder. "This isn't wrong, Nola."

"Oh." She moaned as he shoved her dress off her bosom. "I'm married."

"I know." He breathed, unhooking the front snap of her white, pushup bra.

"God." Before she could fathom it, his mouth was on her breast, tongue stroking her nipple. "I can't believe this is happening." Her vulva pulsated while any reason she should've stopped him vanished from her mind.

Sucking and slurping, Quinn pushed her droopy breast in his mouth and the more he suckled, the hungrier he looked.

"I've never felt so wanted." She pushed her fingers in his hair, surprised it wasn't as greasy as it appeared. "But...we have to stop."

He pulled his drooling lips from her breast. "You don't look like you want to stop." He grabbed her head with both hands and latched his mouth onto hers while that tingle in her crotch grew into a painful throb. "Oh, Nola." He pushed her dress up and snatched at her panties as if he owned her.

She clamped her bottom lip in her teeth. "I love my husband."

"Then you'd be with him now." He sucked her neck. "I bet it's been a long time since Reuben made you feel this way."

"Quinn."

"Sh." He kissed her again, stroking her gold, pendant earring. "I'll take you to the mountain top."

She whimpered.

"Look at me."

She did, batting her eyes.

"I want you, and I'll show you that every day." He went for another kiss when someone knocked on the front door.

"Nola," Reuben yelled. "I know you're in there! Quinn, open this door right now."

"Oh my god." Nola covered her mouth with trembling hands. "It's Reuben."

"I'm glad he's here." Quinn stood, straightening his shirt.

"What?" Nola latched her bra and struggled to pull up her dress. "Are you crazy?"

Quinn's eyes became glossy. "For you."

"Nola?" Reuben banged on the door. "Quinn, you better open this door. You lay one hand on my wife I'm gonna kill you."

"Oh god." Nola covered her eyes.

"We can't keep doing this." Quinn lifted his head, balling fists. "We want to be together and we need to be honest with Reuben."

"Wait, wait." She jumped to her feet. "What are you talking about?"

"We love each other." He threw his chin in the air, squinting. "And, it's about time Pastor Ryder knows it." Quinn marched out the room.

"Quinn, wait." Nola ran after him, waving her hands. "Quinn, don't do this. Quinn!"

CHAPTER THIRTY

"Quinn, wait." Nola grabbed his arm when they got to the front door. "Let me take care of this."

"Are you going to tell him you're leaving him to be with me?"

"What?" She grimaced. "No, look—"

"Figured as much so I'll do it for you." He yanked the front door open and Reuben stormed inside, charging Nola.

"This is the last straw." He huffed and puffed, sweating. "It's one thing to act like this but to embarrass me? The whole town saw you riding around with Quinn. I look like a damn fool!"

"Reuben—"

"Be quiet, woman."

"Don't talk to her like that."

"You stay out of this." Reuben swung around, facing Quinn. "That's the problem; you can't keep your greasy behind out my marriage."

"This is *my* house." Quinn thrust his chest out to Reuben, raising on his tiptoes. "I don't come in your home yelling so I'd suggest you show respect."

"Respect?" Reuben guffawed. "You're trying to sleep with my wife and you want respect?"

"Reuben." Nola sighed, rocking from side to side. "Please, calm down."

"There's no calming down with this, Nola. I'm passed that. You've put my reputation at risk. The whole congregation was just at our house and they're worried about how this impacts the church."

"That's all you care about, isn't it?" Quinn asked. "The church. You wonder why Nola's here instead of with you?"

"Quinn." She glared at him. "You're not helping."

"He's never gonna listen to you." Quinn grinned. "He doesn't pay attention to anything but his beloved church members. You got the best woman in the world." He glared at Reuben, thrusting his finger at Nola. "And you don't even appreciate her. You know how many men would kill to be with a woman like Nola?"

"Quinn, please." Nola got in between them. "Listen, Reuben—"

He grimaced, staring at her hair. "Where is your clamp?"

"What?"

"The clamp that was in your head when you left the house." Reuben's lips tightened. "Where is it?"

"Well, it's a miracle." Quinn raised his arms. "He finally noticed something."

"Shut up, Quinn." Nola touched her hair.

Reuben clenched his jaw, bottom lip vibrating. "Where is your clamp?"

"It's in my den." Quinn pointed at the hall. "I took it out her head." A condescending, boastful smile overtook his lips.

Nola closed her eyes and prayed but wasn't sure even God could stop Reuben's upcoming wrath.

He placed his angry stare on Quinn's face. "You took the clamp out of my wife's hair?"

"You damn right, Pastor." Quinn pushed his shoulders back. "What are you going to do about it?"

Reuben put him in a headlock. "I told you to stay away from my wife."

"Reuben!" Nola grabbed his arm. "Let him go."

"I warned your dumb behind." Reuben tightened his arm around Quinn's neck. "You thought I was playing? You don't know who you're messing with."

Quinn gagged, pushing at Reuben's sturdy arms. "Get...off."

"Reuben, please stop." Nola tugged on him. "You're a pastor! You can't be acting like this."

"And you're the first lady." He let Quinn go. "Wouldn't say you've been acting like it."

Quinn coughed, moving toward the door.

"Look what your actions have done, Nola." Reuben wheezed. "You've deduced me to violence."

"Everything is always someone else's fault." Quinn grunted.

"Shut up," Nola told him. "Reuben, this was a mistake. Let's go home and talk things out—"

"We're past talking." He stood back, looking at her as if she were the most disgusting thing he'd ever seen. "It's over. You won't walk all over me and act like I'm the bad guy in this."

Quinn rubbed under his chin where Reuben had gripped him. "You are."

Nola grabbed Reuben's shirt. "I wanna work things out."

"*What*?" Quinn shouted.

"Why now?" Reuben gestured at Quinn. "Obviously he's giving you something I can't."

"I love you." She pushed her palms together, sniffling. "Let's talk, okay?"

He shook his head. "I'm done."

Quinn moved from the door with his eyebrows raised.

"It's bad enough when you disrespect me," Reuben said. "But disrespecting the church is another. You should be ashamed of yourself, Nola."

His words tore into the base of her soul, bringing a worthless feeling she'd never experienced.

"Twenty-five years, Nola." Reuben held up his index finger. "That's how long we've been married."

She whispered, "Reuben."

He closed his eyes as if daring her to speak. "You say I haven't been listening to you then listen to me. It's over."

"Reuben." She shuddered. "Please."

"We can't keep going in circles with this and I'm tired of shouting." He shrugged with tears in his eyes. "All I've ever wanted was your happiness and if that means not being with me then so be it."

"No." She yanked his hand. "I love you, Reuben. I never wanted to end our marriage. You got this wrong."

"What's wrong is how you've treated me. I admit I haven't been the perfect husband but two wrongs don't make a right."

She covered her face, shaking her head. "Listen, please."

"You want to be with Quinn then you can stay here." He marched past Quinn and to the door.

"What are you saying?" She rushed to him.

"I'm saying don't come home tonight, Nola." He opened the door. "How about that?"

"Don't do this." She sobbed. "The reason we're in this mess is that we never talk. We've got to or things won't get better between us."

"Is there still an 'us'?" Reuben let go of the doorknob. "That ship's passed."

"It'll never pass. I love you, Reuben. We have a daughter together and a wonderful life."

Quinn sighed, touching the bridge of his nose.

"We can't throw that away." Nola reached up and stroked Reuben's sweaty cheeks. "I don't want to."

"You should've thought about that before you let him take the clamp out your head."

"It was a stupid mistake." She bounced in place. "All I've ever wanted was for you to pay attention."

He put his hands out as if he wanted to hold her, but he didn't. "I'm done." He walked out.

"Reuben." She ran to the stoop, sniveling. "I love you!"

CHAPTER THIRTY-ONE

Nola shut Quinn's door and leaned against it, crying. "What have I done?"

"That wasn't what I expected you to say to him." Quinn rocked with a sour expression. "You were supposed to tell him you'd leave him and you want to be with *me*." He hooked his hands on the top of his head. "But, that didn't happen."

She moved from the door, pointing back at it. "I never said I was leaving Reuben."

"You led me on, Nola."

"Quinn, you couldn't have believed I'd leave Reuben."

"Reuben can't give you the life you want. If you stay with him, it'll be twenty more years of misery."

"That's not true. I've had a wonderful life with Reuben despite the problems we've had." She looked at the wall as her mind wandered to the happier times in her marriage. "My goal was to get back to what Reuben, and I used to be. Not to leave him."

"You can't complain about your husband then turn your back on someone who wants to give you what you've longed for."

She touched her wedding ring. "This is my fault, and I'm sorry."

He squinted.

"I've been selfish." She slid her hand against the wall. "I didn't consider your feelings. I was having fun, and it didn't occur how you might've felt until you kissed me at the lake."

"You wanted me to kiss you." He breathed in her face.

"I did." She nodded with her head low. "But, it doesn't mean it was right. I've screwed up on so many levels. I've hurt you, betrayed Reuben, and I've turned my back on my beliefs for what? Sinful pleasure?"

"It wasn't sinful." He held her in his arms. "I love you, Nola."

She did a semi-chuckle.

"I do." He shook her. "Be with me. Forget the church and this town. For once make yourself happy."

"I intend to." She moved from his grasp. "That's why I have to fight for my marriage."

His face deflated.

"Reuben's worth it." She sniffled. "I took too long to realize that."

"Why would this time be different?" He backed up to the wall. "You'll be complaining about the same shit. Is that the life you want? One full of loneliness and empty of desire and passion? I bet I've wanted you more in the last week than Reuben has in a year."

His words stung. "Reuben is the only man I've loved. I've never even kissed another man until..." She avoided his gaze.

"You want me. If Reuben hadn't interrupted us we'd be making love on that couch and you know it."

"Maybe so." A tiny breath lodged in her throat. "But, thank god he came because that would've been the biggest mistake of my life."

"Wow. Thanks for the compliment, Nola."

"I didn't mean it like that." She touched his cheek. "Quinn, you're a wonderful man and you deserve better than being with a woman who can't commit to you."

"We're good together." His nose crinkled. "We've shared and enjoy each other's company. Doesn't that mean something?"

"It never should've gone as far as it did."

"It didn't go far enough." He huffed. "I'm supposed to just walk away and act like we never happened? I'm still going to want you."

"I understand. My feelings for you aren't disappearing just because I walk out that door, but my love for Reuben is too strong to throw away what we have." She kissed his cheek. "I care about you, Quinn. Don't doubt that."

"I feel used, Nola."

"That wasn't my intention, but we can't see each other anymore."

He snorted, eyes watering. "What about the center?"

"I'll change the time I come in so we won't see each other."

He stroked her hand, begging with his eyes. "Does it have to be this extreme?"

"You were right when you said we'd have made love if Reuben hadn't shown up. If we're in this position again, it'll happen for sure and I'm not doing that to Reuben or my daughter or myself."

His shoulders dropped. "Nola—"

"I have to make things right before it's too late." She went into the den.

He rushed in behind her. "What are you doing?"

"I'm getting my clamp." She got it off the table. "And, I'm leaving and never coming back."

"I brought you here. Let me take you home."

"I'm going to Ginger's for the night." She rolled her hair into a French roll and clamped it. "The last thing I want is another fight with Reuben. I'll wait for the bus down the street."

"Nola." He groaned following her back to the foyer. "It'll be at least an hour or two before that bus comes."

"Good." She smiled, opening the front door. "It'll give me time to figure out how the heck I will fix my marriage."

"Nola, please."

"Goodbye, Quinn." She displayed a quivering smile. "Thanks for reminding me how fun life can be."

****

"Holy, moly." Judson walked through the junkyard a few days later, ogling the Camaro parts scattered on the grass. "Sweet Lord." He whistled. "Is there anything left in it?"

"Not much." LJ threw the wrench on the ground and dabbed his sweaty face with the end of his sleeveless, black T-shirt. "This thing is a mess."

"I see that." Judson picked up the carburetor. "Needs a new carburetor?"

"Shit, this thing needs a new everything." LJ grabbed his water bottle off the paint bucket. "A new engine, brakes, gasket, ignition coils, exhaust system." He gulped water.

"Sounds like it'll be cheaper buying a whole new car." Judson picked at the small hairs on his chin. "Why are you fixing this up, anyway?"

"It's a surprise for Ginger. Was hoping I'd have it finished by the time we move to California but with the shape this heap's in might not be finished by *next* Christmas."

Judson released a stiff chuckle. "You'll get it done."

"You all right?" LJ knelt, examining the manifold gasket from the Camaro. "Seems like you got something on your mind."

"I feel horrible."

LJ looked up at him, squinting from the sun. "Why?"

"Because I didn't stand up for you." Judson kneeled beside him. "I should've hired you at the
shop and not worried about these folks."

"I don't blame you. Beluga's got its rules, and I'm not looking to change people's minds."

He grabbed LJ's shoulder. "I'm offering you a job at the shop."

"I appreciate that but no thanks." LJ smiled. "I leave for the job in California in three weeks and my mind's made up."

Judson removed his hand from LJ's shoulder. "You don't want to be with us?"

"I do." He laid the gasket in the grass. "But, it's not my calling. Uncle Jud, I wanna make it on my own with no handouts."

"We're family. Family helps each other out."

"You and Aunt Felicity have done more than I deserve. I'll always be grateful but you don't owe me anything."

Judson chuckled. "How'd you get to be such a proud son of a gun?"

LJ stood, winking.

Judson groaned as he struggled to get up. "Man, I'm old."

"Be honest," LJ said. "You don't want me to go to California."

"Darn straight." Judson straightened his greasy baseball cap. "I've enjoyed you being here. Just need to make sure you're doing the right thing."

"Well, if I make a mistake in Cali I can come back here." LJ walked to the other side of the car. "Right?"

"You're always welcome with us."

He rubbed the trunk. "I'm going to be somebody."

"LJ, you are somebody."

"Beau said I'll be nothing but a felon for the rest of my life."

"Oh, please." Judson scowled. "Who cares what Beau thinks? He can't talk about anyone with the shambles his life's been in."

"It hurt when he said it though." LJ exhaled. "California. Can't believe I'll have my dream job."

"Will you have time for Ginger? With the way you are when you get around these cars you might never see her."

He laughed. "Trust me; I'll make time for Ginger."

"You're in love with her, aren't you?"

LJ's face flushed with warmth.

"Ah, young love." Judson leaned on the car, looking at the sky. "It's a beautiful thing."

"Some might say we haven't known each other long enough to move away together."

"Who cares?" Judson rolled his eyes. "You got to live your own life. That's what I hate about this town, people expect you to be a certain way and all. Shoot, I wish I'd had the courage to leave when I was your age." He lifted the rim of his cap. "I'd have been out this place."

"Ginger's a breath of fresh air." LJ propped his arms on the trunk. "When I first saw her, I was blindsided."

Judson smiled. "She *is* pretty."

"I wanted so much to get to know the real her. I was shocked to see the person inside would be as beautiful as on the outside. What I love is that she *sees* me." He grabbed his shirt. "She sees who I am and accepts me for that. She doesn't want to change me and she understands how I feel."

"That's great."

"I'm glad I have your support in this."

"As long as you feel this is right..." Judson shrugged. "Who am I to say different? If you love her that's all that matters." He poked LJ in the forehead. "I bet she's excited to get out of here. Ginger been wanting to leave Beluga since she was born." He laughed.

"Yeah, it's all she's been talking about, but she hasn't told her parents yet."

Judson winced, making a sucking sound between his teeth. "That ain't good. Pastor Ryder won't be too happy with you taking his baby girl away."

LJ put his hands in his pockets. "Hopefully he doesn't kill me."

"Look at it this way. He can kill you and preside over your funeral at the same time."

"Funny Unc." LJ snickered, scratching his nose. "Dad called this morning. He starts chemo next week. Doctors are optimistic."

"Thank you, Jesus." He slapped the back of LJ's neck. "The family's been praying for him."

"I'm sure he appreciates it."

"What are you doing this Saturday night?"

"What do you mean?" LJ walked away from the car.

"Well, everyone in town will be at the annual Christmas festival. Curious about *your* plans."

LJ scratched his stomach under his shirt. "I'll be there too."

Judson turned his head so fast his cap jumped out of place. "Say what?"

"I'll be at the festival."

"Hold on." Judson held out his arms, batting his eyes. "Did I just hear you right?"

"Ginger roped me into taking her."

"Boy oh boy. You're going to the Christmas festival?" Judson wiggled his eyebrows. "Now I *know* you're in love."

CHAPTER THIRTY-TWO

Saturday Night

LJ and Ginger strolled through the congested Christmas festival, which covered the entire downtown Beluga.

LJ tried to keep his composure but the loud cheers and bright lights reminded him of the times he and his mother visited the Six Flags in Illinois.

"See, LJ?" Swinging his hand inside hers, Ginger yelled over the people who screamed from the Ferris wheel and rollercoasters. "It's the best of both worlds." She bit a chunk of her red and green cotton candy. "We get to celebrate Christmas and go to the fair at the same time."

"Wee!" A skinny, Hispanic boy rode a carousel horse on the Merry-Go-Round.

Everywhere LJ turned he faced laughter, base-filled Christmas music, and the aroma of sweet pastries and corn dogs. Christmas garland and icicles decorated the rides while Santa Claus sat at a huge booth as kids took his lap hostage.

It wasn't easy to stay out of the spirit.

"Having fun?" Ginger skipped through hordes of happy children who ran past her and LJ. "It's so magical, isn't it?"

"Yeah." He looked up, strings of bright lights and red and green tassels blew in the cool night air.

"You okay?" Ginger giggled. "You're blushing."

"Am I?" He touched his warm cheek. "It's so welcoming here."

People waved and smiled at him, which surprised LJ because any other time they did their best to stay away from him.

"You are welcomed." Ginger stuck her cotton candy in his face. "You're a part of us now."

"My stomach's tingling." He patted it. "My nerves are jumping. It feels good."

"That's the Christmas spirit." She put her arm around his waist.

People dressed as Christmas elves danced by the vender booths blowing trumpets as people sold T-shirts and toys.

"It's like a fairy land or something," LJ said. "I knew this was a big deal but didn't expect all this."

"You should see how Beluga gets down during Easter."

"You said your dad's giving a sermon here?" He raised his voice as a vender spoke in a megaphone, directing people to her display of designer purses.

"Yeah." A sugary, cherry smell burst through Ginger's breath from the cotton candy. "The sermon is at the end of the night." She pointed toward the park covered by a Christmas tent with lights and garland. "It'll be over there."

Reuben's grand pulpit sat under the huge tent in front of rows of chairs with red, green, and silver decorations.

Ginger rubbed against LJ. "Sure you don't want anything else to eat?"

"You kidding?" He maneuvered his hips in the snug jeans. "I ate three fried candy bars, two cupcakes, an Oreo cookie ice cream sandwich, three corn dogs, and two funnel cakes." He belched. "I've eaten more tonight than I have my entire life."

"Welcome to the festival, LJ." Ginger jumped in front of him, dancing to the teenage band playing "Let it Snow."

"You've been jumping around since you got here." He laughed.

She twirled him around and dipped him.

"Hold up." He laughed, regaining his composure. "The man dips the woman."

She laid against his chest. "Dip me, my love."

"You're nuts." He dipped her and gave her a tiny peck on the lips.

"I'm so happy!" She grabbed his waist with both hands. "You gotta come to our house for Christmas, LJ."

"Whoa. Now, I agreed to come to the festival, but I didn't say I was celebrating Christmas."

"For me?" She giggled.

"Everything can't be for you." He pinched her nose. "You talk about sacrificing well how about you sacrifice for me then?"

"Okay." She batted her eyes. "I'll spend Christmas with you then."

"I'll be alone on Christmas." Her moved her beside him and put his arm over her shoulders.

"Not anymore." She pinched his cheek.

"You'd skip out on celebrating Christmas to be with me?"

She beamed. "In a hot minute."

Fireworks exploded through the sky.

Ginger jumped in front of LJ. "I can't wait to spend Christmas with you."

"Your parents will flip. Bet you've never spent Christmas apart from them."

"They probably won't even spend Christmas together." She kicked a soda can out her way. "If they're still acting like children."

"Your momma still staying at Paula's?"

She nodded. "She and Daddy have never had a fight this bad."

"Let me win you a toy." He stroked her hair, walking her past the carnival games.

"I don't want a toy." She laid her head on his shoulder as they continued walking. "I want my parents to be like they were before."

Tisha, Da'Kuan and Ronny walked toward them.

"Ah, heck," Ginger whispered. "Da'Kuan might start some shit."

"I can handle it if he does."

"Hey, girl." Tisha ran up to Ginger and hugged her. "Ooh, I love that blouse." She tugged on Ginger's white, draped blouse with the plunging neckline. "Hi, LJ."

"What's up, Tisha?"

"Gotta say I'm surprised you're here." She grinned. "Thought you were allergic to Christmas."

Ginger pulled him close. "He's here for me."

"Merry Christmas, Ginger." Da'Kuan sucked on a green, white, and red candy cane while Ronny snickered. "You don't know nobody anymore or what? Just stopped calling a brotha."

She shrugged.

"I'm LJ."

Da'Kuan's mouth twisted. "I know who you are."

"It's the Christmas festival okay, Da'Kuan?" Ginger exhaled. "Don't cause a scene. Just let it go."

"Hey, I'm cool." He put his arm around Tisha. "Got someone else to fill my time now."

Ginger's mouth fell open. "Tisha?"

"Don't look so surprised," Da'Kuan said. "We been hooking up." He gave Tisha a loud smack on the lips.

Ginger laughed. "I can't wait to see what Deacon Eason has to say about this."

"I have a 'don't ask, don't tell' policy with Daddy." Tisha winked, giggling. "Besides, I'm grown. Let the chips fall where they may."

"Got some blunts." Da'Kuan motioned to Ginger. "We gonna get our smoke on by the trees later. You both welcome to join us if you want to."

"Not my thing," LJ said.

"Weren't you in prison?" Ronny asked.

"That doesn't mean I did drugs."

"You never smoked weed?" Da'Kuan stuck out his lips as if to doubt LJ. "And you from Chicago too?"

"I didn't say I *never* smoked weed. I'm not into it anymore."

"LJ's trying to stay on the straight and narrow." Ginger held a proud smile. "I'm giving up the dope too. If I'm gonna be with LJ I need to be a good role model."

"Dang." Ronny made a face. "Guess he really put it on ya' for you to give up weed huh, Ginger?" He and Da'Kuan laughed.

"We'll see you." Tisha patted Ginger's hand as she and the guys walked on.

"I can't believe Tisha is dating Da'Kuan." Ginger gaped. "Deacon Eason is stricter than Daddy."

"Looks like love is everywhere." LJ kissed her, tasting the sweet candy on her lips.

****

Ginger met up with Nola underneath the big tent after Nola and Paula passed out candy canes to the children.

"How are you?" Ginger asked. "You were working them candy canes."

"Who you telling?" Nola took her glittery Santa hat off and fluffed out her hair. "Been ripping and running all day but it's worth it."

Ginger situated her bottom in the cushion of the chair. "Talked to Daddy?"

"Where's LJ?"

Ginger grinned as Nola tried to switch the subject. "With his family at the Christmas tree lighting."

"You should go over there then." Nola patted Ginger's thigh. "That's your favorite part of the festival."

"You're more important and stop avoiding my question. Have you spoken to Daddy since you been here?"

"He was busy." Nola's face tightened. "He was riding bumper cars with the children from the youth choir."

"Why didn't you speak to him?"

"He didn't seem to miss me." Nola set the Santa hat on her lap. "He's laughing and having a good old time."

"Come on, this can't go on. I demand you two sit down and talk like adults—"

"Ah, hell."

"What?" Ginger turned as Reuben headed toward them. "Momma, be nice."

"Tell *him* to be nice. I'm not the one who threw my wife out the house before Christmas." She perched the Santa hat on her head, huffing. "Why is he coming over here, anyway?"

"Stop it. You know you miss him." Ginger took her mother's hand. "Here's your chance to make things right."

"Merry Christmas." Reuben sat in the row in front of them, facing the women. "You having fun, baby girl?"

"I'd have more fun if you two would stop this nonsense." Ginger dug her fingernails into Nola's hand. "Say hello to Daddy."

Nola shifted her eyes in his direction. "Hello, Reuben."

"Nola." He gripped the back of his chair. "How are you?"

"Okay, I guess." Nola remained allusive. "Would rather be at home though."

"It's been difficult not having you there. The house is too quiet. I miss you."

Nola's face relaxed. "You do?"

"Course." He batted his puppy dog eyes. "Miss having you there when I have my coffee in the mornings."

Nola's face sunk. "Seriously?"

Reuben grimaced. "Yeah."

"Are you kidding me?" Nola's voice rose. "You miss me because you want someone there to have coffee with?"

"What's wrong with that? We always have coffee together in the mornings and I look forward to it."

"Coffee?" Nola shrieked. "Out of all the reasons to say you missed me, you choose 'having coffee in the mornings'?"

Ginger sighed, closing her eyes.

"Why not say you miss me because I'm your wife and you love me and can't live without me? This is exactly what I'm talking about. Reuben, you're pathetic."

"I didn't come over here to be abused." He jumped from the seat. "I can't do anything right and I'm sick of it."

"What you said is the exact reason we're in this mess, because you lack passion. Get out my face, Reuben."

"Momma."

"You don't have to tell me twice." Reuben kissed Ginger's cheek. "I got to practice my sermon."

"Daddy, don't go."

He marched away.

"Momma, that was mean. He was trying to be nice."

"He should've kept his mouth shut and saved us from that stupidity." Nola smacked her lips.

"You don't tell your wife you miss her because you need someone to have coffee with."

"He didn't mean it like that. You're impossible to please."

"Guess so if I need love and attention, huh?" She stood. "I hate to say it but I'm not sure we can fix this."

"Bull. You and Daddy belong together."

"As time passes, I'm not so sure, sweetie." Nola caressed Ginger's cheek. "I'm gonna help

Paula pass out the treats to the kids."

"I'm not letting this go," Ginger yelled as Nola walked toward the crowd. "I'm getting you and Daddy back together if it kills me!"

CHAPTER THIRTY-THREE

Before Ginger left the tent, Beau walked up with a small sack and a handful of red, white, and green candy corn. "Want some?"

She rose, taking her cell phone out the back pocket of her jeans.

"Wait." He groaned. "Can I talk to you for a minute?"

"I have nothing to say to you, Beau."

He blocked her, shaking the little sack. "I got you a present."

She crossed her arms, rocking. "Want me to show you where you can put it?"

"Man." He clamped his lips together, breathing loud. "I can't even do something nice without you hating me?"

"I'm still pissed at how you acted at Capricorn. You spit at me as if I was nothing. That hurt my feelings beyond belief."

"I hated myself the minute I did it." A spot remained on his face from the bruise LJ had given him. "I'm so sorry."

"You dealt with the drug addiction but you've got to do something about your anger before it's too late. Next time you'll get in the wrong person's face and you might end up dead or the other way around."

"My actions were inexcusable. That's why I want to apologize."

"Apologize to LJ and while you're at it give *him* your gift."

"Not sure he'd be interested." He took a medium-sized snow globe out the glittery, red sack. "I ordered it online."

Her heart fluttered as she took the globe that said, "I Love California" on the front. "It's beautiful." She shook it up and snow rained on the miniature beach.

"That's Santa Claus surfing." He grinned.

"I love it."

"You always loved snow globes."

She shook it again, fascinated by the enchanting scene. "It's so detailed."

"It's a three-for-one gift. A Christmas gift, an apology, and a going away present."

"I don't know what to say."

"Let me do the talking then." He rubbed his hair. "I can't let you go to California with this rift between us. You're right, Ginger. I've been blaming you for how my life turned out." He shrugged. "Guess you've been an easy target. But, I was never angry at you. I was desperate to get you back."

She rocked forward.

"Since we broke up, I dreamed we'd find our way back to each other but it never happened. It killed me to know it wasn't meant to be."

"I loved you, Beau."

"I *still* love *you*." He backed up, lowering his head. "I don't like LJ and I don't think he's good enough for you, but I want you to be happy even if it's not with me."

She smiled. "You mean that?"

"At least one of us will get out this town and do something with our life."

"Beau, you're not stuck unless you wanna be."

He shrugged, rolling his eyes.

"It's like what LJ told me, we have to choose to change. Things won't change on their own. I know you're scared." She touched his hand. "Everyone is but either you want something more than working at the gas station or you don't."

"You're right. It's easier to wallow and blame others."

She nodded.

"Can't believe you're leaving." He swayed, sinking his hands in his pockets. "I'll miss the hell out of you."

She smiled.

"I wonder..." He swallowed. "Will I ever stop loving you?"

"We were our first serious relationships." Ginger bounced on her toes. "No one will ever replace what we meant to each other, but that's the past." She watched LJ wandering around in the crowd and smiled. "I'm looking forward to the future."

****

"Ah!" Nola swerved the red and yellow bumper car when Paula sped straight into her. "Girl." She bounced back and forth.

Paula cackled, steering her little car as it backed up on its own. "Shoot, this thing's going crazy."

A man bumped into Paula, knocking her car into Nola's vehicle.

"Whoa!" Nola spun. "Paula, help."

"Ain't this fun?" Paula knocked cars from her path. "We used to do this all the time when we were kids, Nola!"

A blue car shoved Nola's out the way. "Sorry," the man yelled.

"Ooh, Jesus." Nola struggled to control the wheel. "Paula?"

Paula cackled, bashing into cars left and right. "Woo, hoo!"

"I'm done." Nola parked beside the wall and got out, wobbling. "I can't take this."

"Where you going?" Paula drove into a little girl, sending her car flying. "We're having fun, Nola."

"Not me." She straightened her blouse and patted her hair. "I'm too cute for this."

"Girl, come on." Paula slid her bumper car back and forth. "Party pooper!"

Nola stumbled out the exit as Quinn walked past eating a huge funnel cake.

He stumbled, stopping in place. "Nola."

She laughed at the powdered sugar on his lips. "Chowing down, huh?"

"Oh, yeah." He wiped his lips with a napkin and flashed that smile that made her panties melt. "These things are addictive. I've already had three. Want me to buy you one?"

"No thanks. Enjoying yourself?"

"Who wouldn't?" His eyes flashed as he blushed. "I feel like a kid again."

"Yeah, it has that effect on you." She pulled on her earring out of discomfort. "Well, it was nice seeing you."

"Nola. Can we talk in private?"

"Not sure we'd get much privacy here." She chuckled. "Besides, that wouldn't be a good idea. Reuben's here as I'm sure you know."

"Please?" He hurriedly chewed the smidge of cake in his mouth and swallowed. "It'll only take a minute."

"Okay, I guess." Nola followed him to the woods, far from the people but where they could still hear the festivities.

As soon as they stopped, Quinn rushed to her, lips puckered. "I've missed you so much."

"Don't." She backed away. "I told you we can't do this."

"I haven't been able to think about anything but you since you left my place. We can't let things end like this."

She closed her eyes, fighting the urge to kiss him. "It has to be this way."

"Why?" He moved closer, breathing his cinnamon and sugar breath in her face. "You want more than what Reuben can give you. What makes you think things will change if you go back?"

"I love him."

He grabbed her. "You love *me*."

She looked him in the eyes and shook her head. "I don't."

He exhaled through his nose, releasing her.

"Quinn, this hasn't been fair to you. You don't deserve to be jerked around."

"God's a beast."

"What?"

"He puts a beautiful woman in my path, someone I thought understood me more than anyone and just snatches her away."

"That was me, not God. We latched onto each other for the wrong reasons. I wanted to have fun, and you were lonely."

"No." He grimaced, looking at the ground. "I'm in love with you, Nola."

"Listen." She placed two fingers on his lips. "If I wasn't with Reuben, I'd be with you in a heartbeat. You're a wonderful man, Quinn Moretti."

"Then give us a chance." He locked his arms around her. "We could have a wonderful life together."

"I can't." She closed her eyes and laid her nose to his. "I belong with Reuben. I realize that more than ever."

With brute strength, he kissed her, her loins exploding at the slightest touch of his lips.

Nola moaned, hearing something move in the distance. She jerked from the kiss while Reuben peered from behind a tree.

His face contorted into anger she didn't know possible as he marched away in the opposite direction.

"Oh no." Nola pushed Quinn out the way and ran after him. "Reuben, wait!"

CHAPTER THIRTY-FOUR

"Reuben?" She caught up to him, grabbing his arm. "Listen."

"You said this bull was over." He snatched his arm from her. "What is *wrong* with you, Nola? Do you care at all that you're killing me?"

"You've got the wrong idea."

"I saw you kissing him! How could you do this?"

"I never meant to hurt you, but we were having problems before Quinn. Things haven't been fine in our marriage for a while now."

"Then why didn't you tell me sooner?"

"I should have." She inched forward. " You were right when you said it was my fault I wasn't happy. I put myself in this position because I allowed you to ignore me and take me for granted." She pushed her hair behind her ears. "I concentrated on you and your needs while pushing mine away. I didn't share my desires and goals and you got used to that."

His bottom lip jutted out.

"I made the biggest mistake in our marriage by remaining quiet and that's why everything fell apart."

He dropped his head, scratching it.

"It amazes me how you spend your career counseling others about their marriages and have no idea what's happening in your own." Tears flowed despite Nola fighting them. "It was never about another man. I didn't set out to cheat on you, Reuben. My goal was to wake you up and for things to improve between us." Her voice cracked. "You're the only man I'll ever love."

He sniffled, pinching his nose.

"I wanted the fun we used to have." She shivered. "I wanted you to want me again, Reuben."

"You think I don't want you?" He squinted. "For years I've traveled all across the country for my ministry with other pastors. We go everywhere and meet many people. Women." He steadied his eyes on her. "Pastors have groupies too."

She blew a breath. "Don't I know it."

"We go to these places treated like rock stars and we preach the word of God." He jeered. "Then all those married pastors crawled from behind the pulpit and into the motel with any woman who smiled at them for more than five minutes. And, I sit there in amazement wondering how they could do that because in all these years Nola, with all the women throwing themselves at me and all the opportunities I've had to step out, it never once..." His lip shook. "*Once* crossed my mind to cheat on you."

She felt his truth deep within her soul. "Oh, Reuben."

"Not one time, ever. Because why would I risk losing the best thing I have for empty pleasure? No woman could ever compare to you." He raised his hand above his head. "You're up here and these women are down to the ground. There isn't any woman worthy of breathing the same air as you, let alone one worth throwing my marriage away on. Nola, you're all I've ever wanted. My love for you has grown through the years not lessened."

She clamped her eyes shut.

"I'd be a fool to mess with that." His voice muffled from holding in tears. "One thing Rueben Ryder is not is a fool."

She managed a snicker.

"You're a part of me." He drew nearer. "Without you, I'd be so lost even God wouldn't be able to help me. I need you." He lifted her chin with the tip of his finger. "I want you."

"You don't know..." She sucked in tears. "How much I wanted to hear those words."

"You're my world." He pulled her into his soothing embrace and any doubt she had disappeared. "Please, don't leave me."

"I'm not leaving you, Reuben." She pushed her face into his large chest, inhaling the love that escaped his body. "I love you more than anything."

"I'm sorry it took another man for me to see what you needed." He kissed her in a way he hadn't since they'd first gotten married. "That'll never happen again."

She kissed him, acknowledging a fresh beginning to their new life together.

"Girl, you've done it now." He laughed, tears hanging from his eyelids. "I'm gonna show you all the attention you want and then some."

"I look forward to it." She watched him underneath her lashes. "Reubear."

"Reubear?" He gyrated, beaming. "You haven't called me that in years." He touched the curve of her back. "You always used to call me that when you were in the mood."

"I *know*." She turned him loose and lay in the thick grass. "Come here."

"Nola?" He cackled, kneeling beside her. "What if someone sees us?"

She pulled him on top of her. "Who cares?"

CHAPTER THIRTY-FIVE

Ginger staggered up the Ryders' porch, holding her breath the next morning. "I'm nervous as hell."

"You'll be fine." LJ pushed the doorbell. "We have to tell them we're going to California, right?"

"Easy for you to say." She breathed into her hands. "This could be a disaster. My dad will hit the roof and I'll have a panic attack in the middle of everything."

"What about your momma?"

"Momma's cool. She always has my back, but Daddy will freak out worse than you can imagine. Me leaving to be with a man I'm not married to?" She frowned. "You might end up going to California alone once he kills me."

He laughed, kissing her forehead.

"Damn, what's taking them so long to come to the door?" Ginger knocked. "Momma? Daddy, it's me."

Nola popped out the door with her hair wild, grinning from ear-to-ear. "Morning, baby girl," she sang as she gave Ginger a kiss. "Mm. Isn't it a beautiful day? LJ." She pulled him into a soft kiss on the cheek. "I can't get over how lovely it is outside this morning." She stretched. "The birds are chirping, butterflies humming. Everyone is happy, happy, happy."

"*Well.*" LJ grinned. "Had a good night's sleep, Mrs. Ryder?"

"Oh did I?" She rocked with a sneaky smile. "Come on in."

"Ewe," Ginger whispered to LJ as they walked into the foyer.

"What?"

She scowled. "They've been doing it."

He chuckled under his hand.

"I was on my way to the kitchen." Nola fluttered through the hall with her silk robe flowing behind her.

"You just got up?" Ginger and LJ stood in the kitchen doorway. "Momma, it's eleven. You and Daddy are usually up at the crack of dawn."

"Not this morning." She hummed to the cabinet. "Would you like coffee?"

"No." Ginger groaned. "Is Daddy still sleep? LJ and I have to say something important."

"No, *you* have to say something important." He sat at the table, moving the floral centerpiece aside.

Ginger rolled her eyes at him. "Momma?"

"Hm?" Nola directed her little, bare feet to the coffee maker, humming Keith Sweat's "Right and A Wrong Way".

"Oh god." Ginger gripped her chest. "You're humming Keith Sweat."

Nola nodded, putting the contents into the coffee maker.

"They must've really gotten their groove on." Ginger whispered in LJ's ear. "Momma loves Keith Sweat."

"So? Isn't this what you wanted?"

"I wanted them to stay married, not have sex." She shivered, scrunching her face. "Ewe."

LJ snickered as if he enjoyed her being tortured. "How you think you got here?"

"What's up?" Nola stood at the island. "Oh, LJ." She tottered toward him. "I know you're not into God but I wanted to invite you to have Christmas dinner with us Thursday. No one should be alone on such a day."

"That's sweet, Mrs. Ryder. But—"

"LJ and I are spending that day alone together, Momma."

"Oh." She poked out her lips. "We've never spent Christmas apart before."

"Momma, we came to talk about something bigger than Christmas but—"

"Bigger than Christmas?" She batted her eyes. "What's bigger than Christmas?"

"Hey, Nola," Reuben yelled, coming through the hall. "There's still some whipped cream left. Let's get this party started." He walked in wearing blue boxer shorts and nothing else. "Ginger." He fumbled, sticking the whipped cream can behind his back. "I didn't know you were here."

LJ laid his face into the table, laughing.

"*Daddy*. What in the world is going on? Why you got whipped cream?"

He switched his eyes to Nola.

"We were baking," Nola said, wincing. "I had the whipped cream in the living room."

"Why would you have it in the living room?" Ginger bopped. "Daddy didn't even come from the living room. Ooh, this is so gross. You guys been getting your freak on with whipped cream."

LJ guffawed with his mouth wide open.

Ginger clenched her teeth. "It's not funny."

"The heck it's not." He slapped the table.

"Momma?" She glared at her parents. "Daddy?"

Reuben stood beside Nola.

"This is disgusting," Ginger said. "I didn't know you were this freaky."

"Girl, grow up," Nola said. "How do you think you got here?'"

"That's what I said." LJ chortled.

"You should be happy we're back together." Nola put her arms around Reuben. "Ain't that right my little Reubear?" She kissed him.

"Reubear?" Ginger's stomach twisted. "You haven't called Daddy that in years."

"You know about 'Reubear'?" Reuben asked.

Ginger sat at the island. "Look, this is important and I need you to hear me out okay?"

"Okay." Reuben pressed his hands to the countertop. "What is it?"

"Um." Ginger's confidence evaporated. "I...well...um—"

"Spit it out, Ginger," LJ teased.

"Yeah, we ain't got all day." Rueben smirked at Nola. "Your mother and I got things to take care of."

"Church business?" Ginger asked.

They stared at each other and answered in unison, "No."

"Ugh." Ginger gagged. "I gotta get this out before I throw up all over the place. LJ and I are going to California."

The Ryders exchanged glances. "Say what?"

CHAPTER THIRTY-SIX

"Daddy, before you go on a tangent, it's happening. LJ and I love each other." Ginger stood. "We don't gotta know each other a hundred years to commit to each other. I'm a grown woman and Daddy, you can't tell me what to do."

He straightened his posture. "Ginger—"

"We got it all planned out. I've been saving my money from the Icebox and the McCormicks are giving LJ a loan to help until we get on our feet."

"Ginger—"

"Daddy, he got a job in Palo Alto, California and he'll be working at a car place, living his dream." Ginger smiled back at LJ. "He's super talented and he loves cars more than anyone I've ever met."

Reuben's forehead flexed. "Ginger—"

"Daddy, you might not agree but tough. LJ and I can make it work. As long as love is on our side then nothing else matters. So don't try to stop me, Daddy. I'm doing this with or without your approval."

"Ginger—"

"I want your support, Daddy."

Reuben lifted his hand. "Baby girl, would you—"

"But, if you don't give your blessing then that's just how it'll be but—"

"Ginger!" He slapped the countertop. "Please shut the heck up so I can say something."

She plopped on the stool.

"Girl, you won't let me get a word in edgewise," Reuben said. "Bout as bad as your momma. I'm fine with you going to California."

Everyone directed his or her attention toward Reuben. "*What*?"

"You can go to California." He smiled, nodding. "I wish you well."

Ginger slid off the stool. "Okay where is my dad and who are you?"

"Damn, isn't it something how a man acts after he gets some?" LJ asked.

"Daddy, is this a joke?"

"No, sweetie." He kissed her forehead. "You're right. You have to run your own life. It's the only way you'll become your own person."

"Daddy, thank you!" She hugged him. "I'm so happy. LJ!" She ran to him, jumping. "We're going to California. We're going to California!"

"Over my dead body," Nola said.

Everyone looked at her.

"Ginger, have you lost your mind?" Nola propped her hand on the island. "What in the world has gotten into you?"

"Momma?"

"And Reuben you lost your mind too looks like." Nola crossed her arms, wiggling her head left and right. "Ginger, this is the stupidest thing you've wanted to do and trust me there has been a lot of stupid things."

"Wait, wait, wait." Ginger sighed. "You mean Daddy agrees with me leaving and you don't?"

"Why would I want my daughter running off with a man she hardly knows? An ex-con." Nola peeked around Ginger. "No offense, LJ. You're a nice young man but we're talking about my daughter's future. Ginger, you don't know jack about California. You're just a little ole country girl. It'll be too fast for you out there."

"Faster than Ginger?" Reuben laughed.

She put her hand on her hip, cocking her head. "Daddy, what do you mean by that?"

"I didn't mean it like it came out but you ain't the most innocent person in the world." He pulled up his shorts. "She'll be fine."

Nola stuck her nose in the air. "What about finances?"

"LJ will have his job and I'll get something and we'll live together."

Nola screeched. "Live together in sin? Reuben, you hear the nonsense your daughter's spitting?"

"Momma—"

"LJ, would you give us some privacy please?"

"No problem, Mrs. Ryder." He smiled as he left the kitchen.

"What if this job for LJ doesn't work out?" Nola walked from around Reuben. "He's a felon, a thief, Ginger. I'm not saying that to be mean but it's true. It'll be impossible for him to get another job if this one doesn't work out. How will that impact your future?"

"We didn't come up with this out of the blue. LJ and I are prepared for whatever happens."

"If LJ loses this job; then you'll end up supporting him on a seven dollar an hour salary at some burger joint because you didn't even finish one semester of college."

Ginger sighed. "Momma—"

"You'll both end up being bitter toward each other due to financial issues, you'll end up pregnant, he'll become an alcoholic because he can't get a job and you guys will live in a raggedy trailer home somewhere."

Reuben laughed.

"It's not funny," Nola said.

"I'm impressed, Momma," Ginger mocked. "You planned my entire future in less than five minutes. I thought out of you and Dad, you'd have faith in me."

"I do but LJ has too much against him. You can't build a life with someone like that."

"I love him."

Nola poked out her lips. "I don't agree with this."

"Honey, she'll be okay," Reuben said. "We've raised her well and we have to trust her."

"This isn't about trust." Nola held Reuben's arm. "Things could go horrible. What if she ends up without a place to stay or no money? She has no family in California. What will she do?"

"She'll come back here." Reuben smiled at Ginger as he held Nola close. "Baby girl, you'll always have a place here."

"Thanks, Daddy."

"I can't believe you're agreeing with this, Reuben."

"Aren't you always saying Ginger has to live her own life?"

"Yeah, but—"

"Let her then." He swayed Nola in his embrace. "I'm tired of worrying about everyone else's love life and not ours. Hasn't that been our issue?"

"I'm worried, Ginger."

"Momma, if I don't get out of Beluga now I never will."

"What's so wrong with Beluga?" Nola lifted her hands, shrugging. "Your dad and I have been here our whole lives."

"It doesn't fit what I want." Ginger shrugged. "I can't grow here and I don't wanna be forty and still working at the Icebox."

"She's got a point." Reuben stood behind Nola, holding her shoulders. "She could do so much more in California."

"Trust in me, Momma." Ginger kissed Nola on the lips. "You won't regret it."

"But, you're my baby." Nola stroked Ginger's hair. "How will I make it with you so far away?"

"You will." Ginger pinched her cheek. "Besides, you have Daddy to keep me off your mind."

"That's right, baby." Reuben tickled Nola's waist. "I'll keep you busy."

"Since there's nothing I can say then I insist your father and I help you out." Nola touched the belt of her robe. "We'll give you ten thousand dollars to get you started."

Reuben's neck rotated. "We will?"

"We can't send our daughter all the way to California without money." Nola took Ginger's hands. "Never know what might happen."

"Thanks, Momma." Ginger hugged her.

"Promise us one thing." Nola wagged her finger. "When you get to Palo Alto, you find a Baptist church and join ASAP. You understand? I want you to go to church."

"Now I agree with your momma on that one."

Ginger giggled. "Deal."

Reuben's face sparkled.

"When are you leaving?" Nola asked.

"Three weeks."

Reuben sighed. "That's quick."

"That's when LJ has to start the job."

Nola grabbed her into a tight hug. "I'll miss you so much, baby."

"Me too." Reuben smiled.

"I'm off from work today." Ginger bounced, smiling. "How about we have lunch? You can get to know LJ."

"We have plans." Reuben stroked Nola's backside. "Your mother's helping with a sermon."

"Yeah." Nola pinched Reuben's cheek. "We got a lot of work to put into it." She kissed him.

"You got that right." Reuben licked his lips. "It'll be the hardest sermon I've ever written."

Nola's eyes fell to Reuben's crotch. "I bet."

"Oh." Ginger retched, covering her mouth. "LJ?" She ran out the kitchen. "Let's get out of here."

****

Christmas Night

"LJ." A blindfolded Ginger took LJ's hand as he led her into the junkyard. "Can I take this thing off now?"

"Not yet."

They took a few more steps, her foot bumping into miscellaneous items in the dead grass.

"Okay." Her heart raced. "I'm getting scared now. You got a dead body out here or something?"

He laughed, startling her as his arm wrapped around her waist. "You can stop now." He removed the scarf from her face. "Ta da."

Ginger gasped, batting her eyes.

A small, round table covered with a pleated red tablecloth, Christmas tree place mats and a centerpiece made of gold candles and poinsettias sat under the shine of the security lights.

"Don't just stand there." LJ gripped the cloth-covered chair and pulled it from the table. "Madam."

Ginger touched her stomach while taking labored breaths. "LJ, it's beautiful."

He got the radio from the ground, set it on top of the Camaro, and turned it to a station playing "Silent Night".

"That's my favorite Christmas song." Ginger's eyes tickled from emerging tears. "What is this?"

"It's not fair you skip Christmas dinner." He walked toward her with glassy eyes. "When it means so much to you."

"You did this for me?" She got a poinsettia from the table. "This is so sweet."

He gripped her waist. "It means a lot you wanted to spend tonight with me."

"Course I did." She gave him a big hug. "Thanks so much."

"Sit down."

She giggled as she relaxed in the seat. "Where did you get all this stuff?"

"Courtesy of Aunt Felicity."

Ginger rubbed the place mat. "You have a knack for decoration."

He grabbed the plastic sacks off the roof of the Camaro and took out two foam plates of food. "It's Christmas dinner with the works."

She sniffed the celery and onions from the cornbread dressing.

LJ pointed at the items on her plate. "Turkey breast, cornbread stuffing, gravy, cheesy corn, creamed green beans and cranberry sauce." He sat across from her. "Dig in."

"How can I eat?" She chuckled in between large breaths. "I'm overwhelmed."

"Girl, you better eat this food." He laid a napkin in his lap. "Cost me seventy dollars."

She laughed and tasted the dressing. "It's perfect." She got a hint of sage. "Everything is perfect."

The security lights highlighted his memorizing features. "I'd do anything for you, Ginger." He leapt from his chair. "Forgot the drinks." He lugged a cooler from the Camaro. "Grape juice in a can. Enjoy." He tossed her one.

She laughed. "Thank you, sir."

He sat again, pushing his chair to the table. "Sure is hot for Christmas, huh?"

"Always hot in Georgia." She crossed her legs at the ankles, staring at the grayish-black sky lit with stars. "It's so beautiful here at night."

"You're the beautiful one." He doused his turkey with cranberry sauce. "You like your gift?"

"What gift?" She licked gravy from her lips.

He gestured his head to the Camaro. "I'm fixing it up to take to California with us."

"What?" She bounced in the chair. "For real?"

"If I can get it done in time."

"Can I drive it when we get to California?"

"Hm." He squinted, chewing.

"Please." She stuck out her lips. "I'll make it worth your while."

"Since you put it that way." He smiled, eyes crinkling at the corners. "Gotta admit, this Christmas thing isn't so bad."

"Really?"

He nodded, chewing. "Nothing wrong with having faith in something."

"No one's ever believed in me until you came along." She chewed the creamy green beans. "Never been this happy."

"Me either. It's weird to see how my life's changed since a year ago." His stare fell to his plate. "Are you ready?"

"For California?" She sipped the tart juice. "I'm ready for anything as long as I'm with you."

"You won't regret it." He reached across the table and took her hand. "We belong together."

They exchanged smiles.

"Merry Christmas, Ginger."

"Thank you." She pushed her fingers between his, her heart filling with warmth. "This is the best Christmas ever."

The End

To receive book announcements subscribe to Stacy's mailing list: Mailing List[1]

---

1.   http://eepurl.com/dFGzTL

Don't miss out!

Visit the website below and you can sign up to receive emails whenever Stacy-Deanne publishes a new book. There's no charge and no obligation.

https://books2read.com/r/B-A-RTFC-VOJBC

BOOKS 2 READ

Connecting independent readers to independent writers.

Also by Stacy-Deanne

Billionaires For Black Girls
Billionaire for the Night
Billionaire Takes the Bride
Billionaire At 36k Feet
Billionaire's Love Trap
Billionaire in the Caribbean
Billionaire Broken
Billionaire Times Two

Sex in the Wild West Series
Maid for Two
Fling on the Frontier
Favor for His Wife
The Carriage Ride
The Bride in the Barn
The Guest of Honor
Sunday Meal

Stripped Romantic Suspense Series
Stripped

Captured

Damaged

Haunted

Possessed

Destined

Stripped Series (Books 1-5)

Stripped Series Books 1-3

Stripped Series (Books 4-6)

Tate Valley Romantic Suspense Series

Now or Never

Now or Never

Chasing Forever

Chasing Forever

Sinner's Paradise

Sinner's Paradise

Last Dance

Last Dance

Tate Valley The Complete Series

The Bruised Series

Bruised

Captivated

Disturbed

Entangled

Twisted

The Good Girls and Bad Boys Series

Seven's Deadly Sins
Hawaii Christmas Baby
Sometimes Money Ain't Enough
The Best Christmas Ever
Prey
The Good Girls and Bad Boys Series
Bruised Complete Series
Tate Valley Complete Series
The Princess and the Thief
The Little Girl
The Stranger
Oleander
Seducing Her Father's Enemy
Love & Murder: 3-Book Romantic Suspense Starter Set
Paradise
Stalked by the Quarterback
Stripped Complete Series
Tell Me You Love Me
Secrets of the Heart
Five Days
Off the Grid
Sex in Kenya
Fatal Deception
A Cowboy's Debt
Billionaires for Black Girls Set (1-4)
A Savior for Christmas
The Samsville Setup
Trick The Treat
The Cowboy She Left in Wyoming
Theodore's Ring
Wrangle Me, Cowboy
The Billionaire's Slave
The Cowboy's Twin

Everwood County Plantation
Billionaires for Black Girls Set 5-7
The Lonely Hearts of San Sity
Stranded with Billionaire Grumpy Pants
An Alpha For Christmas